Breeds

Keith C. Blackmore

Edited by FirstEditing.com
Proofread by Red Adept Publishing
Cover by Karri Klawiter www.artbykarri.com
Formatted by Polgarus Studio

A special thank you to Ewart King for matters of all things handy and technical, as well as Joe Hart, Griffin Hayes, Brian J. Jarrett, and Miguel Tonnies.

A Cautionary Foreword

Just to let you know—bad things happen to dogs in here. The dogs aren't real, of course, (after all, it's all fiction) but if you're a dog lover, hell, an *animal* lover, you probably won't like what happens in the pages that follow. For that reason and that reason alone, save your cash, and do not buy this book. It's not my intention to upset readers.

Oh, and if you don't care for violence or swearing... again, you probably shouldn't buy this book.

Really.

You shouldn't.

I wouldn't.

For my grandparents; the ones who stayed and the ones who left.

And for the puppies.

1

Footsteps.

The sound of boots chuffing through deep snow grew louder in the gauze of low-lying cloud, coming closer, hooking Borland's attention from the bleary malaise of the wintry morning. He paused in his creation of a knee-deep trench, shoveling through last night's fun from his front door to the storage "store" behind the cabin. He ran a tongue over his upper lip, felt the wiry bristles of the beard he refused to trim, and listened. Smelled.

One man.

All alone.

Heading this way.

"D'fuck ye want?" Borland muttered in his evolved Scottish-Irish brogue, the words becoming vapor. He sighed in annoyance. Whoever it was, he'd give 'em an earful. Most of his neighbors considered him an old bastard to avoid, a reputation he had no problem upholding. He inhaled and tasted the chill on the air, felt the steely ache in his eroding teeth.

A figure appeared, black against the smoky white of the fog and the thick cream of fresh drifts. Borland watched the man struggle towards him and his cabin. The visitor wore winter boots that sunk into the frozen depths up to his knee, and a black and blue winter coat that looked more hip than actually warm. Young gun, Borland mused, though he suspected the visitor didn't actually carry any such weapon.

With another weary sigh, Borland took his shovel and harpooned an untouched drift. Then he turned to his guest, who made no attempt at all to conceal his approach.

Overconfident.

Not giving his senior the respect he deserved.

Young *fuck*, Borland scoffed.

"Hello!" the stranger called out, repelling the black magic of the fog. He slowed to a stop, his arms at his sides. "Hello?" Softer this time.

"Yar." Borland placed his gnarled hands on his hips in a gunslinger's stance. "Who d'hell are ya and why y'here?"

"Looking for a man named Walter Borland," the visitor said. Unibrowed shit, with a bearded face as black as a bear cub's coat and bursting with youth. That pissed Borland off. With every passing second he felt all of his many, many years on earth. Felt it when he got up in the morning, felt it when he pulled on his stubborn, tight, bloods-a-bitches socks. His hips ached constantly, as did both of his shoulders, a deep, penetrating growl that scraped bone. It felt as if he were being stabbed by knives coated in some sinister, half-assed poison. And those were just his joints. He pissed four times a night, which confounded him, as he'd stopped drinking anything after seven, especially his favorite fizzy pops. He'd learned from the news that the carbonated shit increased a person's risk of prostate cancer by thirty percent, and that was *all* he needed with all the other hurts his body was collecting as it passed contrarily through time. He'd once read a t-shirt that read, "Life starts at 70." There'd be no sweeter bliss for Borland than to find the cocksucker who wrote such lying horseshit and wring his goddamn neck. Just strangle the bastard until the vertebrae crinkled and snapped. Growing old sucked *donkey* cocks, and he had the surprising ailments, the wilting sex drive, and the interesting phlegmy rattles periodically issuing from his lungs to prove it.

"You know where he is?" the man inquired.

No more than thirty, Borland figured, knowing he had calluses older than the aborted fuck puppy on his doorstep. That knowledge alone was very hard for him to swallow.

"I'se him," Borland growled, suppressing a cough. "What's it to ya?"

"Was told by a friend to check in on ya. You haven't been answering your phone."

"Me phone?" Borland scowled at the knee-deep Samaritan not twenty steps away. "Y'see any goddamn telephone wires out here?"

The man raised his hands in surrender. "You don't have a cell phone?"

"Dem tings rots yer brain. And no, I don't have one. Can't afford one on me pension."

"They are costly."

"And d'fuckin' companies dat lease or sell dem contracts have all de important parts in fine fuckin' print. Dey see me comin' and dey tink dey can sell me anyting. No sar. I don't give dem Jesus bastards d'goddamn pleasure."

This black bearded little shit smiled, baring healthy teeth. The enamel on Borland's teeth had worn over the years, making eating or drinking anything agony.

"You swear like a sailor," Blackbeard said with some measure of admiration.

"S'pose y'smoked enough of deir cocks t'know."

That made the youngster's face go slack. "Well. Um. Yeah, anyway, swearing doesn't bother me."

"Hey, peckerwood, look down for a second, willya? Tell me what ye see?"

He did so, tentatively. "Snow?"

"More specifically."

"Land?"

"Gettin' close. *My* land. And yer standin' on it. Which means I don't give a tree knot fuck what bodders ye. If I really wanted to know, I'll put me boot a foot up yer ass and watch yer goddamn eyes explode."

Blackbeard's enthusiasm melted like an early spring thaw. "Ah… well—" He paused, deciding on just how to best approach. "I was told to contact you anyway. Wanted to do some huntin' in the area."

"Huntin', eh?"

"Yeah, huntin'. I was given your name. Told to ask for your permission."

"Not much huntin' around dese hills," Borland remarked, suspicion lacing his tone. "Y'sure dat's all yer here fer?"

"I'm sure."

But Borland could see that his visitor *wasn't* sure. In fact, he could smell the uncertainty coming off him as fragrant as fresh shit. That amused him. For all of the youngster's bravado in coming out here by himself, that confidence had been shaken by a few crude exchanges.

But hunting, now. Borland could appreciate that.

"Come on in, den," Borland grumbled, waving an arm. "I'll put a kettle on. Ye drink coffee?"

"Tea."

"Tea?" Borland scoffed loudly and again eyed his visitor with distrust. "Might have a few leaves pokin' around in d'house. Come on in 'fore y'fuckin' freeze yer nutsack off out here. Sure as Christ won't find dem marbles in the snow."

"Cold doesn't bother me," the man said. He looked to the heavens before meeting Borland's face. "Love it."

Love it? Love the cold? Borland choked back a cough. No more than a minute and he despised this prick already. Showing his back, he shuffled to the front porch and stomped his feet on the planks, making them rattle as he cleared his boots of snow. He thumbed the old-fashioned latch on the cabin's door and pulled open the black maw of an entryway. This he disappeared inside of, off to one side. He thumped around for a moment, and then materialized with an armful of split wood before heading deeper into the interior.

Blackbeard hesitated for all of a moment before following.

Inside, the heat emanated from a relic of a potbellied stove with curled black feet. Borland shuffled towards the stove and dumped the wood near a stacked pile beside it. He grabbed two cut junks, opened the polished chrome lid of the stove, and shoved them inside one after the other. Glowing embers flew.

"Chair's dere," he muttered and pointed to an old-fashioned, bare wood seater before shambling off through another doorway. By the time he returned, Blackbeard had sat himself down and was inspecting the ceiling.

"Where'd you get this stuff?"

"Hm." Borland looked up at what hung from the rafters. Axes and old bow saws suspended from wooden pegs and thick nails. Coils of drooping rope. Cast nets with weighted balls dangling like thick, black spider webs. Below this, shelves lined with old cans of nails, all connected by a mesh of dust. And crowning it all, a massive set of moose antlers—a full eighteen points, complete with a scalped section of flesh—spiked to the north wall. Dirt and grease coated the windows, rendering them all but impossible to see through. The interior of the cabin appeared to consist of one room and an adjoining kitchen, along with a closed door behind Borland's back. A broad, white-surfaced table rested against one wall, tucked in beneath a window, the one closest to the door. It was perhaps the only clear pane of glass in the entire structure. It also provided a view of anyone walking towards the front of the cabin.

Borland placed a dented blue kettle on the stove's top and sloughed off his winter coat, revealing thick winter pants held up by a pair of worn suspenders. He stood at about five-eleven these days, shrunken by the hateful snarl of arthritis in his back. An age ago he towered over local folks at six-foot-three and was fearsome to behold. Now, he was balding, possessed old man's skin, and hated every morning for yanking him from his dreams.

He scratched at the thick, gray wool around his jaw while he hung his coat on a wooden peg set into a wall. He then sat down with a groan on a worn, red sofa. Once settled, he eyed his unwanted visitor.

"I'll get d'cups directly," he said and glowered at Blackbeard. "What was it y'wanted again?"

The man flashed those white teeth of his. "Huntin.'"

"D'fuck y'want to hunt out here? Nudding's in season, b'y." He grunted, colloquially meaning *boy*, and saying it as *by*.

"Was told to find you."

"So yer huntin' me, in one way, eh?" Borland rumbled deviously, fixing his guest with a knowing eye.

Blackbeard didn't reply, choosing silence as a defense.

"Y'talk funny," Borland pointed out, filling the awkward quiet. "Yer not from around here."

"From Corner Brook."

"Corner Brook. Yer a goddamn townie, aren'tcha? Dey all talk like ye out in Corner Brook?"

"Most do."

Borland leaned forward, his eyes dangerous. "Ye saucin' me, b'y?"

"No, no, not at all."

"Cause if ye was saucin' me, I'd jack-slap dat Jesus look offa yer townie face right here and now."

In the silent wake of the threat, a breeze gathered itself up and rattled the window.

"Look," Blackbeard said, his voice measured, controlled, but his gaze locked onto Borland like heat seekers. "I was trying to get in touch. You had no phone—"

"No phone here. Got one at d'house."

"This isn't your house?"

"Dis look like a house to ye?"

Blackbeard took a steadying breath. "So I had to ask around and find you on my own."

"Y'asked around about me?" Alarm sounded in Borland's voice.

"To find out where you were."

Borland didn't answer for a few seconds, mortified, staring at the newcomer as if he had two heads. "Y'wanted to find I somethin' fierce. Reminds me of a feller who came here about a month ago. He was over here. Huntin'."

"Yeah?"

"Yeeeah. Proper nuisance he was, too. Seems like dat's all I get dese days. Proper nuisances. De world's gone nuisance. In my day it was do what you do to survive. Now, it's do what you can wit what isn't regulated by government or pissed on by dese self-interest or the animal rights groups. Get on yer nerves all them fuckers will. The whole Jesus bunch. Nosy, too. Whatta world is all I haveta say about dat. And one can't even speak yer mind against dem in a public place as the fuckers'll have someone on ya faster than a morning shit. Just for saying yer mind! Leaders don't like dat. Fights are done in courts and y'can't fight 'cause a goddamn lawyer will charge three or four hundred dollars an hour. An hour! Who the hell can afford fuckin' three or four hundred dollars an hour, eh? You?"

"No."

"Nar I. But y'know somethin'? Somethin' dat really turns my piss cold? I'll tell ya. It's de goddamn private corporations rulin' everythin' behind the scenes. Even de government ain't about doing what dey can for de people, it's about doin' enough to get a fat pension and all dem lobster dinners. Taxes. Regulations. Shit, y'know what happened out in Quebec? Some French guy got tossed off his land, his own fuckin' property, 'cause a company wanted to buy it and he wouldn't sell at their price. So what did de company do? Went to court and got dis guy evicted off his property dat was owned by him and his family for fuckin' years as dey were ah, ah, detrimentialistic and preventin' dese other cocksuckers from makin' money and keepin' deir shareholders happy. Said he was being greedy, too! Can you believe dat? Man owns his own land for a goddamn age and along comes a mining or oil company, says, 'You got oil under dere. We wants it. And we'll give you dis much for it.' Which is only a pissdrop in the bedchamber pot really, and when someone says it ain't enough, well! Yer upholding development so *fuck you.* Fuck you and yer fuckin' land. We'll go to court with our team of bigwig lawyers, pay off de judge and take it anyway, and you can go to fuckin' jail and see how you like a little white room for a year or whatever, playin' pond hockey with de soap in de showers and stayin' de hell outta de corners. Who gives a goddamn ya lived on dat land fer all yer life, eh? Raised family on it. Jesus Christ. Law. Money. Banks. All fucked up. All twisted. People's just as twisted by it, too. Never mind de fuckin' pollution goin' into de air. Goin' into de groundwater. Never mind de open freedom of the wild bein' regulated all ta hell. You know, I haveta start worryin' about cancer now. Cancer! *Me!* Never been sick a day and it's suddenly all pilin' onto me. Biggest fuckin' mystery. And folks don't like it that I talk. I ask questions. I open me mouth. Can't have dat. Makes certain people nervous. Some people like to live in de shadows, know what I'm sayin', eh, b'y? Y'know? Dey're more on living out deir days in secrecy, and keepin' de rest of us in line with threats. Black hearted sonsabitches. Don't listen and look out. Look out. You get a visitor some morning or some night. Low. Underhanded. Like... like fuckin' spiders. Bah. Sick of movin' I is. Don't wanna leave dis land. Not dis time. Can't have dat, someone says. Can't have it. So why I asks, asks 'em straight up. Man to man, like. *Oh* dey don't like dat. Supposed to just fuckin' *take it.* Y'know what dat feels like? Feels like, like an electric eggbeater shavin' at yer prostate. Jesus, Jesus."

Blackbeard's face remained unreadable during Borland's disjointed vitriol. In fact, his youthful, bushy visitor sat quietly with his hands in his lap. Too damn quiet, really. Borland ran a dry tongue across his hairy upper lip, charging himself for the next rant.

"S'like dis place here," Borland continued. "Claimed and bought dis land years ago. Not much, outta de way and all, so I don't have to pay town taxes, right? Still gotta pay property taxes, though. Not dat I do. And the works of 'em are too goddamn scared to come out here to face me. Any day now, some pork-assed municipal spaztic is gonna call de cops. And dey will, eventually. Knows dey will. But you think dey're gonna get me to pay anything? No sir. Not I. Gettin' it from all sides. The locals wantin' their money for land I already own, and dat group of cocksuckers dere dat tink it's time for me to move on. If I dig deep enough, I daresay one controls the other. Da fuckers wants me gone some bad. Some *shockin'* bad. But I ain't goin' nowhares. I'll *fight* before dat happens. I'll *murder* whoever it is coming into me territory. Fuckin' *feast* on deir hearts."

Borland growled the word "feast," his voice taking on a frightening tremble that made Blackbeard straighten ever so slightly. His visitor appeared on guard, yet trying very hard to look relaxed, and that put a satisfied smirk on Borland's own bearded jowls. Young fuck had finally gotten it. Young fuck understood now.

Another gust rose up and clattered against the window, rattling the pane. The kettle shushed Borland with heated impatience.

"Ah," the old woodsman said with a fatigued flail of a hand. "Sorry b'y. Y'don't want to listen to me go on about de ways tings are. I don't speak much to folks. Don't have time for it. And y'caught me at a bad time. Y'want some biscuits with yer tea?"

Blackbeard forced a smile and shook his head.

"I'm havin' some den," Borland muttered. "Only time I can eat d'damn tings. I likes to dunk 'em. Me teet hurt if I chow down on 'em dry."

Borland got up, knees crackling, and turned his back on his unwanted guest.

And in that instant, Blackbeard's face became a shockingly stern thing. His right hand stole behind his back and went up under his winter coat. He leaned forward just a little as he quietly freed the hidden Bowie knife from its sheath, already picking the most critical point to stab in Borland's spine. He lifted himself from the chair.

The kettle's hissy fit heightened.

Borland whirled with a speed utterly unexpected. Three-inch claws flashed across Blackbeard's face, raking hair and meat in a grisly explosion of force and leaving the flesh in fine tatters. The surprise and ferocity of Borland's attack rendered Blackbeard stunned for all of a split second—more than enough time for a second clawed hand to uppercut, swung from the hips, leaving a foursome of lines as fine as gills in his throat, spouting arcs of cherry black. The blow lifted Blackbeard over his chair to crash-land flat on his back. The Bowie skittered from his fingers.

Borland pounced. With unnatural nimbleness for a man his age and size, he landed knees-first on the man's chest, breaking ribs as if they were weak ice, and snatched up the silvery blade. He grabbed the younger man's throat, blood bubbling around his fingers, and positioned the weapon's tip right under the chin. Blackbeard's right eye swiveled around but the left didn't. Borland's claws had sliced that orb open, making it weep an almost colorless jelly that slid into Blackbeard's ear.

"Little shit," a black-eyed Borland hissed through bared fangs. "Tink y'can just walk in heres and *fuck* wit' *me*?"

Blackbeard blinked in terror.

With a grunt, Borland shoved the Bowie's point up through the man's skull, burying the weapon deep and allowing it to shiver just for a second… before twisting.

2

A smoky blanket of cloud stretched across the sky as snow floated down in silent tufts, frosting the land in white deep enough for the need of snowshoes. Ross stopped in his hike and just savored the scene before him, listening to nothing, as there wasn't anything to hear out in the woods at times like these. He scanned the ghost-white hills ahead of him, blinking when flakes drifted into his eyes, and simply appreciated the view for what it was. Snow covered the land in an unspoiled sheet of dull brilliance. A canvas of cold sugar, bordered on either side by stout fir trees left untouched by Christmas. Rocks poked their dark tips up through the fresh sheets, reminiscent of pebbles in the smiles of snowmen. In between some of the smaller trees lurked rising reefs of drifted snow, shaped as fine as any museum sculpture. Some of the larger ones resembled the backs of mighty whales breaking the surface for a quick breath.

Sheer, freezing beauty.

And not a goddamn soul in sight.

Just the way he liked it.

Fir and spruce trees covered much of the land beyond where he stood on a low hill, and he could faintly make out the landfill area that once served as a dumping zone for garbage. The communities of Upper and Lower Amherst Cove, King's Cove, and all the others on the peninsula now sent their refuse toward the new dump near Bonavista. And while Ross hadn't visited it yet, he imagined he would sooner or later. Sometimes he'd find perfectly good items to salvage from the nearby Catalina dump, and for a guy who recognized their worth and didn't mind a little work on the side, it was as good as shopping at any of the bigger chains in Clarenville.

Ross stood and hefted his rucksack on his back, shifting the weight of his water bottle, a wrapped bologna-and-cheese sandwich, and the three frozen rabbits he'd taken from his wire slips. Slips he had to dig down to reach. He didn't mind. He was an outdoors person, a born woodsman, and the land provided a good portion of what he needed. In the fall and winter, he hunted rabbit, duck, bear, and moose. Fished in February if he was bored, but he usually caught his fill of trout during the summer months, and kept them in his freezer.

Freeze.

The thought made him sniff at the cold. He felt his face loosen from the chill that hardened his exposed skin. It was only minus seven today, least that's what the truck's thermometer told him. Moving around in his black-and-yellow winter snow suit, with the weight he carried, kept him more than warm. He thought about heading back to the truck and getting home, starting a fire and heating the place up, but the weather was too fine for that just yet. The scenery too glorious. He wanted to enjoy it as much as possible because, in the spring, chances were he'd have to board up his house and move out west, to the oil fields or some other area ripe with employment opportunities. As beautiful as the land was around here, the economy was depressed. It had already forced most of the younger folks to move, seeking work elsewhere. Ross had held on as long as he could, but the writing was on the wall.

As much as he hated to even consider it.

With another sniff, he got to hiking, making his way over hoary ridges populated with stunted trees and hoping that, in September, the wild blueberry bushes he knew existed underneath would provide a few weeks of uninterrupted picking. The time spent in the outdoors agreed with him. At forty-two, his doctor marveled at his overall general health, telling him he had the heart of an athlete. Tobacco held no interest to him, and he sipped alcohol only in moderation, so he was free of those particular vices… although, after catching a glimpse and a hello from the social worker at the local community hospital, Ross did feel the urge to develop a gambling problem. Not that he would have a chance with her. He wasn't a pretty man. The razor graced his chin only when absolutely necessary, the last time being four or five days ago, so his lower face appeared prickly with stubble. In his usual state, his unshaven beard could skin the ass off a cat if he tried, as his departed grandmother often remarked about his grandfather's sandpapery jawline. Ross also buzzed his hair low if only for the ease of maintaining it. His vision wasn't the best, and in the evenings, when he chose to read by lamplight—just to save a few dollars as the cost of electricity was outrageous—he found he held his books farther and farther away from his face.

Gambling addiction. Damn straight that was a fine idea. Only trouble was the social worker, with her hair done in a golden droop of a ponytail. Couldn't have been any more than twenty-five, if that. Twenty-seven at most. Young enough for him to feel awkward about ever saying anything more than, "Hello."

Then again, who knew who he might meet while playing blackjack? The notion made him chuckle. There were better things to do than play cards online at the local community library. Watching porn came to mind. Alvin knew all the good, virus-free sites.

The wind blew snow into Ross's face and made him squint. He cursed softly for not bringing a pair of goggles. The land dipped into a gulley and he thumped down the incline, keeping his snowshoes apart, careful not to trip. He didn't have any more rabbit slips to check on, and this hike was only because he loved the outdoors. The worsening weather scratched going any farther, however. A short walk and he'd turn around and make his way back to his waiting truck.

Snow whorled around his ankles in white puffs of magic as he descended, accepting help from tree limbs. Even through the dwindling visibility, he had no difficulty spotting the tracks, almost hidden under a low-hanging roof of heavy boughs. At first he thought moose, but upon closer inspection, he could see that they were much wider. Snow filled them at an angle, reminding Ross of loose socks fallen slack upon thin ankles. He crouched down and the chilled expression on his face worked into one of sheer puzzlement.

What the hell?

The tracks weren't fresh, as the stiffness of the bottom layer of snow informed him, but that wasn't the perplexing thing. He'd seen all manner of prints in these hills: coyote, bear, moose, rabbit, and even squirrels—not to mention the boots of fellow hunters and folks who enjoyed the outdoors. But this set made him uneasy. Though the heel was partially filled, the tip of the print could be made out, as could the grainy imprint of toes… widespread *human* toes.

Ross's face scrunched in blatant puzzlement. Who the hell would be running around out here in their bare feet? There were no polar bear clubs around seeking mid-winter dips, and even if there were, the coastline was a kilometer away. So who would be prancing about ankle-deep in their birthday boots? Ross saw where the tracks emerged and where they were going. A scowl hardened his salty face. The wild was an unforgiving place at the best of times. Anyone heading into the woods at extended lengths should be prepared, especially if the territory was unknown. A memory surfaced of a missing person's report about three weeks or so ago—some guy from either the West Coast or out of Province had come in to do a little hiking and winter fishing. Just last year a couple of old hunters up from Maine had flown in to chase moose and ended up blasting themselves in what the cops concluded to be a suicide pact. The Mounties discovered their frozen corpses three months after the closing of the season. Strange shit went down around these hills sometimes.

With some effort Ross followed the tracks, sensing they were heading back toward the highway and hoping they stopped there. Grim images of what might be waiting for him clouded his mind. Dead animals he could handle, but dead people were something else entirely.

"Gonna regret this," Ross muttered and left the gulley behind. He pushed snowy branches from his face as he trudged onward, the chilling dust coating him from head to toe. He stopped every so often to get his bearings, wondering when the snow was going to let up. The highway drew closer, and he expected to hear the wet hiss of passing traffic any moment. A few minutes later, he emerged from the treeline and lost the tracks at a clear-cut incline which was the shoulder of a frosty ribbon of asphalt. The highway department had plowed the snow over the slope, covering the tracks. Ross huffed and continued on, climbing up to the road and peering in both directions, frowning at how the falling snow skewered the visibility a hundred meters out.

Not one for giving up, Ross crossed and descended the other side of the road, approaching the treeline some twenty feet back. He went right, seeking any sign of someone passing through, before turning back to the starting point and going the other way. The treeline led him to an open brook baring ice fangs, drawn back over a chilling rush of water too wide to jump. The sight of the stream flowing into deep woods forced Ross to halt. He sighed. Thus ended the hunt. The only thing he could do now was phone it in and alert the Mounties. Just in case it was a missing person. Or a crazy.

Or just strange shit.

Ross hoped whoever the person was had parked their ride alongside the road, returned after their little jog, and simply driven off. He hated seeing good taxpayer's money go to waste looking for crazy people.

3

With plump snowflakes falling all around, Harry Shea made his way to the rural block of red-and-white mailboxes near the top of the hill. The inhabitants of Upper Amherst Cove had fought for the delivery service, else they'd have to drive down to Bonavista to get their mail. And with his fixed income, it was a challenge every month to keep the house warm and the scattered bit of food on the table. Politicians didn't have that particular worry, not with their fat pensions. Just the thought of their campaign-smiling asses, all understanding when they were looking for the senior citizen vote, only to reveal their true self-serving interests once in power. It made his scrotum and asshole pucker up in a tug-o-war on either side of an angry taint. Soon, very soon, if cutbacks to regular pensions continued, and everything else kept rising, it wouldn't be a challenge of heating the house and having food on the table—it would be a choice. The thought of it made his blood boil all the more and he scowled his angst at the falling snow.

Standing in front of the mailboxes, he got out his key and unlocked his own. Grocery flyers, cable bill, which he'd have to cancel this month. Nothing more, so he slammed the mailbox shut with a muttered curse. Still nothing on his damn colonoscopy either, and that riled him anew. The Canadian health system was another victim of government cutbacks and, while once proudly heralded as being one of the best, was now reduced to shit. A year he'd been waiting for notification—always sent by mail, never over the phone—of his turn to head into Clarenville and have his shit chute plumbed with a camera. A simple cautionary procedure for men of his age, and one he despised having done, but to wait nearly a year on something three years already overdue was something else. His doctor sympathized with him, citing a lack of resources. Shea knew it wasn't up to him, but it didn't make the anger and frustration go away.

Flyers in hand, he took a moment to gaze past the mailbox, where the hillside fell away into an enormous ice-filled bay. The other side of the water lay hidden this morning, lurking somewhere behind a thick, calming snowfall. The view always relaxed him, vented the rage of his memories of seemingly unheeded protests to local municipal town officials, and he stood there and just mentally linked flakes with lowering his blood pressure.

If it didn't work, he had roughly a hundred and fifty liters of homebrew sitting in his basement which sure as hell would. Thirty of which had just reached the bare minimum four weeks of aging, making it just ripe for chugging.

"Lovely day, Harry."

Harry Shea turned and saw an elderly man with a blue snow shovel in hand, a pinched cone of a bright red, homemade stocking cap on his head, and a black-and-yellow snowsuit replete with a reflective orange-and-yellow vest. The figure ambled along a thin path, some fifty feet long, trenched between the porch of a white, two-story house and the main road.

"Lovely day, Sammy," Harry greeted back. Samuel Walsh was another of the twenty homeowners of Upper Amherst Cove, and probably the only true friend he had in the small community.

"Gray, though," Sammy said, poking at his thick bifocals. The brutes almost completely shielded his face from the weather.

"Gray day, yes sir, gray she is," Harry agreed, and studied the red cap with disapproval. "Y'look like a fuckin' simpleton with that."

Sammy shrugged. "Sally knitted it for me, so I wears it. What can I say? If I don't wear it, well, I don't wanna think about that bit."

"Even if it makes ye look like a retarded elf?"

"S'pose so."

"My son. She's got you by the balls, don't she?"

"She does. She does."

"She'd skin ya."

"She would."

"Skin ya proper."

"Yeaup," Sammy agreed again, stretching the colloquial mashing of 'yeah' and 'yup.'

"Whattaya up to today?" Harry asked his friend, to which Sammy held up the shovel. "Gettin' started early, ain'tcha?"

"Naw," Sammy replied. "Exercise. Although I don't know why. All of this'll melt in the spring."

Harry Shea smirked at that little nugget of Sammy logic and looked down over the continuing hill, until he saw white land blur with ice. The whole community had grown on the side of a large hill, almost a stunted mountain, that faced the waters of the Atlantic. Once a small but thriving fishing and farming town, it was now populated almost entirely by the same folks who grew up here, who watched their children move into St. John's, out to Fort McMurray, or elsewhere, leaving the old folks behind. It wasn't that Amherst Cove folks didn't like the cities, it was more like they preferred their little bayside village. It was remote, quiet, and eternally home.

"Snow seems to be pickin' up," Sammy observed.

"Fuck the Jesus snow. All white and shit."

"Gotta clear it, though."

"*You* gotta clear it. On Sally's orders. All I gotta do is watch."

"Hm." Sammy grunted, long desensitized to his friend's bluntness. "Just wonderin'. Why couldn't snow be, I dunno, more green? Or purple? Or even... polka dot?"

Harry made side eyes at him.

"Or even," Sammy continued, "or even white with women's breastuses on it? Just think. If it were like that, every guy'd be out shovelin' it then. Be lookin' forward to it. Course then, it'd only open up another problem."

"Yeah?"

"We'd be all playin' with it."

Shea shook his head in dismayed amusement. "The women folk wouldn't be playing in it."

"Some might."

Harry conceded that point. "Could ye date the snow?"

"Maybe."

"Wedlock?"

"Might be possible. Hmmm, might be a stretch, though. Especially in the summer. Unless you had a freezer."

"Oh, well."

"Best t'keep at just snow tits."

Harry shook his head again. Where on God's earth did Sammy come up with this stuff?

"Perky little snow tits," Sammy said dreamily.

"All right, stop it now."

"Milky, too."

"There's a hockey game on tonight," Shea threw out, trying to change the subject.

Sammy paused and turned his huge, white-flecked bifocals onto Harry. "So there is. Well, anyway, gotta shovel."

"Yer probably gonna make a couple sets of snow tits now, aren'tcha?"

"No, probably not. Sally's got the window open there and she'll be checkin' on me. Don't want to haveta explain it all to her. She doesn't appreciate our little conversations. Or the humor."

"She's a big girl. She can handle it."

"Naw," Sammy whispered as he leaned in. "Most women don't have the same humor as guys do. No matter how funny the shit is."

"Perhaps," Shea said, but he didn't wholly agree.

"Sammy!" a woman's voice bawled, cutting the coolness of the scene. "I told you to clear the driveway so I can get on the road! I gotta be in Bonavista by twelve thirty."

"Yes, me love," Sammy called back. Then to Harry, "I'll be over later on."

"Yeah? Why?"

"You got that batch of Pilsner ready to drink, don'tcha?"

Shea started and shook his head once again. "You remembered that?"

"You thought I forgot?"

"I did."

"Well, now, I didn't. Can't have you drink all that beer alone. What kind of neighbor would I be? You just have the mugs and beer ready. Be over this afternoon, while Sally's in Bonavista. I'll even bring over the nachos and dip."

"What's she doing over there?"

"Gettin' her hair done."

"Ah. Fair enough. All right. Seeya then. You got any of that cheese sauce?"

"Yeaup. The mild kind, too."

"Ah, good. That medium is too damn spicy for me. Wicked heartburn last time. And me ass was on fuckin' fire for half the day."

"No worries of that this time. I'll bring over a tub of sour cream, too."

That did sound good, Harry mulled. "Seeya, then." And he muddled off, heading for the top of the hill where he crossed the only road leading out of Amherst Cove.

Behind him, Sally's high-pitched vocal chords speared the air once again.

From her window, Sally Walsh leaned back and pulled the kitchen window closed. She huffed, smirked, and rested both hands on her sizeable hips, keeping watch over Sammy as he made his way to his parked car. At sixty-four, she had remarkable hearing and picked up the conversation of the two men. Snow tits. She scoffed. *Men.* Talk to them all you want, but the moment you mention tits and suddenly, *magically*, you had the floor. It was Sally's firm belief that the surest way to get a man to do something was to hang a pair of boobs on it. If she could put a set of knockers on the radiator in the house, she'd have to pry both Sammy and Shea off the goddamn metal.

Sammy turned around and waved to her with both hand and shovel, pulling an unwilling smile out of her. Like kids they were, and like kids, life would be questionable without them, if not downright miserable. She maneuvered around the kitchen, the air redolent of freshly baked bread, the buttery loaves laid out over the table. She stopped in front of the one mirror hanging beside the fridge and inspected the graying roots of her brown hair. Her one vanity was her mane. Always had been. The brewing weather wasn't fierce enough to keep her away from her appointment, and she wanted to get it done before anything worse came down the pipe. The weatherman preached on about a blizzard two days away. A monster of a storm crept up the eastern coast after socking it to parts of the states and pummeling Nova Scotia, and was on a collision course with the island. The next few days might see Amherst Cove cut off because of the snowfall, and yet, the thought of *not* getting her hair done today terrified her more.

She could do it. Winter storms didn't bother her. She liked the way the wind blustered off the ice pads of the bay and leaned into the house. The howls and the creaks of timbers lulled her to sleep without fail, and sometimes, if there was a gust on and Sammy was either upstairs or not immediately around, she'd turn off the television or put down the book and just listen to the fury outside, breaking upon the corners of the house, while she remained safe and warm inside her timberframe pocket of memories and dreams.

Winter storms didn't bother her in the least.

But graying hair absolutely *poisoned* her.

4

It took some effort to wrench the Bowie knife free of the skull. Once Borland had the weapon out, he held it before his full black eyes and sniffed. Pure silver. Just holding the lethal blade in such close proximity to his face made his jaws ache as if lit up by a tuning fork. Borland held the knife at arm's length and snapped his fangs, not bothering to withdraw them and perversely *enjoying* how they extended over his human jowls. Going half shape instead of a full-on transformation took many, many years to learn, but with a little concentration, a little willpower, he'd learned how to maintain his biped form while summoning the wolf inside. Something that the Elders probably didn't want him to do, or have the others find out about.

Or anyone, for that matter.

The first time he effected the partial change, he actually gauged his success by feeling and studying his reflection in the bedroom mirror, smiling at the fright framed in glass.

It took even more strenuous practice to change only parts of his body. The strength and power that came with the limited change was almost as seductive as if he'd completely gone over. Almost.

But Borland preferred being man-shaped at times like these. Even though he was nowhere near as fast or strong as a fully transformed werewolf, he was still faster than one in its man suit, and certainly much stronger.

As Blackbeard had discovered.

Borland hissed through fangs at his dead visitor. The *second* werewolf sent his way. He had no doubt that a third would be coming. Perhaps even more. That thought made Borland wrinkle his nose. More visitors. More disturbances. Not even the Elders could ignore this now. All Borland ever wanted was to be left alone. To die in peace. To die *his* way. But the Elders had their own ideas of how old wolves like him should exit the world. Cleaner, less newsworthy ways. Borland didn't want that; he just wanted to run through the wild one last time and let the wolf free, to do as it would. Damn the consequences.

He knew the Elders wouldn't allow that. Thus, they sent the wardens.

The wardens. Every territory had at least one guardian, depending on its size. Newfoundland had a pair. Borland regarded the dead form on his floor. Now the island had only him. This warden had been sent in response to the initial killer the Elders had dispatched to put the rebellious cur down quietly. Probably lied to. Probably was told Borland had gone crazy and butchered one of their own for no reason other than to satisfy a maddening bloodlust. The Elders would make up any story they liked to rally the troops, and they would send another warden with orders to kill him. That thought made Borland snarl at the cold air within his cabin, frustrated and ever so hateful of the lies and bureaucracy of his own kind. He despised their measured, conservative ways of attempting to exist behind a veil of untruths and subterfuge, beneath the human stock which they were far superior to in any form. The wolves of Borland's father's time would not tolerate the shit messages and forked tongued preachings being cultivated and spread across the territories. They'd rip the throats out of the speakers.

Yet, here he was, forced to kill another of his own kind.

Not my kind, Borland seethed, spittle spilling over lips stretched by curved teeth. Droplets speckled the young visitor's lower pants. Refusal to live under such pretenses any longer was only part of the reason Borland didn't care for the Elder's rule. The real reason was something much more frightening. It was previously thought that he or any *Were* was damn near invincible to any disease of man. Yet here, in his twilight years, the onset of cancer in his system filled his enhanced senses like the stench of rotting cheese. Eating the human's food had been the cause of it. If he were allowed to eat what he was supposed to feast upon, *when* he wanted, he damned well knew he wouldn't be as poisoned with chemical toxins as he presently was. That he even upheld the law while suffering in secret only added to his misery.

Upholding *lies.*

But not anymore.

Not while he still drew breath.

There wouldn't be much time, Borland realized, and so he flipped the dead warden onto his front. He raked one claw down the length of the coat, parting the material as if he were tugging on a zipper instead. Borland dug into Blackbeard's exposed back, ripping out the gray stuffing of his winter coat until he uncovered the leather scabbard of the Bowie. Moments later, he stood up with the freed casing and sheathed the knife before sticking it down the back of his own jeans. Borland had his own ceremonial blade, a length of forged death bestowed upon wardens as a lethal badge of their authority. All wolves hunting in a warden's territory recognized the symbol, and adhered to his word before engaging in any hunt. In any killing. To protect their existence from the human herds.

Such… *shit.*

Borland didn't know when, but somewhere along the years, the wolves of the day had lost their balls.

The techno harping that passed as pop music spurted from Blackbeard's pocket. Frowning, Borland grabbed and shook the corpse by the ankle as if he were a doll. The music repeated. Who would be calling this length of pink dog cock? Blackbeard's form shivered violently as Borland continued shaking him over his floor.

Then something hit the wood with a clunk.

A cell phone lay face up, lighting up the shadows with its harsh song.

Borland picked it up with his three-inch claws. He bobbled the device for an instant before transferring it to one hand. With the other, he tapped what he thought was the button to further activate the device.

Cautiously, untrusting of the plastic, he pressed the cellphone to his ear. Listened.

Even territories away, Borland sensed the Elders. Could smell their tainted musk.

"Well?" a voice asked in his ear.

"Well what?"

"Is it done?"

"I killed him."

Hesitation. Then dawning realization, laced with loathing. "Borland."

"Aye, tis I, ye goddamn sack of dog shite."

Silence. The wind rasped against a nearby pane, drawing Borland's attention to the one window he could see out. Snow splashed the glass.

"You killed him?" the voice asked dubiously.

"Y'deaf as well as fuckin' stupid?"

Silence again. Then, from the other end of the satellite connection, came words spoken with hatred as raw and ugly as torn flesh—a tone Borland understood.

"You just killed yourself, you ancient… *fuck*."

More silence, the Elder waiting for a reply. Borland gave one. "No, b'y." His bared fangs warped the words and he exerted pressure around the black casing of the cell phone while injecting red fury into his next breath.

"I've just declared *war*."

The device splintered with a *pop* from the crushing strength of his hand and the line went dead. Borland allowed gravity to take the crumpled plastic from his open palm. It plunked onto the floorboards with a clunk, a surprisingly lonely sound. He stared balefully at the device. Outside, the wind rose to an eerie pitch.

Borland's eyes flickered to the window.

"Bring it, homie," he hissed with a flawless mainland accent.

And crushed the phone under his heavy boot.

5

Snow rasped against the window, but Douglas Kirk paid little heed to it. He sat on his warm sofa, ass deep into cozy cushions, feet crossed and up on a coffee table. The windows to his apartment had been pulled closed, sealing him inside. A lamp shed soft light near his shoulder, which he peeked over to read.

To think.

And to drink.

But more importantly, to drink.

Anyone looking at Kirk's bearded face would place him in his thirties. A lean if not athletic build, clothed in worn pajama bottoms and a t-shirt that read, "Fuck Housework." He lay sprawled on his couch in utter shitfaced stupidity, staring ahead at a wall, holding a paperback in one hand and a bottle of beer in the other. He'd been drinking since early yesterday evening, passed out sometime after midnight, only to wake up just before dawn and continue his beer buzz. Kirk wasn't an alcoholic.

Hardly drank at all, in fact. But some days, like yesterday, he exacerbated the depressing funk of winter by shutting himself off from the world and just lighting up his senses. A damn fine idea. When the night lifted, revealing a hoary morning like a busking magician pulling back a tattered sheet, he'd felt inclined to just pull the curtains closed, lock the world out, and stay in the zone of being pleasantly shitfaced. Read some classic literature, even.

Kirk thought all the classics went down better with beer.

He idly scratched at the overgrown beard hanging off his chin, feeling the snarl of thickening whiskers, and lifted the bottle for a lazy sip. Already he had a warm buzz on. By supper, he planned to be properly fixed with toe tags. No one would come knocking. His neighbors knew better than to disturb him, and the mailbox was on the bottom floor of the apartment building, six levels down. The walls were built solid enough that he could only hear voices if someone shouted just outside his door, and at this time of the day, most folks would be at work.

Not him.

He didn't work. Not like regular people. And he was aware of people in his building who suspected him of questionable activity and income. In their eyes, he was an urban hillbilly. A concrete redneck. A recluse spotted outside of his apartment with as much regularity as Bigfoot and one to observe at a safe, non-threatening distance if at all possible. His questionable hygiene and usual, disheveled attire of track pants and t-shirts reeked of bad news.

He didn't care. His appearance kept them at a distance, and Kirk made it a point not to interact with any of them unless he absolutely had no choice.

They… reminded him of things.

Of different times, long past.

The last two gulps of beer sloshed in the bottle as he drained them down. He dropped the empty bottle into his lap. His head sunk into the couch, coaxing him to stretch out for perhaps another nap. Just a minute between rounds. Blinking heavily, Kirk regarded the dark of the living room, focused on nothing. His eyelids eventually closed.

He felt himself slipping.

Deep forest.

A magical plume of breath on the air.

His muscles ached gloriously as his limbs worked in powerful arcs, racing across a hinterland drying from summer rain. The moon peeked through the branches above, eyeing his sprinting form with white malevolence. Blood was on the air, and the smell of musk. Of heat.

Her heat.

A howl eased through the midnight hour, but he paid it no heed. It was far off. Too far to make a difference, and he knew instinctively she wanted him and only him.

Not the others.

I'm not a monster.

The trail opened and he ran over the ground, keeping low, following the scent. The forest tipped as the path curved and twisted, through rocks and alongside streams that appeared like glacial flows of silver. Closer now.

She barked. Whined.

Ahead, through the trees, he could see her shape.

And she danced, growling, sounding like a machine...

Reality pulled him back, warping the dream in a waking stretch.

The phone buzzed on the coffee table, chasing a non-existent tail. A light the size of a pinhead winked on and off, insisting that Kirk answer it. Kirk didn't *want* to answer it. He felt that picking the cell phone up and bouncing it off a wall would be a better idea. Or just placing it on the floor and crushing it with a boot. Anything would be better than answering the thing. He hated the phone, despised the presence of the thing, especially when he was in his dreams.

But he had to have it.

The Elders made him take it. Ordered him to. Just in case.

One arm lay hooked behind his head like the twitchy half of a set of meaty rabbit ears, while the other, he realized, still held a well-used paperback of *20,000 Leagues Under the Sea*. The book he'd been reading before he fell asleep. An open case of Alexander Keith's Beer lay just beneath his hand, half its soldiers wiped out.

A fifth buzz and the little plastic slab continued to whine.

Kirk frowned, nudging the book where it rested on his chest.

A sixth.

Answering the device seemed to be a very bad idea. The insistence, the urgency of the whine reached out beyond the cell phone's frame, providing plenty of reason to blatantly ignore it. To hunker down and just keep on reading, and get pleasantly shitfaced while doing so.

Until sleep took him. Back to her.

He picked up on the eighth.

"Yeah," he snapped, grimacing, hating himself for giving in.

"We have trouble."

The voice set Kirk's backbone tingling as if someone had just stropped it with a straight razor. He recognized the voice. The brevity of it. His suspicions were correct the first time around. *Should never have picked up.* "What do I do?"

"Go to Halifax Airport. Check in with Porter's airline. There'll be a one-way ticket waiting for you. You're going to Newfoundland. Place called Upper Amherst Cove on the Bonavista peninsula. You do the job, call me, and there'll be a ticket to get back. Understood?"

"Yeah. What do I do there?" Kirk asked, forcing sobriety into his voice and hoping the person on the other end wouldn't detect anything off.

"You find an old dog by the name of Borland. You gut him."

That made Kirk blink.

"He was the local warden," the voice continued. "Now he's gone dark. One of the pack went up there just a month ago to do some hunting. Never came back. We sent the West Coast warden over there to find him, and to check in with Borland. Borland killed him just today. Thirty minutes ago, in fact. We called and he answered the warden's phone. Imagine our surprise. Freely admitted to killing both the hunter and the warden. Actually said he was declaring war. We don't know why, except that he's one of the oldest. Probably the oldest of us *all* out east. Might have gone crazy."

"Crazy?"

"We believe he's gone crazy. Dementia. Alzheimer's."

That slap of cold information made Kirk balk. He sat up, sober in the eye of the storm. "You're kidding. We... we can go *crazy*?"

"Blame it on something in the water, the food, the hole in the ozone layer, whatever. It happens. Rarely, but it happens. And it's happened on the Rock. Easiest explanation. Regardless, we can't have him running wild over there. There *are* people over there. You understand?"

"Yeah." Kirk pinched the bridge of his nose. "Yeah."

"We're sending you over there with Morris."

Well, shit. And that chill rushed up his spine again, like fingers swishing piano keys in a violent flourish. He knew better than to say anything, but he did anyway. "Why two of us?"

"Borland's already killed two, including a warden from the West Coast. He's dangerous."

"How old is he?"

"Old," the voice stressed. "Never mind exactly how old. You just keep in mind he's murdered two who were much, much younger than him. He put them down and *laughed* about it. Laughed right in my ear. He might be old, but he's *dangerous.* You heed that, and you kill him."

Christ, Kirk thought. Right into the fire. "When do I go?"

"As soon as we're done here. And Kirk…"

"Yeah?"

"Make no mistake. You're going over there to hunt down and bleed an old fuck dead. Don't you care one goddamn about how old he is. Or what's he's done. He gets no respect. And don't dare show any mercy. The lines have been drawn on this one. Understand?"

With the phone to his ear, Kirk nodded. "Yeah."

6

Not one for dawdling, Borland gripped Blackbeard by his ankle and pulled him towards the door, smearing the dark elegance of the blood pooled on the floor. Borland retracted his fangs and claws, felt his wereblood ebbing, but he figured he'd have just enough strength to get the body out back. It took energy to force the change and to maintain it. The speed of the change, essentially channeling it where it mattered the most, was his secret weapon. Ordinarily a young wolf had no control over the transformation, like a human baby having no control over its bowel movements. When the moon was full, the *Were* changed, regardless of when or where. He changed. But as time went on, the change *could* be controlled, even delayed a bit on the nights when the moon blazed, and initiated even on nights when there was no moon. A complete change still took time, at most three minutes if one let himself go. Three minutes, Borland had learned long ago, was a long time if one were rushed or pressed. It could mean the difference between life and death. He realized one didn't really need to go full wolf if their life was at risk, and over time, he learned to morph his body in the places where needed, *when* needed. Claws. Fangs. Strength and speed. The final form of the wolf was the purest, the pinnacle of the gift, and nothing felt finer than running through a forest at midnight, with the path lit up by the moon. Nothing could compare to the natural high of being in that state. Borland dreaded never being able to feel that rush again, even after dying. But the *half* form, the 'quick draw' of the change which he could unleash in a very shocking second, was his secret weapon.

In an honorable world, a sane world, two *Weres* would fight *after* their change. In Borland's, his fight started with a hard, unexpected knee to the balls. Honor meant nothing to the dead. And in the coming days, the approaching battle, he would utilize all the tricks of an age to survive.

The door swung open with a click and whine and Borland dragged his victim outside. The cold enveloped him. He should've stopped to gather up his coat, he knew, and cursed because of it. The cold made him yank on his victim in spite. Blackbeard lurched forward and stopped. The dangling leg caught the edge of the doorframe, clogging the entryway with a bunched-up torso and almost toppling Borland with the abrupt halt.

"Y'disagreeable little shit." He jerked the leg hard enough that the body banged against the wood.

"C'mon," he urged, annoyance in his voice, but the body would not right itself of its own accord. "Goddamn little *bitch*."

He bent over the dead form, savagely angry at having to make the extra effort. His back threatened to snap as he gripped the offending leg. A short shake freed the corpse and Borland wrenched it through with a pissed-off grunt. Blackbeard's head bumped off the two steps of the front porch like a bowling ball. Snow speckled his ruined face and eye. Borland didn't pity the dead. Law of the land was kill or be killed, in the wild or in civilization. One had to be on guard at all times. To think that the Elders kept sending in one young fuck at a time to put him down galled the hell out of him. Snarling, Borland bared his old teeth to the freezing breeze. White spattered his face and beard as he pulled the corpse along the partially dug trench, towards his old store.

Already he could hear the dogs. Both furious and scared shitless to be kept within that wooden, single-story bunker of a building. The store he nailed together years ago with no help from a damn soul. The dogs he had gathered more recently.

Above the door hung another imposing set of moose antlers. A piece of wood in the shape of an old-fashioned bed's headboard, nailed through the center, kept the front door of the weathered storage structure closed. Borland gripped this dwarfed Napoleon's hat and twisted it, allowing the heavy slab of wood to be pulled open by a strip of cold-stiffened leather.

The barking intensified.

"Shaddup," Borland yapped back. The lifeless weight at the end of his arm dragged on him, and he jerked the carcass over the three steps. The head rattled across the threshold.

The gray light from the open door and pallid beams illuminated the interior as Borland trudged into this cavern of canine terror, hauling his victim behind him. Crude holding pens constructed of thick planks and chicken wire ran the length of the building on either side. Jaws snapped behind the lattices. Some pulled the mesh inwards. Claws poked and rasped. Growls and howls marred into an unnerving screech of something not yet realized, but suspected. Borland's shadow darkened the caged animals as he passed, infuriating them more. A black-and-orange Rottweiler eyed him with a killer's reproach. A trio of white Shih Tzus bounced in their pens like angry popcorn. A Golden Retriever sang piteously as if staked to the floor. A Siberian Husky flashed teeth and gnawed at the wire, its eyes a haunting ice blue. A whooping cough of a bark erupted from a Bull Terrier as Borland shuffled by, making him stop in his tracks for a moment and turn on them all. He released a flash of the *Were*, and snarled at his captives with his elongated teeth.

The entire pack broke into whines, cowered by a single blast.

Curs, Borland thought with disgusted anger. Nothing but curs. But they were *his* curs, and he would impose his warlike will upon them. Blackbeard's fingers grazed the wired doors of the pens. Noses came forth fearfully, if not a touch eagerly, sniffing at the tips. Borland knew it was the smell of blood, remembered from the last victim he'd cut up in back. Dogs weren't finicky eaters, but if hungry enough, if *starved*, they'd eat damn near anything.

These dogs had been starved. And fed. Fed a rarity in delicacies, a dish no one would ever *consider* feeding them. A feast derived from dark sorcerous arts only recently discovered.

They had eaten the flesh of a dead *Were*.

And they were more than ready to dine once again.

With some effort, Borland finished dragging Blackbeard to the back of the store, onto a wide wooden pallet laid on top of the bare floor. Hateful eyes bore into his back and Borland turned to lock eyes with a German Shepherd, locked away in his prison. That great brute didn't flinch. Didn't break away.

A fanged smile lit Borland's face. "No fear in ye, though, eh?" he hissed. "Not like dese others."

A faint rumble from the Shepherd's throat. A twitch of black lips. What were usually soft, brown eyes now glinted dark thoughts.

Tough, Borland recognized. This one was the most recent addition to his collection, and probably the last.

"Too bad," he sneered and showed the animal his back.

The other dogs started to bark once again. Borland ignored them and took down a sharp, curved knife—a fisherman's filleting tool. The wooden grip felt fine in his palm, and for a moment, he made the blade dance in his hand, flipping it up, down and over with the confidence of a knife fighter. Of all the hand tools known to man, knives were the most frightening, the most chilling, and Borland knew how to handle it well.

A tickle hitched in his throat and choked off his thoughts. He bent over, barking at the floor. When the coughing fit subsided, he wiped his mouth with a sick moan. Yellow-green butter straight from his guts coated his hand. Specks of blood spotted the sample and Borland studied it for only a moment before smearing if off on a leg. He winked at the Shepherd.

"Not finished yet, brudder. Not I. Make no mistake."

Borland turned to Blackbeard. Within the next minute, he cut though the outer clothing and stripped everything off the corpse, paying no heed to the hairy, pallid flesh being uncovered. This was the easy part. The *clean* part. Borland gathered up the shreds of clothing and tossed them into a corner, which he would later use to soak up the remainder of the blood and burn in a stove. Leaving the naked man on the pallet, Borland rolled over a thick junk of birch wood, used for chopping up smaller chunks. Next, he spun about, flipped the lid of a trunk, and produced a compact chainsaw, which would be for the torso. But he wanted to punish Blackbeard a bit first. Rubbing his jowls, Borland reached to the rafters and pulled down a hand axe. He had a chainsaw for the heavier bits but there was something… *personal,* and oddly satisfying, about hacking up a body with an axe.

The last thing he did was pull on a full-length, clear plastic coat which covered him from head to foot, as well as a helmet with a clear, plastic mask. He didn't bother with gloves. This, he wanted to feel.

Borland released another shot of wereblood as he grabbed the ankle of his victim, empowering him to manhandle the limb across the chopping block of wood.

Borland met the Shepherd's hateful eye, only for a moment, before the axe came down and chomped into the ankle. The foot jumped into the air and rattled dumbly off the pallet. Gore splashed planks with rotted knots. Borland worked efficiently, humming to himself at times, and when he'd removed the arms and legs, he dropped the spattered axe to the floor and took up the chainsaw. It screamed to life with one tug on its rip cord, and the dogs howled at its song. Borland hooted back and dug into the head and torso of Blackbeard, who wasn't looking so healthy anymore. The chainsaw smoked, whined, and bubbled. Blood spritzed the old man's plastic coat and mask in ghastly designs as his hands turned a ghoulish red.

Once done with the cutting, Borland dropped the saw and took a deep, mind-clearing whiff of the lingering gasoline smoke. Then he went to work with the knife once more, parting fat and flesh from muscle, removing the organs and guts which he'd later burn outside in a fire. With almost revered satisfaction, he cut out the heart of the ravaged man, and held the dark muscle up to the Shepherd, who finally looked away with a sad whimper.

Borland flipped his visor. He held the meat up to his face, opening his fanged maw and wheezing with feral delight.

"Dis part's *mine*," Borland declared in a vibrating voice as he plopped the delicacy onto a nearby porcelain plate.

The rest of the body he cut into thin steaks, enough for all. He was almost high from the stench of meat and blood.

"Now den," he announced to the waiting dogs when all was done. "Who eats first?"

The store exploded with sound.

Minutes later, after feeding his dogs, Borland faced the cage of the Shepherd. The animal had refused to eat the last time, clearly possessing a stubborn streak. But now it was weak. Ready to be turned. He summoned the wereblood again. It shot through him like a jolt of nitrous oxide, punching the breath from him as the power ripped up the length of his spine, close to splitting. Years ago his body had no difficulty handling this surge of power, but now, even though he needed it and still relished it, a dangerous feeling accompanied each shot when he allowed it to flow, as if something, somewhere might burst from the pressure. His old bones could barely take it anymore.

Fuck it, Borland thought blackly, stubbornly daring something to rupture. He'd go to hell swearing his last breath on it.

Standing before the cage of the Shepherd, Borland basked in the burn, feeling blood-gorged arteries and veins as thick as cables bulge and protrude in his neck and wrists, feeling the growing pressure energizing and *expanding* him.

The trapped dog whined and pressed itself against the back of the cage, searching for escape, brown eyes no longer defiant.

Controlling his change, Borland opened the door with a hand that ended in claws. He flashed a toothy grin at the dog and grabbed it by its leather collar. With a terrified yelp, the Shepherd came free of its cage and Borland held it high, easily, with one arm. The dog kicked and thrashed, cursing the man-thing and raking talons over his plastic coat, but Borland held it up like a fisherman showing off a trophy catch. When he grew tired of the game, he grabbed a foreleg, stretched it out like a chicken's wing, and bit into it. He sank his fangs into the meat of the animal, his mouth salivating in a gush.

The Shepherd wailed in pain, kicked weakly, writhed.

With a roar, Borland threw the near unconscious dog back into its cage. He heaved in a human steak before slamming the door shut. The meat hit the dog in the ribs and it yelped at the contact as if poisoned.

In a sense, it had been.

"Have a taste!" Borland commanded. He locked the cage, lapping at the juices on his lips. The dog found its balls and glared. A saucy look didn't bother Borland. The animal would see his way soon enough. They all did in the end.

Having done that, he paused and listened to his other captives as they fed.

The smile creeping across his face dripped blood.

7

The automated doors of the Halifax International Airport opened with a gasp, flooding the interior with winter air and causing the crowd nearby to shiver. A couple of late afternoon travelers looked to see who was coming in from the outside and saw a dark figure, ominous against the smoking tailpipe of a disappearing taxi. Free falling snow, thick and stomach-turning, coated almost everything except the concrete, completing the illusion of a near-white canvas.

The trapped heat stamped Kirk's face and made him feel uncomfortable. He much preferred the cold to the multi-level oven of an airport. Carrying his small, black suitcase, he proceeded inside and stopped far enough from the sensor to allow the outside doors to roll shut behind him.

The smell hit him like a freight train jumping its tracks.

It engulfed his hypersensitive sense of smell, stopping him cold, forcing him to reach inside a pocket and get out a facecloth. This he slapped over his nose and mouth and held there, though it didn't really help much. The cab had been bad enough with the driver reeking of lunchtime chicken and swine assholes, but *this*... Kirk took a breath and winced. This was olfactory hell. Some people eyed him, bored, while waiting for their time to check in and completely heedless as to how badly they offended his nose with their pissy perfumes and carbonated colognes, coffee breath and all-round rude body odor. Some travelers stood with designer coffee cups and smartphones, oblivious to everything except a glowing screen, idly multi-tasking as they sipped and fingered. Some of the more forward-thinking ones checked in with the automated terminals and nonchalantly punched in codes like quick drawing gunslingers firing from the hip. A pair of young women dressed in t-shirts and stylish pants—unfit for the winter–-cackled excitedly about their upcoming cruise. One of them was on her period. A man dressed in a sharp black suit complete with overcoat sneezed loud enough to draw stares, and Kirk knew there would be people complaining about him on their flight. An obese man protested loudly about being bumped from a flight to an airline representative. Another younger, varsity type guy was trying to jam a carry-on bag into a bin two sizes too small, arguing that the airline allowed him to take the same bag on board last time.

People.

In all their shapes, sizes, smells and attitudes.

Kirk fucking *despised* gathering places like the airport.

Glowering with the facecloth firmly in place, Kirk stomped his hiker boots clean of slush and moved through the masses. Outside, thick clumps of snow flecked the large windows looking out onto the parking garage, while storm clouds blotted out the sky, almost completely obscuring the view. Right season. Angry weather. Furious planet.

Kirk had packed light: just a single change of clothes. He wore a winter denim coat ringed with a thick, white-furred collar. A black stocking cap covered his head. Bright signs of the corporate carriers lay on his right, one right after the other. When he found his airline's check-in desk and saw the dismal length of people waiting in front of it, he sighed and got in line. The middle-age man in front of him had to be coated in a near-nauseating deodorant, and he couldn't help patting his fingers at his bald spot and the feeble comb-over. It surprised Kirk to see it in this age, where head shaving was so much more accepted. A carry-on bag lay at one side of the guy's ankles while a pink plastic carrying cage was on the other. An unhappy looking cat stood behind a metal grate, fearfully studying Kirk, as if it knew exactly who he was and feared for its life.

Great, Kirk thought, eyeing the little furry bastard in return. The animal started to whine as if a blow torch had been applied to its puckered ass. Cats instinctively knew him, hated him. The owner glanced down at the cage and nudged it with his foot, eliciting an indignant feline squeal. When the line moved ahead, Kirk gave it some slack, wanting to keep a gap between him and the cat.

"What's up with you, huh?" the owner muttered, stooping to check on the animal. "What's going on, buddy? You okay? Huh, you okay, buddy?"

Kirk could almost taste bile bubbling at the back of his throat. Cats weren't anyone's *buddy*. Still, he managed to keep his composure for the thirty minutes it took to check into the airline, enduring it all: the sights, the sounds, the monotony, and especially the *smells*. His stomach protested with a nauseous warning, but he avoided a scene.

When the cat's owner checked in, the airline official lifted the traveling cage and plopped it on the conveyor belt, getting a panicked *raow* out of the little feline fuck. It made Kirk feel a little better.

As promised, a business-class ticket waited for him. And Kirk curtly answered all the check-in person's questions.

"How many bags?" the uniformed man asked. "Just the one?"

Kirk nodded.

"Place it on the belt, please."

He complied, thinking about the silver-bladed Bowie secured in the bag. Kirk had gotten a handmade, wooden carrying case, the length of a custom pool cue, to transport the weapon anytime he had to go through security checkpoints, not that he had to go through a lot of them.

Just having the blade in the bottom of the plane in a box satisfied any sniffing security types.

"I'm sorry, sir, but it looks like your flight's been delayed due to the snowstorm."

"Snowstorm," Kirk repeated and rolled his eyes. He glanced over his shoulder, through the thick runnels of people behind him, glimpsing a spattered window beyond, and groaned inwardly. *Weather.* He took the proffered boarding pass from the guy. A bad feeling twisted his guts as he walked to the glass keeping the storm at bay and overlooking the parking lot. It had snowed steadily as he took his taxi in, and he'd heard about the charging storm front on the radio, but at no time did he think the flight would be delayed. The weather would have to be truly wicked. After a second, he decided he might as well get comfortable somewhere.

Deserted seats lined a section of wall well away from the food courts and souvenir shops. Kirk sat down on one end, placing his back to the broad wall of brick and windows, and then bent over as if he were atop his porcelain throne at home. He killed time by inspecting his hands, the floor, and the gathering weather beyond the thick panes of glass. The people he ignored, even when they parked themselves on nearby chairs for moments before moving. And while the airport steadily filled with delayed travelers, not one sat directly next to the large outdoorsman type with the thick untrimmed beard and the polar bear hide collar. There was a wildness lurking there, a primal aura which no one could endure at length or felt brave enough to challenge.

The sky darkened. Night slid in, cold and blowing. Kirk twisted around, one leg up on the next chair, and gazed sullenly out at the weather.

Something kicked the toe of his boot.

Kirk glanced up and met the sullen glare of Morris, the neck of a black Special Forces sweater disappearing under a beard that made his own look like a soggy duster.

"Moses," Kirk greeted warily.

The black-eyed glare deepened. "Hey. Don't fuckin' call me that. Told you last time."

"Last time was how many years ago?"

"Don't remember. But I remember tellin' you then and I'm tellin' you now."

Kirk set his jaw and glanced back at the deepening night.

Morris took that as an invitation, so he lowered himself onto a seat three over from the smaller man. *Moses Morris.* Kirk sensed the deep woods monster behind him and remembered their first meeting ten or twelve years back. A frame heavily corded with muscle. Short, black hair and a wild shovel of a beard, all edged with silver. From what Kirk noticed a second ago, the brute still wore the same clothes he'd picked up at an army discount shop… except for the leather trench coat. Kirk had no idea where he'd gotten that. Wasn't interested in asking him. Wardens weren't the most sociable of the order. None of them were, really. But not only did Moses embody the brooding "don't touch," ass-kicking type, he *oozed* intimidation like bear spray and bad cologne. Even though Kirk had his back to him, he still *felt* the leather-clad Sasquatch back there, and wasn't happy about it in the least. It was hard to relax when a fucking ogre planted himself only an arm's length away.

The Halifax County native didn't fear much, but Morris made him uneasy. He had to admit however, if there ever was a monster Kirk *had* to have along with him on a killing, it was Moses Morris.

Killing.

The word stuck in his craw like a stubborn chicken bone. Ordinarily he did as he was told, but he didn't like the idea of retiring a warden past his prime in unknown territory. The fact that the old man had already killed two of the order wasn't lost on him, either. Could Borland have really gone crazy?

"Whattaya think about it all?" Morris rumbled from behind. Kirk took a moment to realize the ogre had actually spoken. He half-turned around.

"About what?"

"Strawberry picking under the goddamn arctic sun. The fuck you think about what?"

Kirk exhaled, checking his own temper. "You think here's a good place to talk?"

"I'll talk where I fuckin' want."

"We're in a fuckin' airport. Amongst—" Kirk dipped his head at the masses of people in motion.

Morris flexed his jaw as if tonguing gristle out from between his teeth. “They got better things going on.”

Kirk took a few seconds to process this.

“So?”

“So what?” Kirk asked.

“Whattaya think about it all? Jesus,” he grated and shook his head.

Kirk didn’t take kindly to shit. Especially attitude shit from a warden based out in Pictou County. “Hey, you muzzle that shit or you can be damn certain I’ll make calls when this is all over. Damn straight someone’ll be interested how you are on a job.”

Morris didn’t answer right away.

“They know,” he eventually muttered, his words as thick and final as flowing cement. “D’Christ you think I’m here? Though I wonder why you’re here. Regardless, we’re… we’re the fuckin’ back-up in this story. Reinforcements. Power sanders authorized to smooth things out. That’s what I think.”

Kirk thought that, too. “Yeah.”

Morris didn’t say anything more, which left Kirk in a bad mood. *Fucking Moses Morris.* He didn’t need this shit. Didn’t need Morris. It was why wardens operated alone, to avoid the power struggle between two or more pack leaders attempting to establish dominance over the other. Morris exuded hard ass with every click of his motorcycle boots. Kirk sighed. The Elders were sending over a scalpel and a sledgehammer and neither respected the other’s mode of operation. Kirk turned back and stared off into the storm, trying not to ponder too hard about the task given to them both. His feelings were too conflicted on the matter.

They sat and stewed in the airport, hearing droidish announcements overhead. The falling snow drew Kirk's attention, mesmerizing him, infusing him with a longing to be anywhere else.

People moved in a peripheral blur.

Morris sat behind him, breathing like a cast iron furnace about to explode.

8

Snow fell quietly in the dark. A light flurry, really, but Borland sensed it was only Mother Nature biding her time. The old girl was gathering her strength, brewing her storm so that when the time finally came to dish it, more than a few meteorologists would freak out. Not Borland. Storm weather relaxed him. He remembered coming from Ireland, crossing the Atlantic in the summer of 1792, on a merchant marine filled with young Irish Catholics traveling towards a new life on the island. Two storms pummeled the ship during that three-week voyage. Borland had been much younger then, full of piss and vinegar, eager for bloody hunts under new moons. While most of the travelers suffered during the stormy weather, Borland tied himself down and enjoyed the ride, screaming insanely through ferocious dips and rises as the ship rode out mountainous swells.

Memories. He was different now. Older. Had more battle scars across his back and balls than a pack of pit bulls bred for fighting in underground parking lots. But he still looked forward to the storms of most seasons (though admittedly, not so much the winter anymore) as they reminded him of that initial crossing.

Borland sat at his table and reminisced by lamplight. To fill the silence, he growled out low, vengeful bars of *"We'll Rant and We'll Roar"* while he cleaned a twelve-gauge shotgun, relishing the smell of the oil he used. It was an old, close-range weapon, with a worn walnut stock and smooth sliding pump. The gun metal in between the wood gleamed black, showing off fine scratches. He'd bought the shotgun from an old fisherman and, over the years, took the time to modify the firearm as he saw fit. He'd sawed off both ends, shortening the barrel and the stock, and smoothed the rough edges with sandpaper. Then the plug came out, expanding the gun's ammunition capacity from three shells to five.

When he finished with the cleaning, he pieced the weapon back together with the care and patience of a man handling something with great respect. He placed it across his lap and reached for a box of ammunition, feeding the firearm one shell at a time until full. When he finished loading the shotgun, he held it with both hands and admired its lines.

The Elders would scoff at him for owning the cannon. It was beneath them. No *Were* would ever use one. The Elders decreed such weapons unclean and passed their contempt unto the younger ones. Not Borland. He enjoyed the weight, the promise of destruction, and the visual menace of the shotgun. But mostly, he used it because the Elders said not to. And it would be a cruel surprise for any warden coming through his front door.

A tickle in his throat got him coughing, light at first, then hard. He pressed the shotgun into his lap and bent over it, emptying the bile from within his gut. Speckles of fluid burst from his lips with every barrage. The fit subsided, and he wiped his mouth with a shaky hand. He reached for the glass of whiskey he'd poured earlier, and gulped down a mouthful as if it were cold tea. Composing himself, he placed the weapon on the table and stared at the windows of his cabin. He went over a mental checklist. After he'd fed the dogs, he'd reverted back to human form and lugged wooden planks inside the cabin. In the morning, he intended to nail them over the windows, bolstering the defenses of the cabin. A sinister smile spread across his harsh features. It wasn't the only thing he had planned.

Tomorrow night. He'd fire his salvo off tomorrow night, right in Upper Amherst Cove, and wake the world.

A feeling of closure overcame him then, and he held his glass of whiskey in a soft, considering grip. Old he'd become, and many things he'd seen in his years, to all come down to… this. Slaughtering his own kind. Walter Borland didn't regret that. He was never one to back down from a fight. Besides, the Elders had fired first. The memory of the first killer to come for him shimmered in his head. Same story as Blackbeard, just a guy looking to do some hunting. Borland had smelled the lie before it was even on the air, and had killed the young shit pretty much the same way. Had to turn his back to get the youngster to draw, but he'd seen the flash of silver in the dark mirror of his cabin window, had heard the rustling of cloth, and had put the pup down.

Borland blamed it on change. Changing times. And he wasn't willing to change with them. Threw it all back into the faces of the Elders who weren't wise enough to leave him alone.

But that was only part of it, Borland admitted, though he'd never say it aloud. Not even to the walls surrounding him.

Things had become… strange.

Little things, that crept up on him with the years. Thoughts of slaughter, and of harvest, going back to the old days, when they'd all come over on the boats—not only from Ireland, but from England and Scotland as well. No rules existed then. No order. Not for *Weres*. One only had to be careful. He had been but a boy then. A full grown man, but a boy in the ways of the *Were*.

Then in the early 1900s, the Elders decided that change was necessary and brought laws into effect to preserve the secrecy of their existence and to protect the human herds as well. Observing the new ways had been a struggle for Borland. Having to move every twenty years to avoid questions, to avoid suspicion. *Weres* aged slower than regular folks and in his time, he figured he had done perhaps a near dozen tours of the island, living in areas the farthest from the last to avoid any awkward meetings.

Switching places with the other traveling wardens at times. Outliving the humans until none remembered him the next time he walked into town.

Until now. Now he was through with moving. Knew it in his bones. Knew that the Elders would try and put him down when he refused. They couldn't have one old hound go against the grain, go against their law.

Of all the island, he liked this cove best.

Borland sucked in a quiet, reflective moment of melancholy, remembering that his time on this earth was nearly done, of the wild hunts over hills and valleys awash in moonglow. The savage taking of lives.

Nearly done.

The wind picked up, sprinkling the window with snow. Flames flashed brightly behind the grilled mouth of the potbellied stove, its heat throwing back the cold and making the cabin creak. He loved this old place. He supposed if he was going to perish on this earth, it made him content to know he got to choose where, and on what terms.

The lamplight dimmed.

Borland considered it for several long seconds, fragments of time never to be had again, but he wouldn't dare spend them any other way. Then he took his leave and decided to head to bed early. Get a good night's sleep. Tomorrow, he'd finish his work.

And unleash hell.

*

In their cages of wire and wood, the dogs slept in trembling curls of fur and bones, burying their noses under their tails. Some whimpered with nightmares, others shivered in dreamless pits of black.

The German Shepherd lay awake with his nose between his paws, eyes bright in the dark. Every tiny movement placed him a little more on edge, but he didn't give in to fear yet. The rumbling of his stomach made him dread eating what was thrown at him, for he knew he shouldn't have, even as he relented and devoured the meat. The prison stunk with their waste, as the old man-thing didn't clean the cages, ever.

His given name was Maximilian, or just Max. He belonged to a lovely lady right in Upper Amherst Cove. He didn't know where he was, but the last thing he remembered was being let outside for a quick piss and eating some meat that smelled strange. Then he was here, in the forever cold and sometimes dark, without his chew toys. The others had been here much longer, and most of their minds seemed gone. The old man-thing had collected all shapes and sizes in his cages, and while Max had once thought he'd seen most of his kind, it was obvious that he had not. There were dangerous-looking dogs held here, bred for strength and intellect, as well as the half-breed mongrels grown wild. Ones with oddly-pointed skulls and narrow eyes, and great dogs with airs of dignified melancholy. All kept in cages barely large enough to move in. The little ones, one cage to his right, constantly barked and jumped and seemed the farthest gone. Max felt a distinct evil emanating from them, a swelling desire to hurt people. Or any other animal for that matter.

A rumbling across the way cocked the Shepherd's ears upward. He recognized the dog by its voice alone. Even in the cages as they all were, one had already established himself as leader. With a coat of black and orange, the leader wasn't as big as Max, but size wasn't that great of an advantage. The Rottweiler growled again, warning the Shepherd to look someplace else, informing him that, if necessary, if the leader *had* to, he'd shred the wire of both their cages. And rip the dog's throat out.

Max glanced away, but it wasn't from fear. He didn't fear the leader. But he did fear what he'd eaten.

And the evil growing inside him.

9

The plane touched down in St. John's airport a little after midnight, but Kirk had trouble believing they were actually on the ground. The flight had been a sleepless hell. Trapped scents consisting of quietly released gas, bad breath, and overpowering perfumes and colognes. Somewhere halfway over the Atlantic, one stupid bastard, who had drunk too much before boarding, got sick and puked while fumbling to open his barf bag. The vomiting occurred near the rear of the plane, maybe thirty rows away from business class, where both Kirk and Morris sat, but with their heightened senses of smell, it might as well have happened right in their laps. In his seat across the aisle, Morris appeared ready to explode, testing his armrests with death grips.

Kirk didn't know how he had made it himself. Twenty-five minutes earlier, when he'd looked out his window to see the old city, all he'd seen were the flickering lights of the aircraft's wings bathed in clouds. The captain had come on shortly afterwards, explaining that the cloud cover was low and the snow intensifying, but they would attempt landing anyway. He hadn't mentioned the turbulence until the first solid dip that had Kirk tightening his seatbelt.

The pair of wardens led a sluggish stream of disembarking passengers. Both men were bone weary and didn't bother speaking to each other. The arrival terminal glowed with a fluorescent sterility, causing them to squint against the glare. It took another twenty minutes to retrieve their bags, during which both kept quiet and lingered near the back of the assembled crowds. A few people glanced their way, but furtively, fearfully. Kirk knew he looked hard, but Morris was something dredged up from a charred pipeline. The bright lights of the luggage area only jacked up his intimidation level all the more. The way he looked, the cops could arrest the guy on suspicion of murder based on his appearance alone.

Morris got his bag first, a small overnight deal with a padlock on one zippered end, and sauntered sleepily towards the sliding exit doors. Kirk fumed at his companion, partially because he wanted to be the first out of the airport, and because he didn't want to look like he was chasing after Morris's heels.

Five minutes later, Kirk retrieved his own bag and plodded out the door. Underneath the glare of a streetlight stood Morris, breathing in air tainted with exhaust. A line of cabs idled not ten feet away. Snow fell in a thickening sheet, misting the light.

"You get a cab?" Kirk asked, stopping beside him.

"Nope."

Kirk dispensed with airs and glared at Morris. "Why the hell not?"

Morris took his time answering. In fact, Kirk was a split second from marching to one of the waiting cabs when he heard, "Roads are bad. I talked to a driver. No one's heading out to Amherst Cove at this hour."

"What?" Kirk's jaw dropped, mortified.

"In the morning we can get a shared van with eight other people, or we can pay the one-fifty and ride in on our own."

"So what do we do now?"

"Two choices. Sleep here in the airport until morning, or burn through more of our cash and get a hotel room."

"You'll not find a room in d'city this night, sirs," spoke a voice with just a dash of Irish brogue. Both men turned to see a figure hopping up onto the snow-slick walkway. Short, barrel shaped, with a walrus mustache and a blue winter's coat that looked inflated. "Me buddies were just after ferrying a few folks around. She's all booked up. After telling some other people the same thing now, and they're staying here until morning. Seein' if the weather improves any. Surprised the b'ys didn't mention it to ye."

Morris ignored the cabbie. Kirk didn't feel like talking to him either. Sensing dismissal, the driver waved his hand and paced beside his vehicle as if on guard duty.

"We could rent a car," Kirk suggested.

"Nar car to be had at this hour, my son," the cabbie stated with a defiant shake of his head.

"In the morning then."

"Youse's headin' out to Bonavista, right?" the cabbie asked.

Both Morris and Kirk looked in his direction.

"Trouble is, see, there's a storm headin' this way. Big bastard, too. *Big*. Callin' it a 'blizzard for the ages.' Hundred kilometer winds. Temperature around minus fifteen Celsius. Some forecasters say close to forty centimeters o' snow. *Forty* centimeters! It's ravaging Nova Scotia even as I breathe 'afore ye both. This last flight, the one you were on, skirted the edge of that beast and got you here, but you'll have front row seats for the next one. The monster's moving this way. Be here by tomorrow afternoon and it's three hours plus to Bonavista in *good* weather. Yer lookin' at four or five hours in slop like that. And somethin' else I'll tell ye—no driver from St. John's is gonna want to go out there and get trapped. Nosir. Rent a car, sure, but only if you can get one, and I've heard they're all gone, but don't quote me on that. Yer best bet is t'camp out here, get up in the mornin' and get to the local cab headin' out that way. There's a number at the help desk. You give 'em a call tomorrow. Think the b'y's name is Perry. He has a house out that way and once he makes his run outta town he won't be back in until the roads are cleared, and Lord only knows when that could be. They say forty centimeters but t'won't surprise if'n there's fifty that comes down. *Fifty!* Take more than a few plows to clear that shit up!"

Kirk glanced at Morris's stoic features. "Whattaya think?"

Morris didn't answer, clearly not liking the choices.

"I knows what yer thinkin'," the cabbie went on. "But, you go ahead and ask the b'ys around here. You ask 'em. No one's heading out that way tonight or tomorrow and I'll be surprised if anyone heads that way the day after. Yer best bet—" at this, the old cabbie leaned in, glanced about furtively, and whispered "—get yerself a hotel somewhere for the night. Within walkin' distance of George's Street. That place's tons of fun."

With message delivered, the cabbie nodded and winked as if he'd just done them both a favor, and resumed pacing alongside his car.

Fuming against the cold night, Kirk about-faced and went back inside the near-deserted airport. He walked away from the arrival area, boots clicking on tiles awash in a fluorescent glow, and quickly spotted, of all things, a pair of wine-colored vinyl sofa chairs with their backs facing a broad bank of windows. Kirk made a beeline towards the chairs, picked the most comfortable one, dropped his small suitcase beside it and plopped down. It wasn't a bed, but it would do until morning.

Pulling his stocking cap over his eyes, Kirk unbuttoned his denim coat, slid down in the chair, and propped his feet up on a coffee table. A long sigh blew out his nose, and he noticed that the airport didn't smell as bad as the

Halifax terminal. Probably because it was damn near empty. He gave thanks for that little gift.

Boots thumped along the floor, getting closer. A crash of luggage. Vinyl squeaked as a great weight descended upon it. Another sigh, followed by two great intakes of air. Morris.

"So what do you know about this job?" Morris asked in a weary voice.

Kirk exhaled. "Didn't we already talk about this?"

"I did. You didn't."

"We're in yet another public place."

"No one's around."

"We're *in* a fuckin' airport."

"Take a sniff and tell me who's around then."

Kirk scowled and pushed his cap up. Morris was correct on that point, but he waited before answering, making it seem as though he weren't in the least impressed, or worried, about his warden companion.

"What do *you* know about this job?" Kirk countered.

This time, Morris took *his* time answering, and round and round they went. The aggravating unspoken shit of laying down who was the baddest and the maddest without coming to blows. No pack had two leaders, but that's exactly what the Elders had done in this situation—placed a pair of alpha males together. What was worse, they had placed Kirk with *Morris*.

"Like I said over in Halifax. Know that… it must be bad," Morris rumbled in thought. "To send both of us out here. We're fixers."

"Uh-huh."

"Heard Borland cracked up over here. Stopped listenin' to the Elders. Killed two of ours."

"Heard that myself." Kirk closed his eyes and got comfortable once again.

"What do you think?"

"About what?"

"Him goin' dark."

That made Kirk pause. "Good question."

"Open yer eyes before I slap you somethin' fierce."

Screwing up one corner of his mouth, Kirk complied, but didn't rush. "He killed two of ours. Now, we do what we came here to do."

Morris went silent. "Don't like it."

"What're you sayin'?"

"Just sayin' I don't like it."

"You think I do?"

"Why you gotta keep doin' that?"

"Doin' what?" Kirk looked at him.

"Answerin' my questions with questions."

Round and round, the thought flashed in Kirk's head. This wasn't going to work. They were going be at each other's throats before they even got to Amherst Cove. "Gettin' clarification is all."

"Maybe my boot print on your ass will clarify things."

Here it comes.

"Hey," Kirk said in a tone of deep ice. "You secure that shit. Right now. The Elders got us together to do this, and I don't wanna haveta worry about you while goin' after

Borland. We work as equals on this or not at all. And you can bet they'll know what happened if it's *you* who calls them and not me."

"You sayin' I can't talk to the Elders?"

"No, I'm... look. We work as partners on this. You watch my back, and I'll watch yours. Clear?"

Morris gave it a good thinking, his threatening features contorting. When he gave his answer, it was a sullen nod. Kirk returned it, wondering if things were actually better or had just gotten worse.

"He knows we're comin'," Morris stated quietly.

"You don't know that."

The *Were's* eyes focused on Kirk with mocking light. "You think he doesn't think we're comin'? Christ. Expected better from you, *Halifax*."

Kirk bit back his first reply, and thought about what Morris had just said. A warm rush of dread welled up inside him. Morris was right. The old bastard had already killed two of their kind. Crazy or not, there were repercussions to that kind of blood being spilled. The first time might've been an accident. Not likely, but possible. But not the second time. Borland knew the law of the land. Knew the Elders would send someone else after him––would *keep* sending someone after him.

Until he was dead.

"You're right," Kirk admitted, granting Morris the moment. To his surprise, the big man didn't gloat. "He knows we're comin'. But I bet you one thing."

"What's that?"

"I bet he's not expectin' two of us. Maybe one, but not two."

That silenced Morris, as he digested Kirk's opinion on the matter. Then, almost begrudgingly, he nodded.

Kirk felt the reasoning flow into the man's overheated brain. "You're right, though. He knows *someone* is comin' for him. And he knows the price. For doing what he did. And even worse…"

"He's got time to get ready," Morris finished. He regarded Kirk with dangerous eyes.

"He's got time to get ready," Kirk agreed.

And felt the unease sink in.

Sleep didn't take Kirk easily. Even with the minor improvement in the air quality, and the absence of people and cats. The chair fought with him, making it difficult to get comfortable, and he had a natural aversion to sleeping while sitting up, no matter how much he stretched his legs and boots out over the coffee table, careful not to connect with Morris's own cement blocks. The leather-clad ogre overfilled his chair, resting with his bearded chin on his chest, letting out the softest buzz saw whines that Kirk found oddly comforting. He envied Morris's ability to sleep. A large, sun-shaped clock not thirty feet down the fairway kept drawing his attention.

3AM.

3:15.

3:36.

Sleep. Kirk closed his eyes and emptied his head of troubling thoughts. They nagged at him like tiny, biting mouths. *He knows we're comin'.* Morris nailed that piece of truth. *He's got time to get ready.*

He's got plenty *of time to get ready,* Kirk's mind corrected him. The old wolf already had Kirk underestimating his chances and he didn't like it in the least. The others no doubt had taken Borland lightly as well. Seconds passed and Kirk realized he'd opened his eyes again. He forced them shut, struggling with the tension in his chest, convincing himself two wardens could do the job. Borland knew they were coming. They'd be careful going in. They *had* to be careful.

"Hey. Dickhead."

Morris. "Yeah?"

"Time to get moving."

Kirk blinked and rubbed his face. The sun clock showed a little after seven in the morning. Cloud cover prevented the sun from getting through. Morris struggled to his feet and faced the day.

"Shit," Kirk heard, prompting him to twist around in his seat.

Underneath a gray-black sky, snow fell in a slant and plastered the wall of glass and the parking lot beyond.

"Shit," Kirk agreed.

His eyes fell upon the information booth not twenty paces away and the young man just depositing a steaming cup of java on the counter.

Despite the weather, the two men were in luck. Neither Kirk nor Morris carried cell phones, perhaps the one thing they had in common besides their *Were* affliction. The guy at the info booth answered Kirk's questions and gave him access to the booth's land line. A woman answered the phone, took Kirk's information, and promised that Perry—the taxi driver—would indeed be heading out of town later in the day. Perhaps even earlier if he could manage it, to beat the incoming fury of the storm, but that depended upon how many locals would be heading out that way. She informed Kirk that, at the time of the call, there were only two other bookings.

The two men from Nova Scotia went back to their chairs and waited.

Airport staff walked into work and stomped their feet free of snow, but the display boards glared cancelations in red as St. John's battened down the hatches.

Two hours and a couple of mini-shop sandwiches later, Perry's cab service pulled up to the arrival doors. The all-white, ten-person carrier van smoked exhaust in the frosty air, while heavy beards of slushy ice hung off the vehicle's mud flaps. A wooden storage unit for extra luggage sat on the roof and, as far as Kirk could see, they were the only ones waiting for the rig.

Perry appeared around the rear of the van wearing only jeans, sneakers, and a plaid insulated jacket, the kind woodsmen wore in the fall. He checked his tires before walking to the sliding doors and entering the airport. A Winnipeg Jets stocking cap covered his head.

Perry zeroed in on the two men immediately, stopped in his tracks and near yelled, "Youse headin' out to Amherst Cove?"

Kirk and Morris got moving.

10

Alvin Peters woke to the sound of snow scratching at the window. Dread filled him; he didn't want to leave the comfortable cocoon of blankets he'd heaped on his bed the night before, which his considerable body had heated during the night. The clock stoically stated the time as 12:11 PM, which pulled a groan from deep within his throat. He stretched under the layers of cotton, creasing the blankets with his feet before they popped out the bottom end. Cold air made contact with his massive frame.

"Awww shit," he muttered, the fat rolls on his throat giving his voice an interesting treble. With effort, he threw back the mounds of quilts handmade by his deceased mother. Exposing his naked self to the cold air, he labored to a sitting position with a grunt and went through his morning ritual of scratching at fleshy crevices, bulges, and danglers. He pulled the oxygen tube from his pug nose, and jammed a finger up a nostril, performed a quick but vigorous cleaning, and wiped it off on a bedside tissue. He repeated this for the other nostril before he replaced the tube.

Alvin peeled back a curtain and gazed outside, grimacing at the implications. More snow meant more shoveling. Alvin fucking *hated* shoveling. These days it took forever to clear his walkway and driveway. If Santa was ever listening, he'd probably long since zoned out Alvin's incessant chant for a snow blower. Sighing at what appeared to be a day of ball busting, he scratched again at his chin, pulled a loose blanket around his shoulders, and drifted off into a morning stare.

Alvin Peters was the poster boy for a nuclear-bomb-sized heart attack. At six-foot even, he wore perhaps two hundred pounds more than he should've, most of which hung off his gut, forcing him to walk with his spine arched ten degrees backwards, which also lent the façade of pretentiousness. When he was in public, that massive paunch usually jutted over a dam of a leather belt, hanging awkwardly over near non-existent hips. At times, it was said the man didn't need suspenders—he needed an airlift. Townsmen would mutter behind Alvin's back that there were a couple of whole roasted chickens in him not touched.

With a grunt, Alvin got mobile and shuffled across thick mats and cold linoleum, walking a groove to the bathroom. A length of plastic tube snaked along behind him. He moved with all the grace of ancient arctic ice falling into the sea, and if one paused to listen, his joints cracked with the same intensity. Alvin took his time voiding, not seeing his tackle at all when he looked down, taking care of matters by feel alone. When he finished, he slapped water to his doughy hands and face and left his thick turf of black hair uncombed. When he emerged from the washroom, the urge to appease his monstrous belly occupied his thoughts.

He got dressed, pulling on a comfortable pair of sweatpants that stopped somewhere below his gut, and hauled a triple-X t-shirt over his head. His upper arms were like thighs, while his thighs could have been mistaken for stacked tires. He believed, one day, the friction from his thighs rubbing together would produce smoke. Alvin wondered if he should carry around one of the little portable fire extinguishers, just in case. All he needed was a brush fire between his hams.

Breakfast. One of Alvin's eight favorite meals of the day, not counting snacks. Alvin hadn't always been such a meatball. In high school, he'd been a track athlete and bodybuilder. Had a girlfriend but lost her to university. Alvin didn't need university. In his mind, it was a money racket. He got by just fine with his high school education, and, for anything he needed to learn, he ordered the books online, and read them in a week.

He knew he was intelligent. An internet junkie at ten, he quickly taught himself to type, reaching a speed of two hundred words a minute. His aunt, who took on work transcribing medical notes from busy doctors, took him under her wing and introduced him to the self-employed online profession when he was only eighteen. Alvin took to it right away, reading and absorbing the lingo from a medical terminology book in a week, and later transcribing medical notes and research papers with an unprecedented ninety-nine-point-seven percent rate near perfection. He admitted that listening to recordings while his fingers made his keyboard chatter was oddly comforting. Hypnotizing.

It was then that he started smoking in earnest.

He took up the habit at fifteen but, upon graduation, only seriously started converting his lungs into shriveled raisins of tar when he discovered that smoking made him work faster and *longer*. The words truly flowed while he puffed, and after eight years of sucking back three to four packs a day, he chain-smoked his way into the ICU ward in Clarenville. His lungs rebelled with an infection which almost claimed him. When he regained consciousness a week later, a young doctor from Iraq inspected him and gravely informed him that his smoking days were over. He had come so perilously close to flat-lining. The bad news didn't stop there. His weeping aunt sobbed as she revealed that while he was unconscious with a foot of plastic tubes down his gullet, both of his parents had died on the way to the hospital from a head-on collision with a moose, and had been buried only two days earlier.

Looking back, it was the roughest time in his life. Drinking had never interested him, and his doctor forbade him to smoke again, so he coped with his losses the only way he knew how.

He ate.

Alvin walked over to his garbage-can-sized oxygen concentrator (which he called C-Cup), adjusted the flow from a three to a four, and hardly heard the puffing beat as the filtration system drew air in, purified it, and sent it up the plastic highway to his nose.

As a parting gift, his smoking had robbed him of most of his lung capacity, leaving the still young man with only twenty-seven percent. Alvin didn't mind the gray concentrator that ensured he received the purest oxygen. Didn't mind wearing the tubing wherever he went inside his home. And after years of packing on weight, he didn't mind living his days in the house he grew up in, which he inherited from his parents. The house had a wicked view, peering out over the hillside, past black-shingled rooftops, to the pristine blue-green waters of the bay where, in the summertime, whales played.

But Alvin missed the workouts of his youth. Watching instructional videos online, he had trained in the evenings to become a more than capable practitioner of Kempo Karate (at least in his mind) as well as certain ninja techniques. A dented punching bag hung in his workout room, while his high school free weights lay about in an optimal training circuit. He figured he was black belt level before everything changed, and despite his current dismal physical shape, he still lashed out at imaginary foes with straight jabs and elbow smashes. Just to keep an edge.

His doctor had warned him to take it easy. Sure, Alvin looked like shit. Looked like *doughy* shit. He knew it. But if he had to, if he were forced into a corner and before he started gasping for air, he was pretty certain he could fuck up someone's day.

Kitchen. A black, iron frying pan the size of a hubcap slammed down on a propane burner. Ten strips of bacon were laid out with gourmet precision. The air sizzled with the scent of cooking meat. When the bacon reached the crispiness he liked, Alvin transferred every piece to a plate, left the grease in the pan and tossed in six eggs. A handful of sausages joined in the fun. An eight-ounce frying steak made things even more interesting. Two handfuls of hash browns landed on the side, and breakfast wasn't quite breakfast without toast. Two slices of white bread were dropped into the toaster (butter and strawberry jam already on the table). With spatula in hand, Alvin was barely aware of his ogre-like grunting in anticipation of the first feeding of the day. He daintily maneuvered items through the grease pool with a fork, the spatula separating items where needed. The food popped and crackled. Some specks of grease flew from the pan and singed his meaty forearms, not that it distracted him from his task at hand. Alvin watched it all with predatory patience. His doctor would no doubt have a conniption fit if he saw the bubbling of this magnificent feast. Alvin didn't care. He wasn't planning on dying, but if his arteries petrified while eating, jammed up with cholesterol and trans-fat shit, well, then, he'd just have to forego the rest of his jolly life.

When breakfast was ready, he sat at the kitchen table, facing the wintry bay, and fed hefty forkfuls into his stubbly jowls. Snow fell. Winds cut themselves on the corners of the house. When he finished eating, he dumped the dishes into the sink and started washing. Even that minute expulsion of energy got him breathing hard until he was forced to stop and catch it.

Finishing the dishes, he peered out at the bay. This day, with the storm coming on, was a day to grab a few beers, sit behind his deck window, and just watch Mom Nature do her damnedest, while C-Cup thrummed and chuffed in the background. He might even give Ross a shout to see if he wanted to stop by. Of all the inhabitants of the little town, Ross Kelly was perhaps the only one to whom Alvin felt connected. Probably because they were the only two people around who weren't collecting an old age pension.

He spotted Harry Shea and Sammy Walsh having their morning jaw session. Alvin didn't particularly like the hoary bastards. Shea was far too sassy and he suspected Walsh of being a goddamn hippy. If a snow plow ran over both of them, Alvin wouldn't shed a tear. Shea had also cussed him out once when Alvin was just a boy taking down squirrels with a slingshot, a hobby which had delivered him into Mr. Shea's backyard. The crime scene, as it was later re-enacted by his father and the offended Harry Shea, consisted of an open window, Harry himself sitting in his rocker, head back, mouth open in sleep, and a young, impetuous boy suddenly bursting at the seams in angst at seeing a shot he *had* to take.

A fire-spitting Shea later wanted Alvin's *ass* in a sling so he could lob him out over the bay. Many a time since, Alvin wondered how a ten-year-old boy could be so taken with the urge to shoot a dry pine cone into a sleeping man's mouth. It wasn't the deed he so recalled, but the furious indignant state that Shea, of Scot-English descent, had worked himself into as a result. It was a rage that stayed in the back of Alvin's mind into adulthood, one which had made him wary of the man.

If it had been Sammy Walsh who'd been plugged with a few well-aimed pine cones—especially after a session of home brew—well. Alvin suspected his wife Mary would've handed him a prize and a handshake.

Alvin turned away from the window, thinking he'd put an edge to the katana he'd bought online.

And missed the police cruiser creeping along the curve of the road.

*

The cruiser pulled alongside Harry Shea and Sammy Walsh, making both men at once very conscious of their every movement.

The passenger window slid down.

"Morning, sirs," the constable greeted in a raspy voice.

"Officer," Shea greeted. Walsh only nodded, his inherent distrust of the law visible on his face. Both men stood in front of the mailboxes, very still, having seen enough nature shows to know that fear could be smelled.

"You gentlemen wouldn't have seen any roaming dogs, would you?"

"Roaming dogs?" Shea asked. "Problem up here is missing dogs."

"Flossie's German Shepherd's been gone for some time now," Sammy added.

"We're looking into that, actually."

Flossie had a diamond-shaped face, almost blemish free, except for a few lines about her eyes. No makeup. Brown hair, cut short. Fair to look upon, though certainly no beauty, Harry thought. Not by any means. But he'd heard a little about Officer Sheard. The woman was militant enough for Harry to mind his manners, and he hoped Sammy would as well.

"We'd appreciate the public's cooperation on both matters," Sheard said, grimacing in the growing wind.

"Haven't heard of anything," Harry reported.

Sammy shook his head. "Haven't *seen* anything."

"See any strays around here?" Sheard asked, squinting and showing near perfect teeth.

"Not recently, no," Harry said. Sammy rattled his head once again.

Sheard inspected one face and then the other. "You know where Ross Kelly lives?"

The old-timers stiffened in their winter snowsuits as if goosed. Harry then pointed ahead, across the junction. At the top of the hill where the mailboxes stood. Coming out of an old road that might have been cleared by snow scoop and shovel, walked a figure decked out in winter gear. A stocking cap covered its face.

As if sensing his name, Ross raised his arm and waved.

"There he is, officer," Harry said, glad to know he wasn't turning the man in. He liked the Kelly youngster.

Sheard saw him and for a moment didn't say or do anything.

"Thank you for your time. You guys stay out of the storm," Sheard finally said, leaving the window open as the cruiser crackled over the snow-crusted road, towards a waiting Kelly. Harry Shea and Sammy Walsh stayed in place, watching the car approach Ross like a great white sizing up its prey. The young man bent over at the window for a moment and then climbed into the passenger side.

"Stay out of the storm," Harry repeated with contempt, stirring Sammy from his gawking. "She think we are? Couple of pussies?"

*

The cruiser halted alongside Ross, lining him up with the open passenger-side window. He leaned over, smelled an interior steeped in coffee. It surprised him to see a woman at the wheel, but not terribly so. His second reaction was that she wasn't half-bad looking.

"Morning," she said with a friendly frown. "Ross Kelly?"

"Yeaup. That's me."

“I’m Constable Sheard. We talked on the phone last night.”

“Officer.”

Her brown eyes studied him for a moment. “Climb aboard.”

Ross complied, anxious to please. “Never been in a cruiser before.”

“Well, lucky you. You’ve been a good boy then.”

“Or just never been caught.”

Sheard didn’t smile at that, and Ross figured he’d better clarify. “That was a joke.”

“You going to show me where you saw those tracks?” All business. Not that he should have expected otherwise. Ross started to feel uncomfortable.

“Yes,” he answered.

“We’re a little short-staffed these days. The reason why I’m late getting out here.”

“Well, thanks for taking the time. Storm’s coming.”

“A storm doesn’t stop us. Doesn’t stop the job.”

Officer Sheard took her foot off the brake and rolled up a small incline, driving out the washboard of a road that led into Upper Amherst Cove. She stayed well within the limit, and Ross tried not to be too nosy by sizing up the interior of the vehicle.

“So you found these tracks, yesterday?”

“Yes.” They passed thick timberline on either side of the road, proud fir trees older than either occupant. On the right was a path hidden under about two feet of snow that led to a large vegetable garden Ross's grandparents once tended to for potatoes and carrots.

"Well, the purpose of this little jaunt is just to see exactly where you found them. I'll take it from there."

"Be all covered up by now."

"I know that. I repeat. The purpose of this little jaunt is to see exactly where you found them."

Ross glanced over at the police officer, noted her emotionless profile. A fence of dark green and white sped by the driver's side window. Then the car dipped as it went down the sharp incline of the other side of the ridge. When he was a boy, Ross dreaded riding his bike over that frightening strip of road, which felt a few degrees short of a rollercoaster's initial drop.

The car drove by the driveway that led to old man Borland's house, just barely noted through the natural growth crowding over it and forming a tunnel of boughs. Unspoiled snow piled as high as a person's knees would give a workout to the fisherman, if he ever decided to shovel his way out. Ross hadn't seen the old mariner in a while, and a part of him thought it might be best to check in on him on the way back. Just to make certain Borland hadn't collapsed in his kitchen.

Breadbox Pond went by, a broad platter of water that stretched away from the road. Strengthening winds blew a white veil across the ice, hiding everything from fifty feet in. The snow was coming down fast.

"Going to get messy later on," Ross said.

"Mmhmm," Sheard acknowledged.

"Y'know, I tried out for the Mounties once."

No response.

"Didn't get anywhere. Eyes failed me."

"Probably for the best," Sheard stated, slowing the car down at a stop sign, where the road linked up with the Discover Trail Highway. Ross thought about her response, decided he'd stay quiet for the rest of the ride. He pointed to the right and she drove on, the silence broken periodically by humming radio chatter.

Five minutes later, they pulled over just up a straight strip of wet road, across from the wire mesh fence surrounding the Department of Highway depot. Orange highway plows and loaders stood before the green cone of the salt house, almost invisible behind the falling snow.

Sheard put the car in park, switched it off, and got out without a word. Ross sat in the seat for a moment before following. Cold air smacked his face as he swung the door open, jolting him awake.

"Here?" Sheard waved a hand, divining the spot.

"Yeah, this is it," Ross said, pointing to the hills. "I was coming down off there yesterday when I found them. Straight on in, through the brush, they carried on. No hope of finding them now, though."

Sheard studied the hill, then the sides of the road, and finally the tree line and fanged stream, all with an investigative air. She stood in a black winter coat, only a few fingers shorter, and Ross glanced away before she got the idea that he was sizing her up. He *was*, but he didn't want *her* to know that.

"Could've been a person short taken," Sheard finally declared, more to herself than to Ross. That thought occurred to him last night, just before he decided to call the cops, but to run all the way in there, barefoot, to take a leak?

"Or someone's idea of a joke." She rolled her shoulders.

Not his, however, but Ross kept that to himself and waited, wondering what the Mountie was going to do here, taking whatever the cold had to give. Winter clothing protected everything except his face. His stocking cap could be pulled down into a ski mask, but he didn't feel comfortable doing that in front of Officer Sheard for some mysterious reason.

"Well, thank you for taking the time," Sheard said, half-facing him, and only then for a quick two seconds. "I'll make my report and keep an ear to the ground. You say you found them yesterday afternoon?"

"That's right."

"Well, we've had no calls for missing people. Not yet, anyway. Probably something silly. Like a dare. I'll give you a ride back."

She walked back to her door, but Ross felt that vibe of unease once more. "Thanks, but I think I'll just hoof it back in."

Sheard paused. The wind picked up, driving a tattered sheet of white between them. "You sure?"

Ross nodded, only glancing in her direction. "Thanks for your time, Officer."

"Suit yourself. And you're welcome."

She climbed into the car. The parking lights flared to red life, and she wasted no time pulling away, driving back towards Amherst Cove, probably on her way back to Bonavista. Ross stood on the heaped-up shoulder of the road, a dark figure against the thickening wall of white, and watched the cruiser until it disappeared into a haze.

A hike back home would satisfy his need for the outdoors, and the physical activity would burn away the awkward interaction with Officer Sheard. He'd keep mostly to the road, take his time, maybe even venture into the bush a little ways. The two kilometers would be good exercise and he'd be back home just before the shit hit the fan with the approaching blizzard. Maybe he'd even stop in and see what Alvin was up to.

Ross Kelly slapped his thermal gloves together, making them fit snug, and took a deep breath. Two klicks was a walk in the park for him.

He got moving.

11

Perry informed Kirk and Morris that the other passengers had canceled on him, so it would be just the pair of them traveling to Bonavista. That suited the two men just fine, and upon boarding the van, Morris went straight to the rear and made himself comfortable. Kirk tossed in his bag and stretched out in the middle row, leaning his head against the cool glass and listening to grains of wind-blown ice pellets pepper the window. The movement of the taxi quickly lulled Kirk into a restless semblance of sleep, where every bump caused his eyes to open and check on things, before squeezing shut once more. Perry hunched over the steering wheel, the dull beat of the wipers as calming as a heartbeat at rest. A clap of metal jolted Kirk awake and he stared at the empty driver's seat a second before realizing the van had stopped at some roadside service station. He settled back, wary of the thickening snow blanketing the windshield. When Perry returned, he briefly checked on his passengers before starting up the engine and pulling out into traffic. Even though a blizzard was about to smash into the island, people still dared Mother Nature.

Kirk stared ahead with two eyes that felt like dried-out teabags. Soft music spilled from the radio. The snow fell harder, at times reminding him of a feather pillow exploding against the windshield. And in his left ear, the one closest to the glass, the wind groaned like an animal speared through the gut, bleeding out, yet refusing to pass on. It followed Kirk into that state just below consciousness and a toe dip away from sleep.

Morris snored all the way.

Hours later, Kirk woke up and knew he wouldn't sleep any more this day. He straightened up in his seat and wiped away the steam on the glass. White landscape flashed by, broken by sheer rock cuts, hunched over trees, and frozen humps of hills. Grim cloud cover masked the sky and every now and again a gust would strike the moving van and make its shell quiver. Kirk didn't like the mood, didn't like the growing fury of the storm, and each blast of wind hammered home a rising unease. For comfort, he unlocked his suitcase and felt under his change of clothing for the Bowie. He kept his hands concealed just in case the driver glanced back, and drew the weapon from its decorative traveling case.

He leaned forward and slipped its sheath down the back of his jeans, secured it, and leaned back. The blade pressed across his lower spine, but it comforted him. Of all the lore and superstitions, silver was but one of *three* ways to kill a werewolf, and the one most commonly known amongst the human populace. Fire was another.

Kirk didn't want to think about the third.

He glanced over his shoulder at Morris, noted how his companion's black eyes smoldered in his skull. Morris sensed it, too.

They were nearing the end of the road.

Minutes later, the van coasted to a stop. Perry opened his door and jumped out, allowing a breeze to slash through the warm air inside and bring Kirk to full alert. Perry headed around the van and opened the passenger doors from the outside.

"That'll be sixty apiece," Perry informed them, standing on the side of a road and a sign that had been brushed clean. It read *Upper Amherst Cove*, and an arrow pointed the way. Kirk reached for his wallet and counted out the bills, paying Morris's way as he got out of the van. The vehicle seemed to rise an inch when the larger man stepped onto land.

"Here's me card." Perry held it out. "If'n ye need a ride back in, okay?"

"Where's Amherst Cove?"

Perry turned and pointed. "See that turnoff there? Just off the main road? Go on up there and keep walking. Head up the hill that'll feel like a mountain. The roads are getting slick and I doubt I'll be able to get up them anyway."

Kirk listened as he eyed the turnoff. He'd gotten directions from the Elders to get off at this very place, and walk the rest of the way in. The last phone call they'd received from their warden instructed them to get off in Amherst Cove, talk to some locals and obtain directions, and then backtrack to this spot. Borland lived close by, past a graveyard, and behind a pond. A cabin lurked beyond the pond, and that's where Kirk's orders said to go.

Kirk nodded his thanks and stepped away from the van. Perry closed the doors and looked to the heavens. The wind blew harder here than the city, like the breath of a charging avalanche.

"She's gettin' dirty, b'y," Perry exclaimed. "Best get on wherever ye be gettin'. I'll be lucky now to get home in one piece."

With that, he nodded and walked around the front of the van. Kirk watched him for a moment before turning and looking back at the pavement. The van's tracks in the gathered snow appeared an inch deep already, and no other vehicle had passed this way. He reckoned they were in some serious back country. The surrounding hills and forest cowered under the white sheet piling onto them, and a savage chill tightened his face and burned his fingers.

Perry pulled away, tooted once, and soon vanished in a whorl of snow and exhaust. The growing wind swallowed up the sound of the engine, as if the blizzard had gulped the van down. Kirk squinted at Morris, whose head and shoulders were already dusted in snow. Morris met his gaze for a second before hefting his suitcase, and walked headlong into the wind.

With the air cutting at his face and ears like icy razors, Kirk followed.

The pair hiked up a short incline, leaving deep boot prints as they followed the buried country road, past a bleak graveyard on the right, and onwards towards the base of a monstrous hill that loomed ahead, glimpsed only when the wind subsided. Stinging snow strafed their faces, and they squinted against the onslaught. The wind continued to strengthen, forcing them to slow and lean into it as they placed one foot in front of the next.

Minutes later, the men reached a parting between a fence of flailing trees and brush, revealing a frozen pond.

"There," Kirk said, pointing towards the raging gray curtain ripping across the surface. "His cabin's in there."

Morris didn't say anything. His beard and hair were coated in frost.

"Think we should change?" Kirk asked.

"No. Keep your nose open. You'll smell him if he's changing or changed. And if he has, we'll do the same."

"It'll be too late then."

Morris made harsh side-eyes at him. "That fucker's got to be what? Two—three hundred years old? Takes me two minutes to go over. If we can't beat him to the draw, we *deserve* to be gutted."

Kirk mulled that over. "What about the speech then?"

"What?" Morris grated. "That one about crimes against us all? And we're the executioners and fuckin' yadda yadda? I forgot that years ago. Besides, this fucknut's already nailed two of ours. One of them, or, fuck, maybe even both gave him the speech." Morris shook his head. "Look. He's there. He hasn't changed. Let's kill him and get a goddamn taxi outta here in the morning. All right?"

Kirk rubbed his chin and noticed Morris's leather duster was open, his knife sheath jutting from his belt. His own Bowie knife lay at the small of his back, fixed in place by a belt sheath. Apparently feeling the conversation was over, Morris left the road. Kirk followed, and both waded through low drifts that sucked them down to their knees. They struggled to the edge of the pond and dropped their suitcases in the icy brush, thinking they'd retrieve them later. Their hands freed, Kirk and Morris stepped away from each other, and made their way across the icy surface colored in a flat shade of twilight.

Behind them, the road vanished in a violent screen of white.

*

The wind thumped against the side of the cabin and rumbled along its length like a wrecking ball turned aside, causing the timbers to creak, the way ancient mariners' rigging creaked atop choppy waters. Borland sniffed the air, noted the drop in temperature, and sat up on his couch. With the storm building in strength, it was difficult to smell anything, and he wasn't certain if he did catch a whiff of something or not. But this was war footing, so he limped to his door, cursing his joints with every step, and peeked out the window facing the pond, looking past the comet's tail of frost etched across the glass. The distance to the road was equal to a soccer field, Borland reckoned, but today, as he scrunched up his face and sniffed the air, anyone crossing that flat top of icing would think it three times that length. He'd known men who'd gone sealing in the early 1900s who'd been swept off Atlantic ice pans by ferocious gales and plunked into the frigid drink, chilled to their bony marrows before five fathoms down, or crushed into bright jam by closing ice.

He sniffed again, slow and tasting. When the gusts subsided, as if drawing breath for the next barrage, a ghostly hint of *something* reached him. His nose drew in a great deciphering breath…

Leather.

Nylon… Fur.

Skin.

And *silver.*

That metallic tang hung about his own person and burned in his nostrils. Borland shook his head, slowly hummed the first bars of "*We'll Rant and We'll Roar,*" and checked his belt. One knife lay there in its sheath, tucked in tight. The other was firm against his lower back, out of sight. Borland sniffed again and coughed, which erupted into a horrific hacking that lasted near ten seconds. He eventually regained control and glanced outside with his knowing, red-rimmed eyes.

Snow lashed across the cabin in ferocious sheets.

Then darkness festered within the blank purity of the storm's curtain, like a bruise coming to the surface. One figure. Big lad. Striding through the dull glare like an eerie juggernaut.

The enemy.

Borland scowled. He almost got to coughing once more when he spotted the second warrior, smaller than the first, but just as relentless in pushing through the blowing snow. Both men had their hands free and swinging at their sides like gunslingers of old.

With his throat and chest stinging and shoulders hitching, Borland pulled back from the window and went to the table. He grimly picked up the shotgun and loaded his winter coat's pockets with extra shells. Then he pumped the weapon and pointed it at the door, at one section he'd thinned out so that the shot would have no trouble blasting through the sheet of wood, right around gut level. Borland took a steadying breath, suppressing the tickle in his lungs. He fingered the trigger and braced his legs for the recoil.

"C'mon den, y'fuckers," he wheezed with a snarl, showing the worn stubs of his teeth. "C'mon in."

*

The cabin appeared as a square lump at first, but as the two men got closer, it solidified into a squat but stout little dwelling. A second structure fluttered in and out of sight just beyond. The cold seeped through Kirk's jeans and gnawed on his legs, the only place his winter coat didn't reach. His cheeks felt flayed with ice. If the snow bothered

Morris, he didn't show it. The man's hair and beard had gone near white in the blizzard's growing frenzy, while his eyes smoldered with heat.

Two bursts of wind halted their march, nearly blowing them over into the sifting powder that was gathering on the pond's surface. But the wind exhausted itself, not yet powerful enough to whisk the hunters away, and Kirk and Morris righted themselves and pressed on. In time, they crossed the ice, stopping not twenty paces out from the cabin.

"Smell anything?" Kirk drew close and hollered over the wind. He knew he did, but it was strange. More like… dogs.

Morris, however, shook his head and plodded straight to the door with all the subtlety of a bulldozer.

Kirk strayed five steps to the left. The cabin grew darker in the dreary afternoon light, like a face about to spit something distasteful. Ice-glazed planks covered the windows in haphazard fashion. The barest whiff of frozen blood hooked his nose, briefly diverting his attention to the other structure behind the cabin.

Both men drew their knives, the silver as bright as moonglow on dark water.

Morris reached the front step.

*

Borland's snarl hardened into a dead man's grimace. The wood just outside his door gave a wretched squeak, telling him that someone was there. His finger tightened on the trigger.

And the shotgun spoke.

*

Part of the door exploded in a punch of splinters, blasting Morris flat on his back and freezing Kirk in his tracks. The door flew open and rattled on its hinges as Borland, dressed in winter clothing, appeared with a roar of fury. He spotted Kirk, paralyzed like a startled deer, and swung the sawed-off cannon in his direction. Kirk blurred to one side as the shot shredded only air.

Morris groaned and rolled over, revealing a bloody print in the snow the size of a hubcap. One fist held his silver knife. He looked up as Borland leveled the shotgun, pumped it, and fired—destroying the left set of ribs of the hit man and driving him skidding five feet away. Morris gasped in pain and dropped his blade, fingers quivering.

"Hey!" Borland shouted, training the shotgun's barrel at the corner of his house, where the other one had fled. "Come 'ere y'little *prick*."

Borland then fixed his gun on the shaking fingers of his first victim. He walked up to the wincing figure, inspecting how the pellets had shredded a grisly hole of meat and bone in the torso. There wasn't anything on the face of the planet that could shrug off such a wound. Losing interest, he pumped the weapon and crushed the wrist with his boot heel, trapping the hand.

Borland aimed. "Else I get mad."

He squeezed the trigger and destroyed the man's appendage in one blast. Fingers jumped and disappeared in drifts. The black-bearded biker sort flopped about as if he'd been zapped by an over-charged defibrillator. Borland kicked him in the face, flipping him onto his back. His handless wrist hosed the ground in bright scarlet.

"Hey!" Borland shouted again, a gust of wind buffeting him. He racked the shotgun again, sending a blue shell casing flying into the wind. "Get out here ye little shit! And as a man 'afore I truly fuck up yer partner."

Borland pointed the warm muzzle of the weapon into his victim's face. The crippled man's eyes were open, but glazed with shock. Borland waited a few seconds more.

"Fuck it," the old man growled. He pulled his knife from his belt. Time was a' wastin'. Borland eyed both corners of the cabin before dropping to one knee.

Kirk burst out from around the corner, drawing Borland's attention. The Newfoundlander whirled, fired and missed. Kirk charged in, lunging when he got close enough. Borland dropped the shotgun in favor of the blade just as Kirk tackled him. Both men flew backwards and landed hard in a drift, away from the mess of Morris. For fleeting seconds, they flailed at each other, attempting to grab the other's silver.

Kirk gripped Borland's knife hand while Borland frantically grabbed Kirk's. Kirk overpowered his foe, pushing him down. He stabbed and his blade surfed the swell of the old man's forearm before catching on a sleeve with a rip. The tip stabbed deep into snow to the left of Borland's weathered face, drawing a look of fear and fury. Kirk pulled the weapon back, keeping his adversary's blade at bay. The old man hadn't the strength to stop him, managing only to hold on and slow the action.

Kirk took aim, placing his weight behind his knife arm. The silver tip slowly descended once more, like a lengthening icicle, straight for Borland's left eye. Kirk focused on that dark slit, determined to finish his target. The Newfoundlander squirmed to no avail.

Then the unexpected happened.

Borland *smiled*, exposing a mouth of canine fangs. The old man's eyes flickered entirely black and he wheezed out a chuckle as foul as crypt gas. The startling transformation seized all the energy out of Kirk's attack and, for a split second, he made the fatal mistake of being transfixed.

Borland's grip on Kirk's wrist became a vice. Bones cracked. Kirk cried out. Frightening strength surged through the old man, power only a *Were* could summon, yet Borland was neither man nor wolf, but rather an *in-between*.

Kirk had no choice but to release the blade. A hoarse giggle escaped Borland. He opened his maw of curved teeth—and snapped at his attacker's face. Kirk jerked his head back before ramming his forehead down, bursting Borland's nose.

The old man howled and *flung* his adversary away with enough force to nearly yank Kirk's right arm out of its socket. He crashed into snow and jagged wood. The cabin's front steps. Kirk rolled over and struggled unsteadily to his feet.

Before him stood Borland, who threw his arms wide as if flinging back a cape, and hissed in pain. A sheet of blood drenched his winter clothing. Then he giggled, coughed, and snapped those long teeth that much rather belonged in a wolf's head. He still held his knife, and the blade shone with pale menace in the blowing snow. Black eyes fixed on Kirk, nearly mesmerizing him with their evil mirth. Kirk realized then, with a cold knob of terror seizing his guts, exactly the reason why the Elders wanted this man dead.

The young *Were* bolted for the open door of the cabin. He flew over the threshold, grabbing the door and whipping it shut behind him. Possessing supernatural speed, Borland crashed through the planks, wrecking the entrance of his home. A clawed hand lashed out and rent lines through the denim of Kirk's coat and the flesh of his back, strumming his spine in an electric chord that almost paralyzed him. The blow sent him sprawling into a pile of stacked wood. The neat tower clattered to the floor and Kirk went with it all, twisting onto his back. Borland rallied and dove for the floundering youth.

Kirk got his feet up into the midsection of the old *Were's* diving form, and flung the creature over him to crash into a potbellied stove. The funnel broke free of the ceiling with a metallic *poof* of soot and ash, covering the interior in a black veil. Kirk stood up as Borland thrashed around on rolling junks of cut wood, falling to his knees twice before barking a harsh cough. His claws slashed through the gray-black haze, rendering it into coils of smoke.

Borland got one leg under him, but not before Kirk stepped in and smashed his skull with a chunk of firewood, jacking the *Were's* head to the side. Another cracked into Borland's sputtering face. Shards of enamel flew. A third blow pounded into the creature's neck, bowing him at the shoulders.

But Borland stood up with all the power of a rising titan.

Kirk slammed the wood into an ear, half-mangling it from the monster's skull. Then he chopped downwards and sent the Bowie skittering from a clawed hand. The other freakish paw flashed out and grabbed Kirk by his coat. With a hacking, lung-clearing salvo, Borland heaved him though a closed door. The wood splintered into shards and sinews as he passed through and continued on, until a solid wall halted his flight. Kirk bounced on a bed before tumbling off and hitting the floor, rallying through a daze to make sense of what just happened.

Borland stepped into the wrecked doorway, his coughing fit subsiding, and blocked any escape. He held up his hands, shaking out fingers that sprouted ivory knives. Kirk struggled to his feet, using the wall for support as he tried to clear his head. As an afterthought, he flipped the heavy, wooden bed and heaved it towards the door in a powerful skitter, but it was a flimsy roadblock at best.

Taking his time, Borland stopped and rested one hand on the bed frame, claws dramatically sinking into the wood, splintering it with a frightening crack. His curved teeth clacked. Marble eyes blazed in the dim light.

"What have you done?" Kirk asked, fear and awe flooding his words. He wiped his eyes free of blood and took a deep, steadying breath. The old bastard no longer had a knife on him, but he didn't need one. He had his fangs.

Silver and fire were the two known methods of dispatching a werewolf in accepted lore. But a third way existed, unknown by mortals, and feared by *Weres.*

That being the jaws of their own kind.

More to the point, having one's throat *ripped out* by another werewolf.

Kirk swallowed, feeling terror well up inside his chest. He had no time to effect his own transformation, and Borland in his freakish half-mode was infinitely stronger. Then Kirk caught a whiff of something, masked by the smell of soot and blood, but there all the same. Borland smelled it as well and cocked his head towards the outer door. His lips curled back in hatred and he spun just as an enormous wolf crashed into his midsection in a snarl of rage, sweeping both figures out of sight.

12

The wind blowing harder than ever, Ross plodded alongside wispy curls of white snaking over a snowy road. He'd bundled up in his black-and-yellow snowsuit and thermal gloves before getting into the car with Officer Sheard, and even though a few gusts battered his back and hurried him along, it was nothing. He was on his last leg home, perversely enjoying being out in a blizzard that was just beginning to rage.

He envisioned Officer Sheard's profile in his head. The ol' gal wasn't anything to look at, but for some reason, the more he thought of her, the more attractive she became. Had to be the uniform, he figured. Still, he might just call the station a little later, use the weather as an excuse to make sure she got back safely. Maybe even strike up a conversation. It wasn't like he had many other choices of women. Or opportunities, for that matter. Sounded better than developing a gambling problem.

A gunshot jerked him from his mulling, stopping him in his tracks. Staring into the storm and seeing very little, he yanked down his snowsuit's hood to better hear.

Seconds later, a second blast.

Then a third.

Ross stared in the direction of Upper Amherst Cove, knowing the shots came from somewhere between where he stood and the hill, wondering if old Borland had found snow partridges around his cabin. If so, Ross expected the man to be dining only on feathers and buckshot.

He turned onto the road leading to Upper Amherst Cove and trudged through snow already three or four centimeters deep. One set of tire tracks disappeared into the storm, while two sets of fresh boot prints headed in the same direction as Ross. Someone else out for a pleasant afternoon hike.

But the gunshots made him curious.

He walked on, past the graveyard on the right, and stopped when the boot prints departed from the road and went onto Breadbox Pond. Ross stared, feeling the cold creep into his body, and wondered who Borland might have visiting him. On *this* day of days. And why the shotgun salute.

The wind teased him with the ghostly fragment of a shout, too short to recognize. Ross stood there in the forming blizzard, waiting for something. Nothing came. He fidgeted. Borland wasn't a friend, although Ross knew of him and respected the boundaries of the man's property. But three shotgun blasts on the arrival of quite possibly the decade's, mayhap century's, worst storm made him uneasy.

If anything, he supposed a quick check on Borland wouldn't offend the old codger. Just to make sure he wasn't face down dead or dying on his kitchen floor. It was the neighborly thing to do.

The winds lashed about, attempting to twist his head from his shoulders. Snow caked to his sides, taking the brunt of the gale. Ross spied nearby telephone lines bucking, as if twanged by lightning. It was getting right unpleasant out here.

Swearing at himself for unfounded worrying, and knowing it would bug him well until he knew otherwise, Ross started in over the pond.

*

Morris had transformed into a monstrous three-hundred-pound wolf. He appeared like a beast on steroids and he had *landed* on top of his foe. Borland grabbed the werewolf's bloody mane at the last possible second and held the snapping, flashing muzzle at arm's length. A paw and foreleg kept Borland's own teeth back and for seconds, the two yowling beasts wrestled across the main room of the cabin. Wooden chairs crumpled. The table upended. Cups and plates rattled onto the linoleum and *still* they grappled, dusting up the ash and soot and rolling over chunks of wood. Borland twisted and finally got on top of the enormous werewolf, its body four times the size of a normal animal and thick with muscle, but before he could rain down blows, Morris raked the old *Were's* winter clothing to shreds with his powerful hind legs. Another savage kick bounced Borland off a wall.

Righting himself, Morris stayed low to the floor, growling like an idling chainsaw and blocking the entryway. Borland's chest heaved with the effort expended, while his clawed stomach bled and pattered the floor with darkness. One second more and Morris would have disemboweled him utterly. Horribly wounded, Borland hunched over, claws up and flexing, waiting to pounce.

Every movement Morris took, blood leaked from the cavernous hole still in his torso. Paw prints glistened darkly on the linoleum. He hobbled, lopsided from one foreleg that ended in a raw stump. The severity of Morris's wounds equalized the fight. At full strength, the werewolf would've torn Borland apart in any form.

Bleeding profusely, Kirk pressed himself in the bedroom's doorway and met the soulless eyes of Borland. No words were spoken. There was no need. The fight was just about to enter the third and final round.

"*War*," Borland growled through fangs and he made a truly evil attempt at smiling. He flourished a claw at Morris's head, urging him to attack. The werewolf flinched. Kirk saw the terrible, dripping wounds of his partner and wondered how long he could last.

"Morris," Kirk breathed, taking gulps of air to clear his head. "I'll keep him busy."

The werewolf growled.

Borland's eyes flickered between the pair, uncertain. He reached around his back and yanked forth a second knife just as Morris propelled himself forward with whatever strength was left in his hind legs. The great beast plowed its muzzle into the old man's ruined midsection and chomped down on whatever was available. A scream of agony erupted from Borland. He crumpled inwards and a livid torrent of things best kept inside a person spilled over the werewolf's broad head. Borland shrieked and twisted, and brought up his knife, the silver flashing. Kirk leaped for the weapon as it stabbed deep into Morris's shoulder. The werewolf thrashed as if electrified. Kirk slammed into them both, taking them all into the kitchen. Silver scythed out and licked his chest to the bone, opening him up with a hiss. He gripped Borland's knife wrist and twisted it around, glimpsing the evil effort on the monster's face. Kirk forced the blade down, aiming for an eye. Borland dug long claws into his side, groping for kidneys and rendering him breathless.

Then the Newfoundlander was yanked from underneath Kirk like a moldy rug. Morris, far from finished, clamped down on his victim's ankle and pulled back, shattering the bone like kindling, twisting it like a cheap chew toy. The werewolf backed up against a wall, jerking his head from side to side, ripping Borland's foot off. The old man yowled and pushed himself up against the doorframe to his kitchen.

Kirk crawled on hands and knees to put distance from the combatants—and jerked his fingers away from a glowing silver Bowie lying amongst the junks of wood. Energy flared inside his wrecked body as he snatched up the weapon and stood into a knife fighter's crouch, returning to the fray. The old *Were* snarled at them both, livid with pain and rage, frothing at the corners of the bear trap of his mouth.

Morris crept in on the right, his eyes flaring murderously.

Kirk did the same on his left, Bowie poised in an overhand grip.

Then, as if entering the heart of the tempest, where time slowed, Borland's expression softened. He chuckled almost good-naturedly, coughed, and bared stained and broken teeth.

"Wait, y'fuckin'… peckerheads," he grunted and placed a red hand over the gruesome hole Morris had ripped in his belly. "Them I'se killed? The first one. Weren't no warden."

This paused the pair.

"They'll be… after ya, one day," Borland croaked, struggling to form the words around his canine fangs. His eyes flickered from one to the other. "Young shits. Like yerselves. The moment… ye grow a backbone."

Kirk glanced at Morris. The werewolf hunched up, preparing to leap.

"When ye… reach my age. Ye'll see. The lies." Borland licked his teeth, nodded, and winked. "Jus' wait."

He emptied his lungs in a lengthy sigh then, in one final, weary breath of defeat. There was no last stand. No more resistance. Borland simply sat and wheezed, slumped against the doorframe, bleeding, and waited. He looked to the snow-covered window, as if longing to see the ice and snow over the water one last time.

Morris went for his throat.

Kirk charged in and stabbed, pounding silver into whatever wasn't wolf hide.

13

Somewhere halfway across the pond, along twin boot tracks, Ross stopped in the swirling snow and marveled in horror at what he was hearing. Growls and yips of rage and pain stabbed the air—short, discordant notes piercing the ghostly voice of the blizzard. Ross stood there on the ice, sensing he had split the distance to Borland's cabin. He kept trudging through drifts with violently smoking crests, very much aware of the growing unease in his guts… and the budding fear of what he might find.

The winds cut across the open expanse of the pond, raging against him, seeking to sweep him off his feet or freeze his blood solid. Ross disappointed the elements and forged ahead.

Minutes later, the dark shape of Borland's cabin appeared in the heart of the blizzard. Ross halted and grimaced. Wood or rope groaned in the gale and for a moment, that eerie sawing of fibers caused his whole person to buzz with fright. Summoning reserves of courage he didn't know he possessed, he pushed forward, fearful of frost fairies or displaced yeti bursting out from under the snow and grabbing him.

Shredded clothing materialized out of the frosty gloom, clumped around a starburst of blood. A heavy leather duster lay crumpled nearby, along with the remains of what looked to be a sweater and jeans. Motorcycle boots, intact, lay in a heap. The walnut handle of a shotgun jutted out of a small drift, nearly swallowed in white. Ross stared at the gruesome scene, his fear doubling, forcing him to take a moment to steady himself. There was no body, or perhaps it was already covered over by the snow. He decided it was safer not to touch anything, and was goddamn glad he thought of it. Blood, boots and something else all headed towards—

A startling creak of wood spun him around and he fixed on the ruined mouth of Borland's cabin. *Jesus H. Christ.* Ross figured a linebacker must have been fired from a cannon into the door, shattering it asunder. A length of wood dangled from the upper frame, creaking with each gust and tapping out a soft code on the cabin's bulk.

No sound came from the wrecked doorway. The trail of blood and tracks ended at the front steps.

Ross cleared his throat. "Hey!"

And waited. When no response came forth, he called out again. "Hey! Borland! Yer blueberry wine blow up on ya?"

Nothing.

Sweet Jesus, Ross did *not* want to venture into that wooden cave. A good Samaritan he could be, but not a fucking exorcist. And right now, it looked a sure bet that the Devil himself had risen up with a couple of his demonic buddies and kicked the unholy shit out of Walt Borland's cabin. A blast of wind teetered him, chilling him to the bone, and when he righted himself, his attention went back to the destroyed doorway and the cabin's boarded up windows. Alberta was looking better and better to him with each passing second, but Ross Kelly wasn't a person of half measures.

"Borland! Y'old fucker! You in there?"

The wind answered.

If Borland was inside, he wasn't in a talkative mood.

Shaking his head, Ross wished to God he'd picked up a cell phone yesterday. Or the week before. He'd have one surgically implanted after this episode. He highly doubted Borland had a phone. Then he spotted what looked to be a knife in the snow, and again swore off touching the blade.

"Borland!" Ross pleaded and his shoulders slumped. "Goddamnit."

Bending his legs to his will, he forced himself to walk towards the beckoning hole in the cabin, knowing he wasn't going to like what he found. No sir. His fear gauge spiked. His breath came fast and he readied himself to blaze a trail back over the ice if he had to hightail it. Ross wasn't proud. He might be a recluse, but he was pragmatic about situations and knowing when he was in over his head.

He climbed the few steps to the cabin, as reluctant as a child about to cross a darkened bedroom floor, to see if there really was a monster lurking in the closet. Squinting against the crosswinds, he gazed inside.

"Oh… my…" Ross's eyes widened.

With his winter boots pointed to the ceiling, Borland lay on his back and looked as if he'd been the main course in somebody's gory luau. A knife hilt stuck out of his chest, right where his heart would be, but the very addition of the weapon appeared like overkill. To Borland's right, amongst a floor coated in a nauseating soup of blood, guts and wood junks, a stranger lay in a denim coat with a stained polar bear collar. His chin rested on his chest, clothes drenched in maroon.

To the left of Borland…

Well. Shit.

There were no wolves on Newfoundland, at least according to the Department of Wildlife. Ross himself had never come across any sight or sign of the animals in his time outdoors. He recalled the last documented wolf sighting had occurred decades ago, when animal biologists suggested the beasts could have reached the island by floating over on pans of ice. There had been cases of coyote hybrids that resembled wolves roaming the wild, since the two species could potentially interbreed, and it had been only a year ago or so when a local hunter (Ross knew the guy, lived in Bonavista) shot and killed an animal with mixed genes. That specimen had weighed a paltry eighty pounds and, prior to being identified, had sprouted considerable speculation as to whether there were more of the animals on the island.

The wolf before Ross now, lying on its belly in the shadows of the cabin, had to be three to four times that. It was a monster. Its size and the sound of its ragged breathing rooted the Newfoundland man to the spot. The beast's wounds added to the thick designs splashed upon the floor.

"Holy shit." Ross exhaled, pressing himself against the wreck of the doorframe, with the wind blowing past. He stood there and simply stared at the giant on the floor for seconds. Gathering the nerve he never suspected he possessed, he edged inside, smelling that sharp tang of blood and gastronomic juices. He brought his sleeve to his nose and winced at the stink, but proceeded along the wall, distancing himself as far as possible from that motionless horror on the floor. The knife sticking out of Borland captured his attention and he focused on that for a moment, before seeing the old man's face.

And *that* almost cut loose the drawstring of his asshole to shit-spray himself.

Borland was and wasn't Borland. He had... *fangs.* A huge chunk of meat had been torn from the old man's throat, and the fleshy matter remaining appeared to be a boneless pulp. Ross looked away just as his stomach lurched. Terror energized his calves, urging him to burn a path back to the main road. Outside, the wind nailed a pitched crescendo. Then the interior of the cabin spun like a child's top and Ross's legs gave out. His ass thumped the floor. Borland not only had his throat ripped out and a blade in his chest, but his stomach lay all around him in a gruesome tablecloth.

Ross had skinned and gutted enough animals in his time to be used to the sight and smell of blood, even stumbled across the carcasses of dead moose being picked apart by crows and bald eagles. Once in his younger years, he'd even slashed his leg with a chainsaw while cutting up junks of wood. That episode would have killed him if he hadn't had the presence of mind to use his scarf to tourniquet the wound. But he learned an important lesson about himself then—the sight of blood didn't bother him, and if things got bad, he could function with clarity of mind and do what needed to be done.

But this…

He closed his eyes, felt the panic assault his private dark, and strove to hold on, just hold onto his marbles long enough to get a handle on things.

"Hey."

Ross cracked opened his eyes.

The guy in the fucked-up denim coat fixed him with dark eyes. "Don't… do anything."

"Wha?" the Cove man whispered.

"Just… hold on. Wait." Blood matted the dude's hair and thick beard and his skin tone appeared fish-belly white. "Please."

Then he said no more.

Across the way, the wolf let out a weak whine. Ross's eyes bulged to the size of cue balls at the sound. Composing himself, he stood and cautiously regarded it. The thing's right paw had been shot off, and its body had absorbed some wicked blasts. The animal had to be suffering. Swamped with horrified awe, Ross remembered the shotgun out front. His fear nearly took the steering wheel.

But instead of fleeing the scene, he left the cabin on stronger legs than he'd gone in on. Snow lashed his face and, for once, Ross did nothing to stop it, appreciating its grounding effect. The freezing cold whipped reality back into focus, and his strength, physical and mental, returned. A memory came to him, of driving home from Bonavista one night. His headlights had revealed a furry lump in the middle of the road. It was a rabbit, staring straight into his headlights, insane with fear and trying to pull itself out of the way of the oncoming car. Both of the animal's hind legs had been crushed by a car earlier that night, the limbs resembling old socks trailing a dark stain. There had been no hesitation that night and he ended the rabbit as humanely as he could at the time, by running over it and making sure it was dead afterwards. He could still remember the impact as his car rolled over the wounded animal like a speed bump.

The red patch of snow and ruined clothing lay a short distance from the front door. Ross trudged over and located the stumpy shotgun. Knowing it was a bad idea, he picked up the weapon and brushed it off. His brow arched at the sawed-off nature of the firearm, but only for a moment before he proceeded back inside, the weapon giving him fresh courage.

The cabin floor felt sticky under his boots when he stopped just beyond the threshold. The bloody aroma left him near senseless and he wondered how the hell first responders ever got used to the horrors they routinely encountered. The wolf's breathing had slowed, its eyes still closed, while the tip of a red tongue poked out its long, broad snout. Shaking his head and knowing it was the humane thing to do, Ross pumped the shotgun and aimed it at the animal's skull. His finger tightened on the trigger, and before he squeezed with that final bit of pressure needed, he let the barrel of the weapon drop and simply gawked at the beast.

After a moment he found his resolve and pointed the gun at the wolf's face once again.

"Sorry buddy," Ross whispered and started squeezing the trigger.

The creature's eye cracked open. Its lips unzipped with a low, defiant growl.

"Hey," croaked the sliced up guy. "Don't do it."

Against better judgment, Ross eased off on the trigger, his brow creased in thought. "The thing's in agony, man. A sin to leave it like it is."

"That's… that's my animal." The chin rose and a pallid face stared at him. "Don't shoot him. We'll have words if you do."

"Y'want to let the thing suffer?"

The man smiled weakly. "Yeah."

"Y'got a phone on ya?"

A moment before answering. "No… phone. Listen. Listen to me. You wait. Watch. Don't call the cops. Don't… call no one for—" he drew in a deep, shuddering breath "—for the next few hours. Or so. Give ya five hundred bucks."

Ross frowned at the offer. *What the hell?* Flashed through his mind before his attention was drawn back to the mess of Borland's neck, as if someone had taken a huge bite out of a strawberry muffin. Borland's lips were drawn back, frozen in a snarl.

The stranger's chin drooped onto his chest. Ross watched, struggling with his inaction, but resigned not to shoot the wolf.

Feeling nauseous, he stepped back into the blizzard, holding the shotgun at his thigh.

Fucked up, he thought in a daze and glanced back at the horror scene inside the cabin. The speaker looked to be out for the count. The darkening heavens spoke of an aging afternoon, and the storm wasn't about to let any cop or ambulance here anytime soon. Ross scratched at his head in wonder, unable to piece together what had happened here.

Then he heard the barking.

14

The trench went to a store behind the cabin. The barking intensified the closer he got, prickling his skin, making him wonder how the hell they knew he was outside. The vicious sounds got so bad that he stopped right in front of the door, believing the wood itself trembled from the noise.

"Jesus H. Christ and Savior," Ross muttered. He wondered if he should just go back to the cabin, like *that* was a solution. A strong feeling of apprehension grabbed him, as if he was about to see something else that would give him nightmares. That wouldn't do. Not for Ross. The best trick the devil ever did was convince the world he didn't exist, and Ross wasn't one to back down from a situation or turn his back on anyone—or any*thing*—needing help. He took a breath, twisted the piece of wood keeping the door in place, and pulled on the strip of leather.

The door swung out and the breath of the monster itself smacked him in the face. If the cabin had been bad, the store was worse, smelling of rot, blood and shit. His eyes watered despite being outside in the storm. The light revealed rows of pens constructed of heavy wood and chicken wire, and inside each stifling little cage was a dog, eyeing him madly. Desperately. The very sight of the animals nearly broke Ross's heart.

The dogs didn't stop barking. If anything, they went crazy.

A powerful gust slammed into him from behind, hurrying him to make up his mind. Ross rubbed his chin, hefted the shotgun and went inside. He'd heard reports and seen the missing dog posters decorating telephone poles and the windows of local businesses from here to Bonavista. He now believed he'd discovered what had happened to the entire works. Borland had started collecting other people's pets for some unknown reason, and he'd taken that secret with him to his grave.

Jesus, Jesus, Ross repeated, standing between the rows of pens. The dogs yipped, snapped, barked and pulled at the chicken wire, frantic to be released. He'd never seen such a fury to get out. And here he was, gawking instead of doing. No wonder the dogs were damned near crazy.

"All right, relax, willya? Relax!" But the dogs drowned him out. He went to the nearest pen, which imprisoned a trio of those pretty little white puffs he didn't know the names of. Black masks colored the area around the triplets' eyes, lending them the look of bandits with needle teeth.

They freaked out the closer he got, rattling their cage. "I'm gonna let you out, okay? Just stay near the store or the cabin, 'cause there's a storm on. I'll see if I can find some water for ya."

His fingers hovered over the bolt of the cage. Little paws dug at chicken wire. Tiny puffs of dog breath grazed his hand. He paused and the dogs went ballistic at being so close to release, actually grating their dark noses against the wire like bad blocks of cheese. Their reaction startled Ross so much that he almost backed away.

But then he thought of how damn long these animals might have been penned here, starving, in the icy grasp of a winter's night, and these days, the nights were very, very long. Lord only knew what Borland had done to them. No one would be claiming them anytime soon, not with the blizzard on, and he couldn't bear thinking they'd be imprisoned for another day at the very least. He thought of evidence and disturbing crime scenes, but he couldn't keep the dogs in the pens for the hours it would take for the cops to get here, not in this weather. And taking in the interior of the store, there was plenty to see how the dogs had lived. Just keeping them caged up in their own excrement seemed a health hazard.

No, Ross reasoned, it might be a mistake, but the poor animals had suffered enough already. If anything, he could call them back to the house after he'd released them. They probably wouldn't go far in the storm and would certainly come running to the sound of a friendly voice. Or even food, if Borland had something in his kitchen.

Shaking his head, Ross stood to one side and slid back the bolt. The door sprung open with a clatter and three white dogs, barely the length of his forearm, exploded from their cage. Their paws scraped at the old flooring in their rush for purchase and all three soon vanished into the storm, their excited yaps swallowed up by the wind.

Seeing the littlest of them freed, the others doubled their own demands and efforts to be released. Feeling three-quarters pity and the rest fear, Ross got to work freeing the remainder of the pack.

A Siberian husky burst forth when its cage door open, bolting for the open door.

A black terrier blasted out and actually slipped and skidded on the old linoleum as he bounded for the great wild.

All other manner of mongrels and half-breeds went insane upon being released, racing past Ross who drew back and watched in stunned fascination, wearing half a stupid smile.

When he opened the cage of the Rottweiler, the unexpected happened. Definitely one of the largest of the collected animals, the black-and-orange dog walked out, arched its back and forelegs in a majestic stretch, then regarded Ross with a look that almost appeared to ask, 'Oh, you're still here?'

Ross smiled at the dog, which the animal ignored. The Rottweiler showed him its ass as it plodded towards the framed gray light.

For some odd reason, Ross felt the sensation of just being spared.

But then the remaining dogs barked, yapped, pulled and clawed at the chicken wire, shaking him from his thoughts. He released the rest in short time, each one of them fleeing into the white fury of the blizzard.

The very last dog to be freed was a disheveled German Shepherd. The great animal struggled out of its pen, its legs cramped from its time in captivity. It whined at Ross, its huge, black eyes excessively watery.

"You okay, buddy?" Ross asked and got another mournful groan, as the dog felt nothing would ever be okay again.

Then, the Shepherd's strength returned and it padded outside.

"Fuckin' weird," Ross muttered, watching the animal disappear into the stormy light.

All told, he figured he'd let loose nearly two dozen dogs.

15

"...And this low pressure system, well, it's going to make a mess of things for the next twenty-four hours, centering around the upper Avalon and affecting St. John's, Clarenville, and, ah, the Bonavista peninsula before slowly moving out to sea. Folks in those areas, well, you're going to experience sustained winds around eighty, eighty-five kilometers an hour, with blowing and drifting snow, significantly reduced visibility, and a total accumulation of around seventy centimeters. You heard right—seventy centimeters. A little over *two feet* of the white stuff. Temperatures look to be dropping to minus fourteen, but the wind chill is going to make this feel much, much lower. Say around minus twenty-five. So if you have Fido outside, it's probably best to bring the little guy in before you batten down the hatches. It's not quite the shit storm of—oh, excuse me. I'm sorry. Ahh—"

The weatherman fumbled for poise after his very public breach of etiquette as a dirty grin spread across Harry Shea's face.

"Stupid fucker." He smirked. "Actually said 'shit storm' on television. *Ha*." He shook a fist at the flat screen. "Wait 'til I gets you home. Wicked."

He hoped Sammy saw that. Or, if anything, maybe some kind soul recorded the segment and would take the time to upload it up to YouTube. He'd search later. Along with celebrity nip slips.

The wind battered the house, splashing snow against the windows and churning up a cloud of blowing powder that distracted the senior. Harry stirred in a brown sofa recliner, a veritable island of comfort in his modest living room, and felt for the remote. He aimed the device between his raised feet and muted the broadcast, wondering if the weather guy had Tourette's. Another gust, stronger than the previous one, leaned into the picture window and made it flex, hard enough for Harry to notice. She was coming on, this one. The sky beyond the glass was a low-hanging opaque gray. On a clear day, he could see the other side of the bay. Today, Harry would be lucky to see the mailboxes some fifty feet from his front door.

But he didn't worry. This house could take whatever Mother Nature chose to sling at it, no matter how pissed she got. Harry and his wife of thirty-two years raised the family within these very walls—that is, until she passed on. Every fall and winter they'd listen to the strong timbers groan under dying hurricanes and snowstorms much stronger than the one overhead. The house had seen them through to the next sunrise. Now, however, it was only him in the old homestead, but that didn't bother Harry. His son worked out in Fort Mac while his daughter would be calling soon enough from St. John's, ready to wrangle with him once again about moving into the city to live in her and her husband's downstairs apartment. No, thank you. As much as he loved his daughter, his grandkids, and the idiot son-in-law whose forehead he sometimes yearned to hammer a nail into, Harry couldn't shake the coves. He'd lost his virginity in them. Married here, even. And goddamn it, whenever the Lord was willing, or the Devil got anxious, he'd perish here as well. Toes up, cold junk dead.

Preferably not while ogling online nip slips.

The wind played the glass pane like a stiff drum skin, rolling powerful pressure off its milky surface, and sounding hungry.

"Bawl all ye want, ye savage," Harry whispered, staring at the thrumming glass. "Bawl. I'm ready."

And so he was.

He'd learned long ago the wisdom in being prepared for storms. Out back in a shed, he had a small generator with enough fuel to run for two days if necessary, and a wood stove with a cord of split wood at the ready. Candles, toilet paper, bottled water and canned goods, including a huge can of coffee, and fistfuls of Halloween candy from October were all cinched tight into a closet.

Flashlights had new batteries and he even had the newer ones that only require a few moments' squeeze to shed a sufficient beam. Two fire extinguishers hung in their wall mounts upstairs and down, along with detectors. Entertainment consisted of two forty-ounce bottles of rye whiskey, a forty-ouncer of rum, and a bottle of Macadamia nut liquor that tasted as sweet as vanilla but could probably burn if lit. Then there was the remainder of the Pilsner he'd made, which he and Sammy failed to entirely consume the night before. Finally, he possessed a collection of yellowing action novels written in the 70s and early 80s.

All told, he actually looked forward to being isolated for a day or two before digging himself out. Even better if the power went out. Nothing he liked better than getting shitfaced and reading a cheap paperback without interruptions.

Blizzard? Hurricane?

Not a problem. Not for Harry.

Ice particles scratched at the glass while the wind's timbre rose like an opera baritone. It felt like a tome of music was slamming on his nuts, riding high before a breathless peak.

Harry snorted. *Little pig, little pig... kiss my ass.*

16

He ran through the Halifax County hinterland, across breaking trusses of moonlight. Pumped legs powered him over fallen trees, through near-skeletal bush, and back into a nexus of forested halls. Leaves and broken brush crackled underneath. His heart ached comfortably, welcoming the rush, pushing blood through his body. Paws pounded the ground. Mounds rose and fell but he slipped through it all with no more effort than a breeze. Then he heard it again.

One howl. Long and haunting, cutting the night.

He didn't stop to get his bearings. He knew where she was.

I'm not a monster.

"Hey, you there?"

Kirk's heart skipped, swelled with longing. And just like that, the October night slid away, the air crystallized, and the dark chilled until it hurt.

"Hey? I see your eyes movin'. Y'must be in there somewhere."

"I'm here." Kirk lifted his chin, wincing. He smelled the man before he saw him.

"Good. That's good. Look, we might have a problem."

Kirk opened his eyes. The Newfoundlander before him wasn't a figment of his own subconscious, and he took a moment to realize it. Black hair, just turning gray around the edges. Unshaven stubble about his chin and cheeks. Rough looking, but not unkind. Fear lingered around him, but it wasn't overpowering. This one had himself under control. All anyone could ask for at the moment.

And he had Borland's shotgun, not pointed directly at the Halifax native, but ready if needed.

"What?" Kirk groaned and lifted his arm from the floor to his chest. Blood made his hand sticky, and his coat had a sword's slash right across his chest, leaving a memory of flesh parted by an edge finer than a razor.

"Oh. Goddamn," he muttered. A knife had done that. A silver knife. *Christ,* he grimaced.

"You okay?" the man asked, his face contorted with the question.

"What's the problem?" Kirk repeated as he slowly peeled back the edges of his shirt and denim, grunting when the saturated cloth stuck to his skin parted. A black gill, deeper than he expected, cut across his grizzled chest, slicing his right nipple and just missing his left. The line oozed blood and it stung like a blowtorched bitch.

"Christ," his rescuer hissed, grasping the shotgun with both hands. "That's still bleeding. Hold on. I'll find something to patch it."

"Wait." Kirk clenched his jaw. He saw the potbellied stove on its side. The funnel descended from the ceiling, unattached. A fresh blast of freezing air came through the ruined front door, where smoky dervishes whorled upon a mat of snow. Beyond, the blizzard's breath took the remnants of the door and slapped it repeatedly against the cabin's hide like a drummer going insane.

"Can you hook that up?"

"What? The stove?"

"Yeah."

"You wanna get a fire going?"

"Yeah."

The Newfoundlander held his eyes. "Yeah, I can do that."

"Please."

"But what about…"

"The problem?" Kirk cut him off. "Is it bad?"

"Well, yeah. Well, more strange if anything, really."

"Worse than this?"

A thought. "No."

"Then, later, okay?"

The man rubbed a hand over his chin, nodded, and got busy, leaving Kirk to examine his chest once again. Cut by silver. *Right across the* tits, *of all places.* His other wounds, while hurting, debilitating even, could be shut out. Borland had thrown, beaten, clawed, and stabbed him, but the slash made by that evil length of metal had to be addressed first. That one would *not* heal on its own, which made silver so feared amongst the *Weres*. Its cut was like acid, rendering flesh near incapable of healing.

And, interestingly enough, the only thing to seal a wound made by silver… was fire.

The unmoving bulk of Morris's still furry ass lay across the mess of a floor. Ghoulish swirls, paw and boot prints covered the white floor in a collage of evil art. Kirk leaned forward, felt the claw cuts across his back. Those were healing, however, so he relaxed. Blood clotted around his butt and legs. If he shifted, getting away from the uncomfortable edge of the doorframe, he'd be depositing himself in more of his own plasma. Or Borland's. Metal clattered. The stranger swore several times, the sound echoing.

"Hey."

Kirk felt a hand shake him until he opened his eyes.

"You okay?" Concern in the man's voice.

"Yeah," Kirk lied.

"You passed out."

"I was—just restin'."

The Newfoundlander pulled back, allowing Kirk to see the stove magically put back together. Flames blazed orange behind its missing tooth grill. The doorway had been partially blocked with a chair and an upended table, keeping the storm at bay for the moment.

"You got it goin'."

"Yeah."

"Listen," Kirk said. "Next part's going to hurt. You gotta cauterize this cut, see."

"It's not that deep."

"*Listen,* it's—it's not going to stop bleeding until you torch it. Get something metal. A knife, anything. Something to get hot. And fry this. Burn it. Seal it across."

The man frowned in horror. "You're crazy."

Kirk flashed teeth as he chuckled. "Yeah. Yeah."

"You really—"

"What's your name?" Kirk cut him off.

"Ross."

"Ross. I don't have… time to talk any more. Do me a favor. I'm a—" Kirk took a deep, clarifying breath. He really didn't have the energy. Felt the dreamy tug on his awareness. "Hemophiliac. This. Will bleed for days. I don't *have* days. Understand? By the time you reach a phone… I'll be gone."

That sobered Ross. Focused him.

The blood loss pulled Kirk back then, deep into his skull where only a portion of Ross's woodsman features were visible. The Newfoundlander spoke to him, but the sounds reached Kirk like underwater bugle blasts. Then he felt the sensation of moving, and when he regained his senses, he was on his back, gazing at a bare timber ceiling covered with disturbing saws and cast nets. The nets in particular frightened him. Spiders the size of muddy baseballs crept along their strands, stopping with a predator's pause when he eyed them.

Ross's head blotted them out. He now held, of all things, a metal spatula. The edges glowed and smoked.

"You ready?" he asked, sounding a day away.

The utensil hovered over the cut. Kirk felt its magma heat. "Yeah."

The spatula descended. The first explosive contact made Kirk scream and rattle in place, until the dark grabbed his consciousness and yanked him down.

The smell of flesh and blood sizzling followed him.

Patting.

On his cheeks. A worried Ross playing patty cake.

Kirk held up a hand. "I'm awake."

"You scared the shit outta me," Ross admitted, his face paled by the encroaching dark. Kirk looked to the doorway, saw a worn two-seat sofa reinforcing the barricade, its red velvet cover shining in the dim light. Through the gaps of wood, daylight faded. He inspected the welding job to his chest and winced when the pain assaulted him anew. A horrific grove of burnt meat went deep, into dark and roasted pink where only a veneer of tissue cloaked the bone. If he had the capability to do a cross section, one could probably label each layer of his skin. At least he wasn't bleeding anymore, though he didn't know how resilient that last barrier of sinewy flesh might be… or stay.

"What time is it?"

"Huh? Ah, I don't know. Old Walt doesn't have power hooked up here. Say it's close to four-thirty."

"All right." Kirk struggled to his feet.

Ross stood back and watched in horror. "What are y'doing?"

"I'm okay," Kirk muttered, as far as bleeding was concerned. He took a moment to do an internal check. Each breath informed him his back had been royally stomped on. Probably a few busted ribs from where Borland had thrown him. A sharp tweak of pain shot up his spine upon straightening. He slipped a hand underneath his coat, which hung off him in tatters, and felt for places where the old bastard had clawed him. His palm came back a patchy red, indicating his other wounds still bled but were closing up. A day, he figured, with an ample supply of food and rest, and he'd fully regenerate with only a few scars. The silver cut was a prize, though. No way he'd be able to take his shirt off at a public beach. Not ever again.

He felt for a pocket and produced a shattered cell phone.

"Thought you didn't have a phone," Ross said.

As an answer, Kirk turned his hand over, letting the smashed device fall to the floor.

Then he saw Morris's unmoving carcass. His physical misgivings fled.

Borland, give the old bastard his due, had fought dirty. Street style. Using a shotgun to level the battleground and punching home the notion that, in a fight to the death, rules didn't exist. Honor didn't exist. And desperation justified anything. Borland had gotten the jump on them both, and damned near finished them. If Morris hadn't turned when he did… that made Kirk focus on his companion in this killing. The Pictou County man-wolf was a mess. The devastating wounds he'd absorbed in human form carried over into wolf, and just looking at him would make a person's eyes hurt.

Kirk knew better.

He went to the animal's side and stooped to better inspect it, cringed at the missing paw and the huge hole between the lower ribs and the pelvic bone. Both had congealed. Then he found blood seeping from Morris's shoulder. Stab wound. Poisoned with silver.

"You got that spatula handy?"

"Yeah," Ross said. "Why?"

"Heat it up."

"That thing's still alive?"

"Barely."

Kirk got on his knees, hating the touch of cold blood, feeling it stick to his jeans. A moment of dizziness made him pause. He'd have to be wary of that. The blood loss wouldn't allow any quick movements for a while.

Ross appeared behind him. "Here."

Kirk took the hot spatula. He smoothed back the fur, locating the drooling cut in Morris's shoulder. He cauterized the slit, hearing the hiss of blood and flesh over the wind and the pieces of wood speed-smacking the cabin outside. When finished, he handed the instrument back to Ross and tentatively ran a hand over the werewolf's back.

"He alive?"

Kirk nodded, rearing back and studying the animal's face. Morris didn't worry him so much right now.

The question of what to do with the human did. He hated making heavy decisions like this. It was situations like these that almost stopped him from becoming a warden. He was more of a follower. Then he saw the gleam of silver amongst the wood on the floor. A knife. Kirk stepped over and stooped down to pick it up, feeling the air pressure in his ears drop from that simple movement. He straightened and waited for the moment to pass.

"What was that problem?" Kirk asked, facing the man. "You said earlier?"

"Out back in his store. Damnedest thing. Daresay all the missing dogs were back there."

"Missing dogs?"

"Yeah. Been a weird few weeks. Never really noticed it before. I mean, folks knew some pets were missing from signs posted around town, but no one really thought twice about it. Not me, anyway. Old dogs get old. Sometimes just get up and walk off out into the wild and that's it. They're gone. They know their time. But there had to be two dozen in Borland's store, all in cages."

Kirk didn't like the sound of that. "Show me."

"They're gone now."

"Gone?"

"I let them go. The place they were in, it was too much. Figured it was better to release them and call them back later. Better than where they were. That's the problem. I tried calling them when you were out but they never came back. Anyway, you'll see. You sure you can move around? You look like shit."

"I feel like shit. But you better show me."

"Hold on a sec."

Ross pulled back the furniture and a great gale flooded the cabin, nearly flash-freezing Kirk where he stood. The Newfoundlander picked up the shotgun where he'd placed it amongst some wood, an act very much noticed. Both men bent forward as they stepped outside, into a cold that stunned them with its depth. The blizzard buffeted them, shrieked, flung stinging snow into their faces. A ferocious, near constant gust made Kirk's ruined coat flutter in a rage of dark flames. The approaching night pressed in all around, reducing visibility and casting a blue, deep-freezer hue over the snow.

"This way," Ross roared, pulling the hood of his snowsuit over his head. Amazingly, Kirk realized he still wore his stocking cap and wished it was thicker. The two men walked through the darkening trench towards a huge storage building rising out of the gathering gloom. Ross got there first and opened it, waving his companion inside.

Kirk smelled it from the cabin's doorway. He knew then that he was right when he had caught a whiff of it earlier.

But inside, he had to lift his sleeve to his nose.

Blood. Offal. Bodily waste. Soaked hair. A brutal cocktail that smashed into his senses.

"Pretty bad, eh?" Ross said from behind. "Think I almost puked in here myself once or twice."

Kirk ignored the man and walked between the rows of cages, inhaling ghostly traces of the released dogs. Worse, men had died here, the residual scent of their deaths teasing his acute sense of smell.

"Something wrong?" Ross asked.

Kirk didn't answer. There *was* something wrong, lingering beneath the telltale vapors of fear and madness, for he could smell that rotten taint as clear as decaying meat.

And yet he hadn't a clue as to what it was.

Lying on the bottom of a cage, a brass tag gleamed off a length of worn leather. Kirk picked it up, and read the name *Brutus* etched upon the surface.

"Whattaya think?" Ross asked eagerly.

Kirk tossed the collar and studied the floor, the ceiling and the cages before answering. Tufts of hair decorated wire mesh. Teeth fragments gleamed on the floor. Part of him could almost hear the mournful cries of animals trapped and suffering. Something god awful terrible had occurred within these isolated confines, and what bothered him the most was he could only discern a hint of it.

"I don't know," he finally answered.

"What should we do?" the Newfoundland man asked, holding the gun across his pelvis.

Kirk just didn't know. He wished he'd never answered his phone in the very beginning.

Ross fidgeted uncomfortably. "Look, back at the road and halfway up the hill is the old guy's house. We can head there and use his phone. Sound good?"

It sounded just fine, Kirk thought miserably.

And yet it bothered him because of what he might have to do.

17

Freedom.

But after being imprisoned for so long, freedom from Borland's store didn't just fill them with relief or elation. Not for what had been done to them, the things they'd had to endure. If anything, it only made them… crazier. The wind and snow and cold whipped their rabid enthusiasm to mindless heights. At first, they scampered past the cabin, headlong into the blizzard without a thought other than the frantic, mind-numbing impulse to *get away*. Their paws ripped up pristine walls and mounds of snow. Their voices almost frazzled in the afterburn of their escape. They ran, over the frozen pond and into the tree line, low hanging boughs exploding into falling plumes of white as they sped past.

They smelled each other in the storm, and eventually, each dog ran across another's trail, until the pack centered on one trail in particular—one that led them all away from the cabin. Max wasn't sure where he was going, nor did he like the scent he was following through the brush, but all around him he heard the whine of the other dogs who were wondering the same thing. The pack clambered up through a frozen timberland close to impassable. At times, Max saw dogs to either side of him, plodding in the same direction. He didn't go anywhere near them. Badness lurked within those animals.

The badness lurked within Max, too, for that matter.

The forest grew colder as the sky pressed further down upon their flattened ears and skulls.

Then a cabin appeared. A different cabin, situated in a patch of woodland where tree stumps poked up through the wintry surf like dead volcanoes. Old and decrepit, with cheap plastic curtains that fluttered in smashed windows and long-graying planks that might have been someone's first attempt at building a dwelling. Max saw the lifeless place from its rear, smelled the decay, and powered through the deep snow leading to it. He was far from home, weak, and nowhere near his full potential, in desperate need to find shelter from the night. Fear gave him energy and his heart burned with it.

Cold, everything was so cold.

Dogs barked and gathered around the sides of the cabin. As much as he loathed to, he recognized strength in a pack. Max approached the structure once realizing that no one lived there. He searched for the entrance desperately, to escape the dropping temperatures.

He rounded a corner and halted in his tracks. There, standing directly in front of the open doorway stood a dog. Max had never seen the animal before, but it was large and powerful, and it snarled at the assembling pack like a gatekeeper ready for war. Some of the bigger dogs barked and snapped at the black beast with orange flares about its jaws and paws, but Orange hunched over and stared them all down, threatening them with a gnashing of its frightening teeth, warding most away from the entrance.

A husky breed with beige and white fur crept forward, tired of the snow and the cold and seeing Orange as nothing more than a fleshy barrier to be pushed aside.

The growl from Orange's throat made Max back away, sensing something sinister about the dog.

*

His owner called him Brutus, and to that name he answered. He didn't care for his owner, an ungentle sort who would punch him at times, for no reason other than to beat him into submission. His owner fed him scraps from the table whenever he felt like it. Sometimes Brutus would go a week without being fed at all. A few instances, Brutus could even remember being fed pans of animal fat, which, in his hunger, he gladly scoffed down. In the winters, he would actively hunt rats or rabbits and devour them, when he had free run of the outside. That didn't happen very often as most times he would be tied to an outdoor post. He remembered that dreadful stump of unyielding wood, a six-foot long chain that ended in barbed wire, and nothing more than a strip of cardboard as a bed. Even in winter. Rarely was he warm in winter.

When Borland took him in, it wasn't a kidnapping.

It was a rescue.

Brutus was used to pain. Used to suffering. From his owner. He would take what his owner gave and try harder to please. That mindset didn't extend to strangers, however. Or other dogs. Brutus saw no need for such efforts towards any of his own kind or any of the lesser species. Other dogs had it much better than him, and he knew it.

He hated them for that.

Borland wasn't so bad. The cell was small, but the store was warm. The other dogs irritated Brutus. They frightened easily and they never stopped making noise.

Now that they were free, Brutus sensed things were different. Something had changed him while in Borland's store.

Something… for the better.

And there, on the step of a deserted cabin, Brutus decided that he wasn't going to be owned ever again. He hunched over and growled, staring down the biggest of the lot with murderous intent.

The husky with the beige and white fur didn't back down.

That suited Brutus just fine.

Other dogs backed away, not wanting any part of what was about to transpire, allowing Brutus to focus on the approaching husky with its fangs bared. Brutus had found this cabin on his own and the others had followed his trail, drawn by forces none of them understood or ever would. Drawn to *him*. Unlike the mongrels before him, Brutus knew he was a Rottweiler as plainly as he knew his given name. He'd heard his owner repeat the word enough to make the association. Knew instinctively what he was capable of.

Knew only he could lead this pack.

The dog, a thick-haired animal, leaped for his face. Brutus sprang off the threshold of the cabin and crashed into the challenger. A whirl of savage wrestling ensued, much to the excited chorus of the others.

Then Brutus clamped down and yanked back, ripping out the other dog's throat in a vicious fan that dappled the snow surrounding the front door. The challenger died slowly, on its side, legs kicking weakly. Steam rose from its raw gullet.

Brutus backed away from the dead and stared down the others, baring a snout colored scarlet, showing teeth traced in dark lines. Sending a message.

That's one.

A mongrel, thick with muscle and possessing a long, black head and narrow eyes, separated itself from the pack. It lunged forward in a flash of teeth. Brutus stopped it in midair and bore the animal to the ground with muzzle and claws. They rolled in the snow, snapping for each other's throats. The remainder of the pack watched and waited.

The new dog was powerful, and soon bore the Rottweiler to the powdery ground. Brutus twisted out from under the challenger and counterattacked, his jaws crushing the throat of the animal. Brutus forced it down, shaking his head, working his teeth in deeper.

Until bone cracked.

The strength bled out of the mongrel, and Brutus regarded the others while he finished killing his adversary, black eyes daring them all. When the dying dog finally grew still, Brutus released it and backed up, red tongue lapping at his blood-spattered muzzle, this time out of necessity rather than spectacle, but sending a second message to the curs before him.

That's two.

The tall one in the rear bolted. Brutus didn't care. He'd made his point. He barked several times, snapping reports as clear and frightening as gunshots. The other dogs were now curiously solemn. No other dog would challenge Brutus's claim that night. Another barrage of barks burst from the Rottweiler, laying the law down thick.

No reaction from the cold-weary audience.

Sensing no further threats to his leadership, Brutus turned his back and plodded inside the deserted cabin.

The others piled in after him.

They padded and thumped about, tails wagging, seeking the most comfortable spot before lying down on bare wood floors. Before too long, the need to feed came upon them.

Brutus would never have considered eating his own kind, but something had happened to him during his imprisonment with the man-thing and his cages. He didn't understand what it was, and the meat was right *there*, outside, in the snow.

The others watched him when he went outside. The snow wrapped around Brutus, absorbing him, making him disappear. The Rottweiler appeared seconds later, dragging the carcass of one of his challengers.

The other dogs lifted their heads in curiosity.

Brutus didn't see the dead dog as anything else but meat. He'd changed, somehow, that much was clear to him, as clear as the food lying just outside in the storm. Ignoring the others, Brutus pulled apart the dog, stretching out hairy flesh until it snapped, gnawing it free from bones. The smell intoxicated him, as did the taste, and he gulped down his fill. Other dogs approached curiously while he gorged himself on meat and cracked bones, but he put them in their place with a growl.

One of the pack went outside and dragged in the second body. Several of the bigger dogs tore into it while the smaller ones circled, waiting for scraps.

When Brutus had eaten his fill, he backed away from the ravaged dead, and lay down in front of the threshold of the door. He gazed at the storm with the air of a weary soldier on guard duty, narrowing his eyes at the darkening tempest, barely hearing the sounds of the pack devouring the bodies in the background. Bones cracked. Marrow licked out. Growls punctuated the air.

Brutus knew it wasn't enough, would never *be* enough. They needed *more.*

Staring out at the storm, the Rottweiler wondered where he could find it.

He eventually stood up, earning the fearful attention of the others. Without hesitation, the lead animal walked out into the blizzard.

The pack followed.

18

The blizzard parked itself directly over the peninsula, weaving a mighty spell of snow that blew and blustered around the two figures shrouded by the dying light of the day. The temperature plummeted. Flesh and bone stiffened and slowed. One man staggered under the brutal gales summoned by the storm overhead, bare hands plunging into snowbanks that froze his unprotected skin. He floundered to his knees and squinted ahead. Though only separated by five paces from the other man, the attacking snow intensified to a maelstrom of bewildering white, erasing all existence of a world.

"*Jesus Christ*," Kirk swore into the blizzard, fighting an external and internal battle. Never had he been outside in such voracious elements. And never had he been so utterly smashed in a fight. The after-effects grated more on his nerves than anything else. His battle with Borland would leave him pissing blood for at least a day, and now this frigid bitch of a winter storm was stomping on him.

A hand gripped his shoulder and he looked up to see first the shotgun, then the Newfoundlander's cringing face.

"You okay?" Ross bellowed, making himself heard over winds seeking to suck the breath out of his lungs.

"Just pissed off," Kirk roared back. "*This* is fucking *mental.*"

"Cabin's right there."

And like magic, the wind dropped out just enough to allow the snow screen to falter. The cabin lurked not ten feet away, and threatened to disappear any second.

"Move on then," the Halifax native said as he climbed to his feet.

Ross did and Kirk followed, but when he reached the front of the cabin, he paused and motioned for the Newfoundlander to keep moving. Kirk looked out into that swirling, stinging wall of dark white, to where he'd first wrestled with Borland. His knife was out there, not ten feet from the entrance. He fumed for a moment, and then started his search. Ten seconds later, with his hands feeling as if they had been fused into crystal, he located his knife. There were blades inside the cabin, but they weren't *his* blade, and a warden's knife was his badge. He stooped, picked the weapon up and slipped the length into its sheath, still fixed to his belt behind his back.

Ross yelled above the savage wind. "You all right?"

"Yeah," Kirk shouted back, approaching the cabin.

But Ross lifted the shotgun and didn't look so helpful anymore.

"Y'know, when I walked in here," Ross began, "I saw a bloody mess in the snow, a shotgun, which I have, and a big ol' knife."

"That's my knife," Kirk told him.

"And where is it now?"

"I have it. In a belt sheath, behind my back."

Ross watched him, wrestling with the best course of action. "Get in here," he finally said.

Relieved, Kirk entered the dwelling and stomped his feet clear of snow. Ross kept one wary eye on him as he arranged the furniture against the doorway, shielding the interior from the brunt of the storm. Kirk's attention was divided among several things, until his eyes fell on the prone form of Morris.

"Well, what do y'think of it all?" Ross eventually asked.

Kirk sighed. "Don't know. But that shed's fucked up."

"This whole place is fucked up. Which leads me to something else, since you're feeling better. Maybe you can explain what the hell happened here? And why is Borland dead, 'cause right now, you're looking like a murderer."

In the shadows of the cabin only dimly illuminated by the orange, skull grin of the stove, Kirk faced the man. "I can't tell you anything right now."

"Why?"

"Look, you want to call in the police. Let's get to that phone you wanted. You keep the gun, too, if it makes you feel better. And here."

Against his better judgment, Kirk pulled out the Bowie and offered it.

Ross eyed it for a moment before cautiously taking it from the man. "It's gonna take a lot more than just this—" Ross stuck the weapon down his boot "—to make me feel better. You said it best. This is all fucked up. And look..."

Kirk did, in the direction of Borland. His fangs and claws had disappeared, and his face had taken on a pasty gray that, in the growing dark, looked absolutely morbid. Ross moved around the cabin, bending and picking up scattered, red-cased shotgun shells, keeping the weapon lowered but pointed in Kirk's direction at all times.

Careful. Not that Kirk blamed him.

"Leave the knife," Ross said, nodding at the weapon jutting from Borland's chest.

"Wasn't going to touch it."

"Your prints on that?"

Kirk exhaled and chose to not say a word.

"Silence admits guilt, or something or other," Ross stated.

"There's more to it than what you're seeing."

"Yeah, well, I'm seeing a goddamn eyeful. He wasn't a favorite around here, but he was a member of the community, and here he is stabbed to shit and his throat chewed out. And then finding a shitload of missing dogs out in his store, which makes him look pretty fucking guilty of something. I'd say you owned a couple of them animals, faced off against Borland, and things got dirty. Am I close?"

Faint ribbons of light flickered across Kirk's face. "Something like that."

"So then," Ross's face became pensive in his attempt to sort things out. "Why the hell did Borland have... *fangs* and claws? And where the hell are they now? And what the sweet Jesus is *that* thing doing here?" He gestured at Morris.

The questions fell into a void of silence, filled by the dreary caterwauling of the wind.

"Let's go make that call," Kirk said.

"You think that's going to help? 'Cause I'm not sure you'd be too hot to get to a phone. At least, *me* getting to a phone. And calling the cops."

Though his face didn't show it, Kirk winced inside.

"Let's..." He faltered and took a deep breath as his blood loss took him for an unexpected ride. "Look. Look at me. I'm shitbagged. I can barely walk right now and you have my knife. We can't stay here. Let's just get to that phone. It'll make you feel better, right? Bringing the cops in on this? Get them to sort things out?"

Ross nodded. "Yeah."

"All right, then." Kirk hesitated. "When you're ready."

"I'm ready. You go on ahead. I'll be right behind."

"Storm's whipping up shit out there."

"Yeah. I know."

Flipping up his collar and fastening it in anticipation of the cold, Kirk pulled down his stocking cap with red hands. He cursed himself for not bringing gloves. Ross pulled the furniture away from the door and gestured for Kirk to get moving.

Outside, the storm enveloped them with an unbelievable fury. They sunk into the swelling layers of snow. Kirk stopped and glanced back, swaying in the wind.

"Go straight!" Ross shouted.

Kirk did as told.

They walked away from the battlefield of the cabin, and when Kirk looked over his shoulder after a dozen paces, the structure was nowhere to be seen. Ross stood only five steps at his back, but the stormy twilight almost rendered him invisible.

"Go!" he repeated.

Kirk got to walking, plunging his hands into his ruined coat. At least Borland hadn't sliced up his pockets. He struggled through drifts up to his knees, trying to ignore the chill gnawing into his limbs.

"You know where we're going?" Kirk yelled over his shoulder.

A snow-blurred shadow stepped in close. "Hell no. But we're on a pond. A small one at that. Sooner or later, we'll hit shore and from there we follow it 'til we see the road. It's close to the edge. No problem there."

"Unless we get lost."

"Lost?" Ross asked with a trace of dismay. "How can we get lost?"

The woodsman stomped forward then, taking the brunt of the blinding snow, ignoring Kirk for the moment. Perhaps he saw something the Halifax man didn't. Kirk set his jaw and tried very hard to ignore the smoldering pain in his chest and ribs. He struggled to keep close to his companion's back, to utilize the slipstream. The woodsman plunged into the heart of the maelstrom. Being out in a storm of *this* magnitude, with Kirk's own senses whirled by a field of freezing, stinging static, suddenly gave him a begrudging appreciation for the Newfoundlander.

Kirk hoped things would work out for them both.

Lashing sheets of gray obscured Ross's back at times. The man was only five feet away, but visibility was next to nothing. Kirk stumbled at times, hands ripping from his pockets to plunge into the freezing snow, gnarling them into flesh knobs. He got to his feet with effort, noting that Ross waited for him like a black beacon, near invisible in the storm.

Relief surged throughout Kirk when they finally reached the road.

"Was that hellish or what?" Ross asked, standing in snow just past his ankles.

"That was something."

"Gets better," Ross said, straining to be heard. "Uphill from here a little ways, but the trees along the road will break the wind."

Looking in the direction of the pond, all Kirk could see was a wall of harsh smoke.

"Almost dark," Ross declared. "Let's get going."

This time, he waited until Kirk got beside him, and both men walked abreast of each other up the easy grade. Neither spoke, and for that, Kirk was thankful. It took most of his energy just to keep on walking. A craving made itself known. His body needed fuel to complete its ongoing repairs. He needed to eat. Preferably meat.

He tried hard not to look at Ross.

I am not a monster. I'm not.

The hill steepened while a thick, natural fence of timberland rose with gothic might on either side of the road. Minutes later, Ross pointed with the shotgun. There, almost hidden by the storm's breath and choked with snow, was a small lane, almost undetectable. They forged ahead and it eventually opened up into a small clearing. A stark white house squatted in the middle, and an old shed stood on guard to the left of the single-story building. Blowing snow raged across the scene like tattered flags.

Full dark was no more than ten or fifteen minutes away.

"There she is," Ross exclaimed and motioned Kirk to keep up. He did, out of fear of developing frostbite.

It appeared as if Borland hadn't visited his home in a while. The bottom half of the front door was partially buried. A bleached blind had been pulled down, leaving a gap only a few fingers wide.

Ross tried the knob. "Locked." He glanced back at Kirk. "Is breakin' and enterin' still, like, illegal when the guy's dead?"

"Good question. I don't know."

"I'm hearin' a lot of that from you."

"What do you want me to say? Break in the window?"

Ross considered it. Then he shrugged and stooped to peer inside the house.

"Hey…" he eventually said, snow blowing around his head. "There's something in there."

Kirk sniffed the air. Dog. And that crazy underlying taint he'd smelled at Borland's cabin. "Might be a dog."

"No…" Ross trailed off. "It is. I can just make it out. A little one. Damned peculiar, though."

"Why is that?"

Ross grimaced as he cupped a hand to the glass. "Little fella is just watchin' me. Not makin' a sound."

A bad feeling uncoiled itself in Kirk's gut. "Maybe it's just friendly," he said, not believing his own voice.

"Maybe, but—" Ross backed away. "Take a look."

Kirk replaced him at the door and peered inside. Two rooms just inside the entryway, and a short hallway leading straight to the archway of a kitchen, as a blade of light on the other side of the house bounced off a countertop. The place appeared all but empty and sterile, like an empty morgue.

Then he spotted the animal. A black outline of a dog—a little one as Ross had said—just below the countertop. Kirk almost missed it. The animal stood motionless, as if sculpted from hardwood, watching the strangers just beyond the front door.

"You see it?" Ross asked.

"Yeah."

"Small dog."

"Yeah, small," Kirk agreed, recognizing the animal as a breed of terrier. But it wasn't barking at them, and the scent from the thing rankled Kirk's nose, even behind the frosted door. His eyes told him it was a regular dog… but it didn't entirely *smell* like one. The thing could be growling, but he wasn't sure, not with the winds raging around them.

"We can head on down to the next house," Ross suggested.

"What?"

"It's not far from here. Fifteen-minute hike through this slop."

Kirk straightened. "But this is Borland's house."

"Yeah, but I'm not comfortable with breaking in. The law's so fucked up I don't know if breaking into a dead man's house and calling the cops will get me arrested. Regardless if he's been stealing dogs."

"I'll do it then."

"You'll break in?"

"I don't care." Kirk shrugged. He truly didn't, except for escaping the weather. His hands were forming into blocks of ice.

He peeked inside once again, searching for the dog in the shadows.

It wasn't there anymore.

Unsure if he should be worried or not, Kirk started for the work shed.

"Might be an axe or something around the woodpile," Ross shouted after him.

Kirk stomped through drifts and halted after passing the corner of the house. The strange smell had suddenly grown even stronger. He turned towards the backyard of the house.

There, standing in the growing darkness, was a short, stocky man.

A short, stocky, *naked* man.

Kirk blinked at the freakish sight. Steam issued from a mouth swathed in shadow, and the guy's eyes gleamed eerily even at this distance. His upper frame heaved with exertion, and even draped in snowy gloom as he was, there was no mistaking the solid musculature.

Without warning, the brute charged.

Kirk took two steps back, spreading his hands for the potential tackle. "Hey! *Hey!*"

The human cannonball bounded across the snow, ripping up the windswept designs with every step. Kirk's voice left him in a gasp of horror. His legs weakened. Thoughts stopped. The stampeding attacker closed in, facial features becoming visible in the evening's dying radiance. For an elongat second, Kirk beheld the wide, insane eyes—golf balls of blackness pricked by needle points of light and malice. Below this, lips were pulled back in a snarl, revealing a set of long, canine teeth.

And hands ending in curved claws.

"Jesus—" Kirk sputtered.

Just as the monster leaped.

*

Ross wasn't sure what the hell was happening. The guy—he realized didn't even know his name—stopped and stared just before a little naked dude barreled into him. Both figures launched into the air and landed in an explosion of white powder. They wrestled. Someone screamed, long and hard, just as he heard the chuffing of snow to his left and the ragged, if not *excited,* expulsion of breath.

Ross jerked the shotgun up into the face of his own attacker a split second before he crashed into him. Both rolled into the snow, the freak on top, actually trying to bite through walnut and steel with a set of teeth that belonged in a vintage bear trap. Ross pushed, forcing the face back, energized by a jolt of fright when he saw the shocking eight balls that served as the thing's eyes.

Bright orbs that fixed on him.

19

The creature crashed into Kirk and landed on top of him in the snow. He lashed out with his arms, pushing the thing's fanged maw back, screaming for Ross to *shoot it, shoot it*, but Ross wasn't shooting, so Kirk took matters into his own hands just as the monster clawed at his face. He trapped the fright's left wrist in a joint lock and twisted, forcing it nose-first into the snow. Stretching the trapped arm out, Kirk fought to get his legs under him while the *Were*—as it could only be some fucked up breed of *Were* he was fighting—struggled to get free. Kirk wasn't about to let that happen.

He got to his knees and threw his weight onto the elbow of the extended arm, breaking it like a meaty icicle. The *Were* freaked, thrashing so hard that Kirk felt his numb grip weakening. The Halifax warden released the beast, scampered backwards to his feet and into a fighting stance.

The *Were* stood, its evil eyes burning in the failing light, mouth split into rows of fangs. Its left arm hung like a broken length of wood, a jagged point protruding from the crook of the elbow. It shrieked. Kirk reached behind his back and flinched with shock.

Ross had his knife.

The monster lunged.

It flew through the air, sweeping both arms for Kirk's head. The warden ducked under the flailing limbs, utilizing strength and speed he didn't think he possessed in his current state. He stumbled towards the front of the house and spotted Ross wrestling with a naked figure, just as the Newfoundlander pulled the shotgun's trigger and blew the *Were's* head apart.

Kirk flinched at the blast.

Behind him, the other *Were* screeched.

That sound spurred Kirk forward. "Ross!"

The man turned around at his name and his eyes widened. Kirk knew what he saw. Ross pumped the shotgun and aimed as Kirk dove in a splash of powder. The gun barked, catching the rushing *Were* full in the chest, flinging it back as if it had been yanked from behind.

The creature landed in a heap. It groaned, rolled over, and struggled to rise.

"Shoot it again!" Kirk yelled.

Ross considered this with a look of horror, but primed the shotgun once more, the ejector spitting the spent cartridge into the snow. He braced himself for the firearm's kick.

The *Were* rolled over and sat up, grinding its teeth.

"*Shoot!*" Kirk shouted, shaking with effort.

Ross blinked, hesitated. The *Were* stood, further defying the killing blow. A crater spilled blood from its chest, the body heat sending a wispy plume of steam into the frigid air. The beast cradled its wound, its arms covered and glistening with sticky scarlet. It opened its mouth and a whistle of insanity piped from its throat and ruined lungs.

And stepped towards them.

Kirk freaked. "*Shoot, Goddam—*"

Ross fired again, his arms absorbing the kick of the weapon. The *Were's* midsection exploded and it backed up a pair of steps.

Kirk crawled to a stunned Ross. "Knife!" he cried, and pulled the blade from the horrified man's boot. The Halifax warden got up just as the *Were* charged them, bleeding every step of the way.

The warden set his feet and punched his blade through the thing's eye. The monster's feet flew out from under it, ripping the knife from the warden's grasp, and crashed on its back. It bucked once where it fell, claws clutching at the hilt but unable to pull the weapon free, and relaxed with a softening grimace on its face.

Breathing hard, Kirk retrieved his blade and staggered back, taking in the grisly scene, just as the Newfoundlander sank to his knees.

"Jesus H. Christ," Ross moaned, staring at the dead thing. "Jesus H. *Christ.*"

"You okay?" Kirk asked.

Ross's head turned about as if possessed. An expression of shocked revulsion marred his woodsman's features. He didn't answer and his eyes blinked and sparkled like a shorting fuse box. His snowsuit had been rent about the sleeves. Kirk slowed down, dread flooding his chest upon seeing the mess covering his companion. The *Were* had been looming over Ross when he blew its skull apart and a considerable amount of dark matter had splattered the man.

"Hold on," Kirk said. He stumbled to the headless body. The carcass lay off at an angle on its side. Kirk dropped into the snow to study it. He needed to be sure, so he cleared away the white flakes already coating the torso before stabbing his knife deep into the ribs, hunting for the heart.

"The fuck you doin'?" Ross asked in horror.

"Makin' sure it's dead."

"I blew the goddamn *head* off the fucker."

"Yeah, so—" Kirk grimaced and shrugged. "Gutting it won't hurt, right?"

Ross didn't answer. Kirk twisted the knife and held the pose for a moment. Then he withdrew the silver and stuck it into the snow. He studied the Newfoundlander, noting he'd dropped the shotgun by his leg. "You okay?"

"Yeah."

"What about your arms?"

As if awakening from a dream, Ross held up his forearms and inhaled sharply. "Oh Christ."

"All right, don't lose it," Kirk coaxed. "Let me see."

"That thing," Ross muttered, "had claws. Just tore through the sleeves."

"Hold them out for me."

Ross did as he was told. The snow swirled savagely around them as Kirk rolled back the sleeves, revealing deep, bleeding lines. For a moment, the Halifax warden could only stare, shocked at the implications.

The solemn pause was not lost on Ross. "What?" he demanded.

"Nothing."

"Fuck nothing, y'look like you just took the world's bloodiest shit. So you tell me."

Kirk felt his companion's arms tremble. He took a deep, sobering breath and lied through his teeth. "These should be… disinfected. Soon as possible."

"Or what?"

"Or you risk infection."

"You mean *die?* I could *croak* from this?"

"Only if we don't clean them up. I mean, look at those things."

Ross did. "Fuck. What the fuck *are* they?"

Kirk couldn't answer.

"Are they zombies?" Ross wanted to know. "Oh Jesus, tell me they aren't zombies."

"Zombies?" Kirk cocked an eyebrow and almost barked a laugh. "No, they aren't *zombies.*"

"The fuck you know? They *could* be zombies. Oh shit! Holy shit, shit, *shit*. Look at me! They got me! That means I'm gonna turn into one of them *things*. Oh my sweet Christ. This is unreal. All I need is to be runnin' around with my junk hanging out, tryin' to fuckin' eat people."

"You ain't gonna turn into a zombie," Kirk grated, avoiding a much worse possibility. "Look, those things jumped us. Can zombies jump people?"

"Depends on the fuckin' zombies."

"There's more than one kind of zombie?"

"Course there is. I mean, you got your dead Romero-type, slow-moving sonsabitches. Then you got—"

"Okay," Kirk interrupted, "but do they *look* like zombies to you?"

A mortified Ross blinked and shakily answered, "No."

"Well then, there you go."

"I blew the head offa one to stop it."

"That doesn't mean anything. Anyone will die after a round to the head."

Ross seemed to consider that. "They moved pretty fuckin' fast, though. There's fast moving zombies."

"Jesus Christ, they're *not* fucking zombies," Kirk snapped, stunning Ross into silence. He picked up the shotgun and knife and held the firearm out to Ross. It took him a moment, but the other man grasped the walnut grip.

"Come on, before I freeze my balls off out here," Kirk said and walked towards the rear of the house with the knife in hand.

"Where you goin'?" Ross asked.

"To check on something."

Ross caught up just as Kirk rounded the corner. In the dark blue, the outline of a back door could be made out. At its base was a dog's door. Kirk stopped before it and peered into a kitchen. It didn't surprise him that the dogs were nowhere to be seen. That revelation sent another chill through his guts.

How long?

"How long from the time we saw that first dog to when those things jumped us?"

"I..." Ross shook his head. "I don't remember."

"Thirty seconds?"

"Maybe."

Way too fast, Kirk mulled, eyes darting around the dark kitchen. He tried the back doorknob and found it locked. Not caring in the least now, he jabbed his Bowie knife through the pane with a tinkle of glass, noting that Ross seemed to be fine with him having the weapon. He put his elbow through the hole, widened it, and stuck his hand in, wondering if something would leap from the shadowy interior and bite it off. It seemed like the run of luck he was having.

Nothing did, however, and the door opened with a soft click. They entered the house.

"That thing loaded?" Kirk asked Ross.

"Huh? I don't know."

"Well, make sure," he ordered and stepped around a table. Outside, the wind screamed, making the house cringe on its foundation. The place felt like a meat locker and that stink of something, which Kirk suddenly realized might mean *Weres*, permeated throughout. Kirk flicked a light switch on, revealing the interior in a flash. Kirk gripped his knife and held it close, ready to stab, and proceeded down the hall, turning on lights as he found them.

"I've seen these things before," Ross said from behind, to the rhythm of shells being fed into a tubular magazine.

"What?"

"Yesterday. I think… I think I came across the tracks of one of those things while in the woods. Tracks of bare feet out in the snow. Wicked. But—but where did the dogs go?"

Kirk ignored that question for the moment, concentrating on making sense of it all. He peered into a near dark living room. A pair of slept-in bed rolls lay next to a sofa and an easy chair. Paperbacks lined a small set of shelves. The single television was the old kind with a fat ass. Seeing it was clear, he checked out a bedroom with its single queen-sized bed, neatly made. The whole house appeared quite clean. As crazy as he was, Borland kept his house in order.

"Anything?" Ross asked, shotgun pointed at the floor when Kirk stepped into the hall.

"No, nothing. Hold on." Kirk went into the bathroom and checked the medicine cabinet. "Come here."

He pulled out a box of cotton swabs and a bottle of peroxide, which he prepared to dab onto his companion's wounds.

"You think this'll work?" Ross asked as he placed the gun down and pulled his sleeves back.

"Better than nothing," Kirk replied. He saturated one swab before applying it to the claw wounds.

"What's your name, anyway?" Ross asked.

Kirk hesitated. "Doug."

"Thanks, Doug."

Kirk glanced at his earnest face before getting back to work. "Listen. Once this is done, you and I have to head back out there. There's something we need to check on."

Ross nodded, making a face at the peroxide's pinch when pressed to his flesh.

"All right," Kirk declared once finished. "Give me a minute."

He went into the bedroom and tore into a chest of drawers, pulling out white undershirts and even a sweater, all of which he sniffed. Clothing in hand, he returned to the kitchen and found a pair of scissors and got to work cutting the shirts up, knotting some together, and making pads with others. His coat came off then, as did his shirt.

"Okay," Kirk said, grimacing as he peeled away his blood-soaked shirt. The charred line across his chest looked worse in the light, like an unwashed grill after a weekend of barbecuing. "Ross, get over here and help me patch this up."

Ross had just completed his first knot on Kirk's chest bandage when the lights flickered and died.

20

Alvin sat in near total darkness.

He glanced up from his monitor which, only seconds before, had served as a first-person window to a beautifully rendered, post-apocalyptic world ruled by aliens, and he was the cleaner, delivering mini-gun justice to the invaders. Or at least he *had* been delivering. He'd been slinging hot tracers at a particularly troublesome knot of attackers, coming close to finishing them all where he'd failed a dozen times earlier, focused entirely on laying down a hail of punishing fire into the multi-tentacled fuckers, and just about to send them packing with a bon voyage of lobbed frag grenades…

When the power went out.

Leaving him with a black screen and the lingering after-aroma of the three cheeseburgers he'd consumed for supper.

"Well… *goddamnit.*" He hadn't even gotten the chance to *save* the game. That pissed him off. The thought of having to replay the whole damn episode made him fume right down to his short n' curlies. Alvin sucked in a great, clarifying breath from his air tubes and realized then that the concentrator had stopped as well.

"Shit, fuck, *damn.*" He stood up from what he affectionately called his captain's chair, and immediately rapped the small toe of his right foot into the corner of the desk. The sudden crackle of pain bent him over at the waist.

"Shit," he squeaked, mentally transporting himself to an internal panic room to dampen the hurt. When it finally passed, he suppressed the urge to softball pitch things around the computer room. The last time he'd done such a thing had cost him a monitor, and no matter how hard he'd played the sympathy card, PC Land hadn't been convinced the damage had occurred during delivery.

Snow caked the smaller windows, so Alvin limped to his living room and peered out at the shivering scene. He had the best view of the hillside, he figured, and right at this moment, he couldn't see shit. Not another house could be seen beyond his picture window. There was the main road out there somewhere, a mere forty feet from his front door, and the mailboxes another fifteen feet behind that. He couldn't see that asshole Shea's place or his buddy Walsh's house either. All gone. A complete whiteout in the dark, which made him wonder if there was any irony there. He discovered seconds later that the land line had no dial tone and his cell phone was just as dead.

All of this was not to his liking.

Grumbling and recovering from his limp, Alvin went to his back porch. He'd grab a portable air tank, suit up, and head out to his work shed, where he had a small four-thousand-watt gasoline generator hooked up to the house. It would keep the concentrator going, as well as the computer. Oxygen wasn't a huge concern as he also had reserve tanks in his bedroom closet. Heat, well, he had a wood burning stove in the basement and vents cut into the floor.

He'd be rocking in less than thirty minutes.

The blizzard could kiss his fat ass.

*

The farthest house on the northeastern edge of Upper Amherst Cove belonged to Clifford and Marie Spree. The Sprees had moved to the island back in '89, as an early-retirement home from their life's work in designing and redesigning kitchens, based in Boston. It wasn't a difficult decision to make. They had visited Newfoundland several times before in their Winnebago, and fell in love with the rugged coastline, the sentimental matchbox houses, and the clear air. Contrary to their family's beliefs in New York, the weather was milder in the stormy seasons, with Hurricane Igor being the lone exception to the rule.

Upper Amherst Cove, with its single, rustic road and excellent view of Bonavista Bay, was the ideal place to steal away and live out the rest of their gluten-free lives. Clifford occupied his time with a myriad of hobbies, including learning the guitar, while Marie set about growing and cultivating potatoes, spinach, carrots and other vegetables in a small patch of land behind the house.

Clifford gazed out through a window that framed a picture of absolute midwinter darkness.

"See anything?" Marie asked, taking small steps about the kitchen, feeling her way before stopping at the large, hardwood table and lighting a row of candles.

"Nothing," Clifford mumbled. He turned to his wife of near forty-nine years and watched her putter back to a row of cupboards. "Where's the flashlight?"

"What flashlight?"

"The big one."

"Care to elaborate?"

"You know, the big one with the–the–the battery fixed to the bottom there. One flick and *whoosh*. Damn thing could direct in air traffic. The space station would call down and ask 'what the hell's that?' when it's turned on. *Blind* people see the thing. I'm a regular one-man light show with that beast."

"Ohhh, *that* flashlight." Marie smiled evilly, and Clifford knew she had the goods on him for *something*, but damned if he could remember exactly what. At seventy-four, he'd thus far managed to stave off Alzheimer's, or at least so he thought. Though there were moments of irritating memory lapses, like going into the kitchen for something, forgetting what that something was, then remembering it once back in the living room, only to forget yet again upon returning the kitchen.

Clifford hated when that happened to him.

But Marie, like any good woman, kept him mostly on the straight and narrow. Right now, however, her tone suggested they had addressed this very subject earlier, but he couldn't recall when.

"All right." He stood and waited with hands on hips.

"All right what?" she replied sweetly. That was the final telltale hint. Yep. She knew, and she was torturing him with it.

"Where is it?"

"Where do you think it is?"

"If I knew, I wouldn't be asking."

"You don't remember." Marie smirked. She turned her back on him. "You know what this reminds me of?"

Clifford didn't want to ask, but he did. "No. What?"

"The time you forgot where New Delhi was."

"Aw, c'mon, that just slipped my memory. Stop bringing that up."

"But you're so cute when I do."

"You're being a hard ass," Clifford pointed out.

"What's it look like out there?" Marie asked, changing the subject.

"Like shit. Now where's the flashlight?"

"Power's gone out everywhere?"

"Long gone." He snapped his fingers. "Flashlight?"

"I could use a massage tonight." Marie straightened and placed a hand to her cheek, striking a pose of deep thought.

"If I had that flashlight I could find you and give you that massage."

Marie shook her head, making her short bangs bounce, and pointed to the countertop barely glazed in candlelight. "Never mind about that thing. Look. We have these flashlights."

She pointed at a handful of smaller, hand-generated units.

Clifford frowned. "Those are… birthday cake candles. Where's the beast?"

"You won't like where you left it."

"How do you know?"

"It's outside in the shed."

Clifford balked. "Well, shit. Why the hell did I put it there?"

"How often have I asked the same thing?" Marie remarked with a saucy look down the front of his jeans.

"You're telling the truth now?"

"Yes," Marie said. "Leave it for tomorrow. It's too cold to go outside tonight."

Well, that wasn't going to do in Clifford's mind. He did grab one of the small flashlights before exiting the kitchen and descending a short flight of steps to the back door. He flicked at the light switch to confirm the power was still out, then fumbled with his boots and a heavy coat.

Marie leaned against the wall at the top of the stairs, a lit candle perched astride a wooden holder in her hands. "You'll freeze your ass out there."

"Then *I'll* need the massage." Clifford pulled on a John Deere hat. "Preferably with the happy ending."

"At least put something warmer on your head."

"I'll be back in a minute. I remember where it is. Right on the workbench. I'm opening the door now." Clifford winked. "Best stand back else you get party darts."

"You *wish* I get party darts."

Cocking his head at what wasn't a bad idea at all, Clifford powered up the flashlight, opened the door, and headed outside.

The blizzard swallowed him whole, chilling him almost immediately. He closed the door as sixty-mile-an-hour winds crashed into his back and nearly tossed him off his deck. John Deere flew off into the depths of the night, eliciting a short but emotional curse. His hand latched onto an icy length of wooden railing and he pulled his way to the first step, tucking his head down to split the killer wind. To his left, the bay, glorious in the summertime when the sun turned cloudy ribbons into salmon pink, was now a black maw devoid of the usual lights on the other side.

Fifteen feet. No more than that.

Clifford set his jaw and made his way to the shed.

Ten minutes.

He'd been gone only ten minutes. Ordinarily, Marie wouldn't worry about her man in such a way, despite him getting on in his years. But there *was* a blizzard outside, gnawing on the house, and there *were* no lights to see his way back. She'd returned to the kitchen just after Clifford had left, to take further inventory of what they had for light. They had a fireplace, but she suspected the winds might be too harsh to light it. She then returned to her oversized sofa chair in the living room, drew her legs up under her, and gazed out at the black, shrieking weather beyond a finger's width of glass.

When she realized he'd been gone for a while.

Ten minutes? Could have been longer? She retraced her actions in her mind, mentally checking them off, and by the time that was done it had to have been fifteen minutes.

All that time to get to a shed and back? Her legs unfolded, her feet touched the rug underneath, and she held that pose for ten more seconds, listening to the roof creak in the ferocious gale, hoping that, any second, she'd hear the back door open and Clifford thump around in what he called the "home again two-step."

But he didn't.

Marie stood, gathered up her candle, and gravitated to the top of the steps leading to the back door. Snow raked across glass, raising her unease. The house was an old, two-story job, partially renovated when they bought it, but it suddenly felt disturbingly… creepy, and Marie scoffed at her unease. The original builders had situated the house at the very edge of Amherst Cove, only fifty feet away from a thick wall of forest. After the residential squeeze of New York, the lack of neighbors had been a delight, and in the many years they'd lived here, even on the nights when she'd been alone because Clifford had gone off camping or something or other with one of the locals, she'd never felt the way she did now.

Twenty minutes. She leaned against the wall and *willed* Clifford to stomp through the door. He couldn't have had a heart attack. So maybe something in the shed kept him occupied? The fucking question was *what* was so damned important in the shed that would keep him out there, in the dark, in the middle of a shit-kicking blizzard?

She descended one step and paused, holding the candle up, its golden reflection bright in the frozen pane of glass set in the door. Jesus Christ, she'd let him have it once he got back. She'd give him a massage all right.

Two steps now, and she could almost see her worried reflection in the window, a perfect movie poster of a character heading into places she should stay clear of. Right now, she smirked, everyone in the theater was telling her not to go out there. Don't go *any* farther. In fact, she should go back and load up Clifford's .30-30, just to be ready.

A powerful gust sprayed snow across the window, its wail growing with eerie might, only fully appreciated on nights without power, or when one's man is missing.

Three steps, and she was halfway down the stairs. Through her sweater she felt her skin crawl in that subconscious way of knowing something was off. Ridiculous, she knew, but *where was he?*

Something scratched at the door.

The sound startled her enough to halt her breathing. She scanned the entryway for the source. No one pressed their face against the glass, and if they did, Marie reckoned her resulting scream would strike dead a banshee.

But the scratching continued, insisting, right at the seams of the door. At first it was one hook, long and purposeful, but then others joined it, creating a sound like gouging nails, digging, digging away, all to the grim chorus of the blizzard's winds.

"Clifford?" Marie called.

The scratching didn't lessen. "Clifford? You all right?"

Some woman she was being. If it was anyone at all, they would've been inside already. The door was *unlocked* for God's sake. Frowning, Marie composed herself, straightened her back, and went to the kitchen where she exchanged her candle for a flashlight. Thus armed, she took the last few steps to the door.

The scratching persisted, determined. The window remained a dim mirror, framing her anxious reflection.

"Clifford?" she asked again, softly, and placed her hand on the doorknob. Looked out.

Blackness. Snow rasping glass, so thick she couldn't even see what was below the door. She frowned for a moment, thinking she spotted something down there, just outside.

"Who is it?"

Answered by the relentless rake of nails on wood.

Marie held the doorknob. It was too stormy outside for anyone. Anyone except Clifford. Her husband was out there, had been for more than twenty-five minutes now. Something had happened and she needed to find out what.

She turned the doorknob, opened it only a crack.

The cold air charged into the house, washing over her.

A presence moved beyond the door and a second later a frosty looking paw stabbed inside, along with the muzzle of a dog. Sad, muddy eyes implored her. The creature whimpered, a long violin note of mercy, and Marie felt her stomach and nerves all unclench at once.

"Ohhh, what are you doing out there?" she baby-questioned, opening the door just a little further, and placing her hand, palm out, to the dog's cold nose. The animal sniffed eagerly at it. Snorted even. The winds blew into her face and body, freezing her, as she opened the door an inch further and shone the light down.

A bloodhound, she realized, recognizing the face.

The dog regarded her with those sad, sad eyes.

Then it opened its mouth to pant, revealing teeth stained in blood.

Marie's breath glowed on the air just as a terrific force smashed the door aside, flinging her back against the steps. The hard edges stabbed her back, bringing her to the edge of blacking out. The flashlight rattled on the floor, bleaching it. Bare claws scuttled across, white in the light's glare.

Marie screamed just as a mass of fur plowed into her face.

A second before teeth fastened on her throat.

21

"Phone's dead," Ross reported after replacing the silent receiver on its cradle.

"Yeah," Kirk acknowledged from Borland's washroom, pulling on a fresh undershirt and sweater taken from a chest of drawers. He hunted about for a new coat, but resigned to wear the one with the slashes in the front and back. Troubling thoughts darted about his mind, and the course of action he was forced to take.

"Listen," Kirk called out. "Take a peek outside and tell me what you see, okay? Check on those two guys."

"Okay."

Kirk wandered back into the kitchen and opened the fridge door, inspecting the almost unseen contents. He was weak, near faint from blood loss, and the only thing he could think of that would rejuvenate him was food. Half a roast chicken lay splayed out on a platter and he scooped it up without a thought as to how long it might have been in there. The leg came off in his hand with a twist and he stuffed it into his mouth, rubbery skin and all. He then found a plastic jug with about a liter of water, a half loaf of homemade bread, a little stale but edible, and a few containers of peanut butter which he knew from smell alone. All of this, he tore into.

Ross entered the dark kitchen and heard Kirk devouring the food before he saw him. "The hell are you doin'?"

Kirk glanced up, jowls working on a chunk of chicken thigh. "Hungry."

"Y'picked a fucked-up time to eat, y'freak."

"Suppose so." Kirk swallowed. "You check on them?"

"Yeah." Ross sounded dazed.

"And?"

"They're dogs."

Kirk stopped eating.

"Yeah, they're fuckin' dogs, man. I even went out and kicked them. One even… one even had its head blown off. I mean, what the fuck is goin' on here, Doug?"

Kirk cleared his throat. "I'm… not exactly sure. Just listen for a minute. I can't tell you everything. I shouldn't be telling you *anything*, but I figure I have to tell you something. You a superstitious man?"

"Huh?"

"Believe in vampires, werewolves, that kind of thing?"

Ross didn't answer. His shadowy outline merely stood and stared.

"Look," Kirk started again, "there are things out there that mortal man isn't supposed to know about. There are places where no one human should go, phenomena which science will never be able to understand. Okay? Still with me? Okay, now… Borland was one of these things you or anyone else should never have run into. I don't know everything, so a lot of what I'm saying might be wrong, but it's clear to me that Borland was, or had somehow become, for lack of a better word, a monster. I mean a full-on, tooth and nail monster. Worse, I think he was doing things to those dogs he had in the cages. Things he wasn't supposed to be doing…"

"Like little Joey and his pet hamster?"

"Little Joey?" Kirk asked, befuddled.

"Yeah, you heard that joke before. Mom and Dad comin' home early and findin' little Joey with his finger up the hamster's ass?"

Kirk blinked, totally thrown off and no longer concerned about his appetite. "Where the fuck you hear that?"

"Around. A kid's joke. Teenagers tell it all the time."

"Oh. Well, no, not like that. But, well, yeah, he was doing things he shouldn't have been doing."

"So he changed them into werewolves?" Ross asked.

Kirk waved his hand as if clearing bad gas. "Not werewolves. Those things go from being human to wolves. *These* things are going from *dog* to *human*. Which, in my mind, is pretty fucked up."

"Y'got that right, my son."

"Now, there's good news and bad news."

"I think it's pretty much all bad at this point."

"Yeah, well, yeah. I guess so."

"Out with it then."

Kirk took a breath. "We have to find those other dogs. The ones you released. We have to find them fast."

"Fast. All right. Or what?"

"If..." Kirk took a deep breath, fighting off a spell of dizziness. "If they're still dogs, then everything's fine as pudding. If Borland's done something to them, if they're more than just dogs now, then we have to kill them. Every last one."

"Why?"

"Because they're going to want to feed. And they won't be too particular about... what they eat." Feeding was only a portion of it, Kirk feared, but it would be enough to motivate his human companion.

Ross rubbed his head. "What are you saying?"

"I just said it," Kirk insisted. "You saw how those things outside came at us?"

"But," Ross sputtered, "I let those dogs go—the ones in the cages. They didn't come after me."

"Yeah, I've been thinking about that. I think they were just too freaked out by that point. Too eager to get away from the whole cabin area. Right now, I can tell you, they're forming up. Somewhere out there. And they'll be looking for food. Meat, in particular. People, for example."

Ross let his breath go, a picture of disbelieving horror. "This—this is freaky. This whole town. There's only like, maybe, thirty or forty people living here. All senior citizens. I'm forty-two and I'm a *kid* around here. We gotta call the cops."

"Phone's out," Kirk reminded him, grateful for the convenience. Under no circumstances did he want the police involved.

"Well, we gotta do something!"

"Yeah, we do." Kirk locked a dark gaze upon the man. "And this is what we're going to do. We're going to head back out there. Me and you. And we're going to look for these animals—these things. And if we find them, and if they're anything like the fucking house pets that tried to gut us outside, we kill them."

Memories of Borland in his semi-form hounded the warden's mind. He'd been much stronger than a human, but not as strong as a fully changed werewolf. And in human form, the dogs would smell Kirk, even sense he was different from other people, but they probably wouldn't run from him. Dogs barked a good fight, but in the end, they wanted no part of a werewolf. Nothing did. He'd stay camouflaged, act as bait, and draw the beasts out.

Ross thought about it. "Okay. I'll help. Until we can call the cops, anyway."

Kirk knew there would be no calling the police. "How're your arms?"

"Feel fine."

At least that was something.

"You know a lot about these things," Ross pointed out suspiciously. "An awful lot."

"Yeah."

"Should I be worried?"

Kirk wanted to lie, felt the *need* to lie, for the greater good of what had to be done. "Maybe," was as good as his conscience would allow.

I'm not a monster.

"Well," Ross stated, "I got this." He held up the shotgun. "This sure as hell stopped them."

"Seemed to."

"But you stabbed them, too."

"Yeah, I did. To make sure."

"That knife of yours, that's silver, ain't it?"

Kirk didn't answer right away. "Yeah."

Ross stopped and turned around, perhaps fearful of where his line of thought would take him. "All right. When do we go?"

Kirk paused. Then he drained the water, snatched up the remaining chicken, and headed for the front door. Ross followed.

"You tell me," Kirk said in between his final bites. He stopped at the closed entrance and sucked the meat off the bones. "This is your town. We'll need to alert people to stay inside, and to not go around saving any stray dogs that come poking around."

"Jesus, they'll do that?"

"I think they will. What's the layout of this place?"

"We're on a hillside, overlooking a bay. One road in, the one we followed. Up over the hill, then across the flat part of it, say a hundred meters, then down the other side to a cliff, a thirty-foot drop in places if you don't take the pathways, and then a rocky shore and sea. Whole town is surrounded by trees."

"Where's Borland's cabin in relation to the town?"

"Ah, below the hill, of course. Back a ways."

"Can they circle around? Get to the town?"

"Yeah. They can. But in this weather…?"

Won't slow them down. Kirk sighed. "All right. We get to the houses closest to the tree line, any of the ones facing Borland's house and cabin, on this side." He chopped the air with his right hand. "Get those people to lock their doors. Then we can wait for the dogs to freeze. Maybe catch them near frozen out in the open. That's where we'll meet them. And kill them."

"Not save them?"

"I think this way's best."

Ross nodded grimly. "Let's do 'er then."

They opened the door and the storm rushed in, reminding them just how balmy the house had been, and the interior's temperature couldn't have been more than zero. Both men exited, leaning into a powerful air current hitting them full on. The bodies of the dogs, already coated in white, held Kirk's interest only for a moment. Something else got his attention then, a feeling that took him every cycle, and he looked up into the storm's low ceiling.

The moon.

There was going to be a fucking full moon tonight.

Well, *shit.*

Wide-eyed and glorious, rising behind the back of the blizzard. Kirk knew it was up there, felt that familiar tug it had on him, urging him to embrace the change. As if the freezing temperature wasn't cold enough, this new potential problem chilled and rattled him.

A moon was about to rise into the night sky, hidden above the blizzard, but it was still up there, still exerting its influence. Calling. To new *Weres* on their first moon, when the "pups" had no control over their change, the moon not only birthed them, it brought out the worst. They were devoid of rational thought, at the mercy of their bestial urges, and very much ravenous. Entirely id.

Unsupervised *Weres*, ruled only by their appetites and heedless of consequences, would be a disaster Kirk couldn't allow.

And here, on this island, on this *night*, a potential pack of freakish half-breed *Weres* were on the loose.

"Hurry!" Kirk shouted to his human guide.

Somewhere beyond the black and blowing snow, a most wicked moon crept above the night's horizon.

22

Back in Borland's cabin, Morris stirred.

An eye cracked open and rolled around in its socket, taking in the absence of light in the interior, and the snow blown onto the floor. The door was gone and a heap of furniture lay piled to the side. Morris groaned, feeling the cold despite his thick, natural coat. A cruel lance of pain skewered his brain upon moving his pawless leg. Then even more agony, as the sections that the cocksucker Borland had blasted away started crying out, damned near paralyzing Morris to the spot on this bloody floor. He moved parts, feeling strands of fur pop loose of frozen blood. The scent of raw meat assailed his sensitive nose and his muzzle split into rows of curved teeth a great white would consider impressive.

With effort, Morris sniffed the air and listened, his two greatest senses. He was alone, the cabin and nearby grounds, deserted. Not even *Halifax.* Part of him remembered his voice, remembered hearing it in that black, soupy vat of semi-consciousness. *That's my animal. Don't shoot him.*

Morris groaned again. Goddamn Halifax. Calling him *his* animal. What made it really sting was that Kirk practically saved his ass from having his head blown off. That shaved his balls. All Morris needed was to be indebted. To *him*. Still, he had to begrudgingly admit, Kirk had saved him. He'd even helped kill Borland.

That made him think.

Morris wasn't one for people and he certainly wasn't one for other *Weres*. He'd supervised enough wild hunts in the past to eschew the company of anyone not a warden or an Elder. Elders were easy to avoid as no one really saw much of them. Wardens were also easy to steer clear of, since they didn't venture beyond their territory unless ordered to do so.

When he'd gotten the call to go to Newfoundland to kill Borland, Morris had his suspicions, but kept them to himself. When the Elder informed him Kirk would be accompanying him, he felt insulted. Demeaned.

Morris didn't *need* any help in a killing, especially not for an ancient dog crazy, and not from some warden who clearly had identity and perhaps even—Lord forbid—*moral* issues. The wild was black and white. Predator and prey. There was no room for gray. Gray would kill a person.

A warden firing on only four of six cylinders mentally could potentially cause problems. Morris didn't like Kirk, because he was a question mark. He wasn't even sure how

Halifax even became a warden. For this particular hunt, he'd convinced himself from the start he wouldn't allow Kirk the opportunity to fuck up. There wasn't going to be a partnership. Not in his eyes. As far as he was concerned, he was pack leader and Kirk followed.

But since he was lying in a stew of his own blood, still alive because of Kirk, Morris was inclined to rethink his opinion about the Halifax warden.

He regarded the still boots of Borland and growled in satisfaction. Dead as dead. The old man had fought dirty and there was no give in him. Morris allowed him that. If their positions had been reversed and he'd been the one facing down two wardens, well, he would've gone for a shotgun himself, or something else.

Morris tried moving, felt the scorching burn in his shoulder where the knife took him. Stabbed with silver, the absolute *worst* metal on God's earth, and about eight inches of it fucked up his shoulder. He sniffed at it, smelled the burnt flesh, and groaned another curse. Kirk had put fire to the poisoned wound, sealing it up. It would never heal properly, but it wouldn't bleed. Another thank you he'd have to repay. Christ, at this rate he'd be buying the man a Christmas card next year.

With the wind in his ears, Morris reflected on what to do. He was far too weak to track down Kirk, wherever the hell he'd gotten off to, doing whatever. That puzzled him as Borland lay on his back, tits up, right here. What could have happened for Kirk to leave him? For all of his dislike of being paired together in a unit for this trip, Morris didn't believe the man would desert him, especially after patching him up. No, something was in the wind, and Kirk was responding, allowing Morris to heal in the meantime.

He shifted, feeling the blood lose its grip, and inspected his body. There was no way he could change back with all these goddamn *holes* in him.

Then, of all things, his stomach rumbled.

The smell of freezing blood made Morris lick his lips, flex his muzzle.

His eyes fixed on Borland. Mission accomplished there. He'd taken out the *Were's* throat, and in the excitement of the fight, Morris thought the chunk of meat got spattered amongst the junks of wood. The rest of Borland lay right before him, just waiting, *daring* him even to partake. Morris closed his eyes, willing the image away. All werewolves adhered to one important rule, a rule enforced by the appointed wardens. Regulated hunts. Those hunts targeted wild animals and not people, unquestionably the veal of all game. Sometimes, renegade *Weres* broke the law and hunted people, resulting in wardens having to kill the offenders. The punishment brought most of the pack into compliance. Once a year though, for one sacred night, the ban on people was lifted, and all *Weres* could hunt whatever they wanted. While police forces never released the frightening data, this one night of killing occurred during September's Harvest Moon and significantly contributed to the worldwide number of missing people. It also sated the hidden *Were* population.

But occasionally, some went crazy for human flesh, regardless of the season.

Or, as in Morris's current situation, they found themselves shredded and left for dead, needing sustenance to heal. Needing *meat* to just get moving. And having meat just a few feet away.

The most forbidden kind.

Jesus Christ, Morris realized, the old man's corpse tempted him. One great big steak right ready for the eating. He'd only have to drag himself two feet to be within snacking range of a leg. The thought of Borland with those unnerving eyes, claws, and teeth in human form made him hesitate. What the hell did he do to himself? And if Morris decided to chow down on the remains, what might happen to him?

The wind sank into his flattened ears, warning him: *forbidden. Forbidden.* There was a reason not to feast upon another *Were.*

The smell lifted his nose and, as sure as Pavlov's dinner bell, Morris felt his mouth water. His stomach—or whatever was operating as his stomach down there—rumbled again. Anything he ingested would aid in the recovery process. *Two minutes to change,* he remembered telling Kirk. Well, if he ever spoke to the man again, Morris planned on telling him he beat his own personal time. He forced the change, knowing the dangers of doing so, understanding the high chance of personal injury.

But in the heat of battle—more to the point, when some old fucker blows your *hand* off— well, some things just get forgotten and rage takes over.

Morris didn't know exactly how fast he'd changed. He'd been in agony and pissed beyond belief. He'd gotten his fur on pretty damn quick in the past when properly motivated, but this time, damage had been done. Internally. He could feel something wrong.

The rising wind stole his attention and he listened to its song, muzzle on the floor, between his paw and stump. Blizzard wasn't going to last forever. They'd find Borland eventually. They'd find him.

Morris thought he heard the old man chuckle, an unpleasant sound echoing somewhere just underneath the winds. Damn straight. Borland's corpse knew the play. Practically *dared* him to do something.

The Pictou County native couldn't afford to be here. Not in wolf form, and not in his current fucked-up state. Food, forbidden as it was, lay nearby.

Evil. Borland had been straight-up evil. And the old bastard tempted him from beyond with his dead carcass.

Morris sighed, a purely wolf sound. He had choices, but they were all bad.

The weak growls emanated deep from his throat and he winced because of it. The smell lured him closer, his paws scrabbling on linoleum, digging in and leaving grooves. He didn't look at Borland's pallid face. Instead, he dragged his mutilated self towards a motionless boot of the dead *Were*, smearing the chilled blood on the floor.

With a grunt and a whimper, he relented far easier than he could ever have believed.

The fact that he was salivating even more did not escape his attention.

23

With the blizzard only just getting started, Ross pounded on Alvin's door, peered through the dark window, and pounded on it again. A five-minute walk in clear conditions had become a ten-minute-plus march of endurance for both him and his companion, Doug. Twice Ross had stumbled on the way to the nearest house through the freezing winds trying to rip his snowsuit from his hide. Then he realized who lived here. The power had been out for a short time, so he supposed chances were good that he and Doug wouldn't catch Alvin watching British porn on the internet.

The repeated heavy knocking summoned Alvin's sinister lump into view. The big man paused in his hallway, before shining a light into his visitors' eyes.

"Open up, Alvin!" Ross shouted, making Doug glance about, squinting against snow and seeing no more than five feet.

Alvin took his time.

"You know him?" Doug asked.

"Yeah," Ross nodded. "This is the other kid in town."

The door cracked open. A blob of an individual sheepishly edged just enough of his face out to inspect them both. The man wore a headband with a flashlight affixed to it, bright enough that Ross had to shield his eyes. Plastic tubing ran over Alvin's huge shoulders and stopped at his nose.

"Christ, Rossy," Alvin muttered, cringing in the gale. "D'fuck is you doin' out in this shit?"

"You okay in there, Alvin?"

The big man scowled and held the door open with a paw of a hand. "Ah, yeaup. All's cool in here, b'y. C'mon in 'afore yer asses freeze off. Don't mind yer boots."

Alvin backed away. There was very little room for him to turn around. The pair entered, stomping and wiping snow off their frames. Both men looked tired and exceptionally cold. Frost gleamed in the glare of the head lamp.

"Wonnerful weather, eh?" Alvin asked.

"Yeah," Ross agreed. "Turn that light off. Yer blindin' me. Look, Alvin, you got a phone we could use?"

"All down, b'y," Alvin reported, hunching up his shoulders. He looked at Doug and raised his hand. "Alvin, by the way."

"Ah, sorry," said Ross. "This is Doug."

"Alvin."

"Dougie," Alvin greeted.

Doug winced, probably not entirely pleased about being called 'Dougie.'

"Listen, you got any way we can call the cops?" Ross asked.

"Call the cops?" Alvin exclaimed. "No b'y, not at all. Taught you came over to pass the time. I got some black rum up in the cupboard. Powerful shit that is."

"No time for that."

"Wha'? There's always time for a little—" and at this, Alvin tipped his hand back, crossed his eyes, and stuck the tip of his tongue out before lapsing into a sloppy grin.

"Not this time," Ross said. "We got a situation."

"Wha'? Someone die?"

"Yeah, someone did."

"Praise Jesus if it's that old cocksucker Harry Shea."

"No, it's—" Ross scrunched up his face. "That's a bit harsh, ain't it? What's old Harry done to you?"

"Ross," Doug prodded, getting him back on track.

"Right. No, it's old man Borland. Got himself dead."

"Walt Borland's gone, eh?" Alvin stated, half-surprised, half-thoughtful. In the background, the big man's concentrator inhaled and thumped with mechanical irregularity. "What happened?"

Ross looked at his companion. "What *did* happen? You never did fess up."

Doug exhaled mightily. "Wild dog attack."

"Wild dog *attack*?" Alvin exclaimed. "Holy shit fingers. Wild dogs? Around here? D'fuck the wild dogs at around here? D'fuck they goin' at Borland for? Jesus, that one had to be tough as all—"

"Alvin," Ross interjected, knowing his friend easily got off track when he got excited. "You hear anything in here? See anything outside?"

"Y'mean like wild dogs rippin' people apart. That kinda shit?"

"Yeah."

"No, b'y. Nuttin' 'cept the computer."

"All right, then stay inside, okay? You stay in here and lock this door. Y'still got that double barrel of your father's?"

"What for?"

"To shoot."

Alvin's face grew concerned. "Jesus, yer fuckin' serious, ain't cha?"

"Like a fist up your ass, I'm serious."

"Christ, Rossy, no need for that kinda imagery. Gross. Anyways, nah man. I mean I have the shotgun, but I haven't fired 'er off in ages."

"Y'got any gun in there at all?"

"Whadda I need a gun fer? I'm a fuckin' weapon, ol' man." Alvin drew his mass up, eyes crinkling in mock seriousness. "Lookit me. Gaze upon this prime physical specimen and know terror. Lo and be—"

"I'm fuckin' serious here, Alvin."

"All right, all right. No, I got nuthin'."

"You got that ninja shit," Ross pointed out. "The shit you got online. That's a fuckin' arsenal."

"Right, yeah, there's that."

"Then have it handy."

Alvin nodded, all humor leaking from his face.

"You got air?"

"Yeah. C-Cup's powered by the generator now."

"That all?"

Alvin shrugged, seemingly touched by the concern. "Got another two back-up tanks in me bedroom closet. They look like a couple of torpedoes. About eight hours' worth in each. I'm okay."

"We gotta head back out," Doug said quietly, distracting both men and already turning around for the door.

"Yeah," Ross agreed. He fixed Alvin with a steady gaze. "Lock the door. Don't open it for no one. Especially wild dogs. And keep your ninja shit handy. All right?"

A confused Alvin nodded, and Ross could see he was wondering what to make of it all. Doug opened the door, and Ross put his shoulder to it so the wind wouldn't grab it. Cold air flooded the entryway with arctic clarity.

"Mind yerself," Ross shouted at Alvin.

Alvin numbly nodded back.

The wind threatened to slam Ross against the gleaming porcelain hue of the house. Doug was already descending to the road, his silhouette winking out in the dark weather. Ross almost didn't want to go after him. The dog-things had freaked him out more than he let on. Killing one of them disturbed him. It was one of those decisions that had to be made in an instant, life or death in that case, and even though Ross knew he chose correctly, it still unnerved him that creatures like the dogs actually existed.

Standing at the bottom, his deep tracks stopping right in the middle of the road, Doug had turned around to see what kept him. Ross didn't entirely trust the guy. Too much had happened too fast, and while he didn't sense Doug was lying, Ross was pretty sure he wasn't fessing up to everything. At least, after the thing at Borland's house, the man wasn't trying to kill him.

Promising himself he'd be careful, Ross adjusted his snowsuit hood and stomped down over the embankment, towards the road. He glanced back once at Alvin's house, its shape shimmering in the vortex of the storm, and thought maybe he saw something standing in the picture window.

Then another bone-chilling gust and the house disappeared.

*

Alvin breathed hard on his air tubes as he watched the blizzard swallow the two men. Wild dogs. The notion left him a bit breathless. How any wild dogs could be roaming out and about in this hairy shit was beyond him, but then that was the difference between him and the animals. They were stupid *animals*.

Alvin chuckled nervously and felt the bravado pump into him. Wild dogs his ass. The snow scraped across the glass of his picture window as he continued staring out into the savage night. This old shack had been in his family for two generations, and if he could convince an online Estonian honey to move in with him, there would be a very good chance the house would be around for a third generation. Wild dogs didn't bother him, even if they'd offed old Walt Borland.

If they came around, they'd find Alvin Peters's meat a little tougher to choke down.

He switched on his head lamp and walked into his workout room while the concentrator continued drawing in air, purifying it, and pumping the finished product through ten meters of plastic tubing. The walk-in closet loomed before him. A long stretch of cloth hung from the top, Japanese kanji written upon its length. Alvin opened the heavy door, stepped inside, and studied the wall-to-wall collection of sports gear and sparring equipment cluttering the interior. He'd bought everything over the years, the most recent being the sparring gear about two years ago, custom made and practically costing a testicle, but here it lay, and now was needed. Bending over and ignoring the crackling of his knees, Alvin got out his thick chest pad, shin guards, his old minor hockey gloves and helmet with face cage, protective cup, and a set of custom-made leather bracers for his forearms. He pulled out padded boots for his feet, even though his kicks couldn't get any higher than a knee, but in a real fight, a solid boot to the knee would put down any attacker. With ritual solemnness, he put everything on, mumbling queer syllables that passed as Japanese in his mind.

Having armored himself thusly, he stepped to a second inner closet he'd built, situated at the back. He undid the padlock and threw open the doors.

Metal shone in the light of his head lamp.

Alvin had actually hoped for a day when he would get to use his toys. Any scenario would have done—a home invasion, couple of rowdy tourists, even the granddaddy of them all, a zombie apocalypse followed by house-to-house looting. The apocalypse he figured wouldn't happen in his lifetime. Rowdy tourists hadn't happened either, for that matter, and as for home invasions, most folks knew of his eccentric nature and stayed clear of his property. Including the paperboy. The little bulbous shit.

He ran his hands over a set of *kamas*, single-bladed weapons resembling the forelegs of a praying mantis, or whacked-out gardening gear. These he stuffed onto his padded person. Star-shaped *shurikens* shined in the lamplight, and he grabbed eight from his collection, their pointed tips wicked sharp. The wooden *tonfa* remained on their hooks, as did the set of nunchucks.

The katana, now, he considered. The weapon's steel arc shimmed like the prow of a majestic yacht. Deadly sophistication, the katana. Edged poetry. But it wasn't the right tool for wild dogs.

The broadsword, now…

With narrowed eyes he brought out the fearsome, four-foot length of razor badass pleasure. Fashioned by a dealer out in Regina, Alvin had bought the sick sword online (of course) and worked a respectable edge to the blade. Some of his online SCA friends would've called it something utterly lame, like "The Song of Atlantis" or 'The Wish Blade of the East" or some such noble, elvish sounding shit. None of that nonsense grabbed Alvin. So he christened the weapon 'Ass Fucker.' The blade would—when swung with the kind of authority he possessed—fuck up someone's ass. He even planned on scratching or stamping the very lettering into the metal, just so people wouldn't forget.

Just beholding the weapon would shrivel up some scrotums. And intimidation was half the battle. Simple but true.

He slipped Ass Fucker into another custom-made sheath and belt and strapped the sword around his waist. *Goddamn*, he felt impressive, and felt like a shot of anything eighty proof. Even that rocket-fuel moonshine he'd picked up from a cousin in King's Cove sounded good, though he suspected one sip of that diesel blend concoction would permanently blind him.

Still, armed as he was, Alvin felt ready. He played with his air tubes through the face cage, adjusting them as best as he could.

Wild dogs, he thought, and snorted.

Alvin hoped the bloods o' bitches stopped by.

24

Flossie Jones sat by the glow of candlelight, listening to the wind cut its teeth on her roof. The larger, battery-operated flashlights she'd bought only a few months ago lay in the kitchen drawer, as backup only. The candles took her back to the days when she was only a girl growing up in this once strong outport community, and the memories of her and her sisters crowding around the wood stove in the kitchen, listening to stories told by her grandmother. Flossie periodically glanced out at the stormy dark, in the direction of the lower road where, long years ago, parades would march by on Christmas Day.

When the wind dropped, the pop and sizzle of wet junks of split wood thrown into the stove distracted her. She glanced at the candles: snowmen with their heads and shoulders long melted off. They'd been untouched leftovers from Christmas. At first, she was hesitant about lighting the top hat wicks since their portly shapes simply radiated a festive jolliness. When she did apply fire to their noggins, the snowmen's smiles stayed firmly in place, as if swearing it didn't bother them in the least. That odd little act of defiance struck her as cocky. There was no hesitation at all the second time she lit them up, setting their heads on fire. Watching their button grins sag into a grimace under the terrible heat filled her with wicked delight.

For some reason, Flossie enjoyed this immensely, knew it was probably wrong, and still made a note to look for more candles molded into characters. *Any* character. She wasn't picky.

The window pane thumped when the blizzard leaned into it, hooking her attention. As far as storms went, this one was bad, but not the worst. She and her family had survived the beasts of the last century, grown accustomed to the forecasters' dire sensationalism of weather systems. There had been a time when they dreaded the winter months, but that was when her Rufus had been alive, before the kids had all left for St. John's or the mainland. Now, at her age of eighty-two, it was more like *show me what you got.*

Bitch.

Flossie sighed and rocked in the chair that Rufus had made for her sixty years ago, still doing its job. Love held the thing together, or so she told her friends, not mentioning the fact that a few times love had to be reinforced with dollops of super glue. But the chair still served her, as did the old house. She defied the norm, staying under the roof that had sheltered her and her own for decades when so many had moved into retirement or nursing homes. She cut her own wood, shoveled snow at her own pace, walked laps up and down the hillside in the warmer seasons. Rufus was always proud of her for that, and she knew he waited for her on the other side, with that little chiding smirk that leaked the deepest affection.

She liked to think of him when he was tall and strong, in his thirties. And not the last phase of his life, where he'd shriveled up like a raisin in the sun. Done in by cancer of the stomach.

The blizzard rapped her window once again, causing Flossie to clear her tightening throat. Her face hardened when she gazed out the window.

Bring it. Slut.

As if hearing her, the storm did just that, tackling the house with enough force that it made the timbers squeal. And for a moment, she expected to see God's hands rip the roof from overhead.

All this suddenly seemed secondary when she heard scratching at her front door.

Flossie stopped rocking in her chair and looked towards her porch area. A wooden bin lay to the right of the door while pegs for her winter clothes and boots were to the left, all smothered in shadow. But the scratching didn't stop.

In fact, it grew stronger. Urgent.

Flossie knew her way around firearms. Still had Rufus's old peashooter mounted above the fireplace, retired but still capable of putting a second asshole in someone if needed. She waited for a minute, the scratching coming in bursts, then subsiding, before starting up in earnest once again… but becoming weaker now.

She stood up, took a moment to steady herself, then forced blood into her limbs as she walked onto the porch. The front door could have been taken from a vault. There was no window in the heavy wood, so she had no way of looking out without actually opening it.

But she had a feeling—one of hope.

Releasing the inner hooks of the door, she gripped the old-fashioned latch and pulled.

A near frozen snout poked its nose inside, that of a German Shepherd.

Flossie Jones stood there, frozen for all of two seconds, before her heart near exploded with joy. She widened the door, bent over, and embraced her Max, finally come home.

*

At another household, the knocking at the door broke the tension between Sammy and Mary's game of a hundred and twenties, played by candlelight and the warm glow of a fireplace. Sammy got up to see who it was, glad to be distracted from the current ass-kicking his wife delighted in giving him.

"Who could that be?" she asked, half in annoyance, the other in wonder.

"I'll find out," Sammy muttered, leaving the candles and groping for a flashlight, spitefully intending to open the door wide enough so a good blast would blow the damn cards all over the place.

He peeked out the window before opening it, waved the light and saw the dark figures standing outside. Sammy pulled the door open. "What in the name of Christ our Savior are you two doing out in this?"

"Can we come in?" Ross asked as a gale shoved snow into Sammy's face. "It's important."

"Close the door, Sammy!" Mary squealed from within. "Oh my Jesus! The *cards!* The Jesus *cards!*"

The outraged cries of his wife lit up Sammy's face and improved his disposition considerably. "Come on in, b'ys. Just stomp yer boots, is all."

"Everything okay?" Ross asked once inside. His face appeared near frozen in the meager light.

"Oh, pretty good," Sammy replied, eyeing the shotgun in the man's hands. "Yourself?"

"Been better. Look, I need you to lock up yer doors when we leave here. Wild dogs tore up old Walt Borland. They might still be on the prowl. Maybe even in town."

"What? Wild dogs?"

"Yeah." Ross nodded. "Just keep yer eyes and ears open. Keep a gun handy, too, just in case. And Sammy, do me a favor and go on over to yer drinkin' buddy Harry, okay?"

Sammy turned to see his wife in her warm housecoat, face contorted with worry. "I can do that," he said, facing the men again.

"The storm will probably kill them if anything," Ross said. "But now y'know."

"Walt Borland's dead?"

"Yeah," Ross acknowledged. His silent companion opened the door then, and left. Ross took the hint and backed out himself, adjusting his hood. "Keep everything locked down tight, Sammy."

With that, they left the couple, closing the door tight.

Sammy had no intention of going back to the cards.

*

After getting back on what Kirk hoped was the road, he turned to Ross. "What direction's the woods?"

Ross pointed.

"All right, we go that way now. Give them people a heads up."

"Then what?"

Good question, Kirk thought. "I'll let you know."

Ross's near black shape stopped in the bluster of the storm, his frame unsteady in the gale. "You do that. Stay behind me, then. We'll keep to the roads. Cutting over will only beat us out. Snow's too deep."

"Lead on," Kirk muttered through wind-lashed lips. Snow clung to his beard. Every breath expanded his ribs, stretched his chest wound, and nearly drove him to his knees. The weather made his cuts ache, and he dearly wanted to be out of the cold. Someplace warm.

Instead, they trudged down the hill towards the beach, through a landscape of shifting snow, until the obscure shape of the next house materialized out of the night like a creaking monolith. A car wearing a fat beanie of white was parked in the driveway, submerged in cream to its windows.

Ross started to climb the drifts when a dog's yelp pierced the storm's voice. Ross stopped dead in his tracks, head lifted in the direction of the sound. Kirk gazed into the swirling, killing dark as well. Both waited, but the noise didn't repeat.

His face swathed in night, Ross turned to Kirk.

"Lead on," the Halifax warden repeated.

The owners, Kate and Karl Gibbs, were mousy people in their seventies, who appeared jacked up on coffee and caffeine pills. Their eyes widened impossibly when Ross conveyed the warning. Nodding they would indeed ready a gun, just in case, and yes, they would certainly be on guard, they closed the door in Ross and Kirk's faces.

"Friendly people," Kirk observed drily as they walked out the driveway.

Ross leaned in close. "Yeah, not really. They're assholes. Keep your eyes open and stay behind me. There're ditches on either side."

"How far to the next house?"

"In this weather? Ten or fifteen minutes."

Kirk looked to the stormy heavens. The moon called. He knew how to resist it.

But the others…

25

Something pulled Ben Trakers up from his sofa, where he lay nice and snug under a mound of warm blankets. He sat up, smelled the air as if he could detect danger, and got to his feet. The wailing storm and the creaks of the wood blotted out his efforts to hear anything. Snow peppered glass in a harsh sprinkle as Ben turned his flashlight and shone a beam on the huge pane in his living room. His picture window faced the bay, but the blackness lurking beyond could just as easily have been deep space. He walked over, feeling the grind of his arthritic hips, and peered outside all the same, switching off his light to improve his visibility. Or so he thought. In reality, he couldn't see squat with the tempest raging. Mother Nature was having her period tonight.

But he couldn't shake that feeling of having heard something. Hearing a *scream*, of all things, and not just the wind. He thumbed the switch on his flashlight and shone it around his living room, poorly kept since his wife

Agatha's passing, or so he thought. In reality, Ben did quite fine with the housekeeping, keeping the dust from settling, though no one could convince him of that. Agatha had done all the housework for them both, mesmerizing him with a tireless energy in maintaining their home, while he did his part with the outside. A retired fisherman by trade (and not a goddamn 'fisher' as labeled by government heads), he'd married Agatha, a marine biologist five years graduated from MUN. The next forty years had been, in retrospect, the sweetest of his life, and he knew it.

Goddamn right he knew it.

Ben shuffled into a short, dismal hallway, the flashlight beam sweeping this way and that, uncovering piles of books stacked against rich panel wood walls. The decapitated necks of winter boots appeared, reminding him of mouths, and he slipped a bare foot into each, appreciating the warm insulation. He only wore pajama bottoms, the insulated kind, but he had a heavy enough coat to protect him from the worst of the elements. It wasn't as if he were going any farther than the back deck. He wasn't. The lure of wanting to clarify and perhaps get a fix on what the hell he'd heard while dozing on his couch was too great. Agatha always said that his curiosity bordered on being outright nosy. Cherished dear.

With fingers made thick and achy from arthritis (he was polluted with the shit), Ben got into his coat, pulled a stocking cap down over his head, and cracked open the door. The intake of wind teetered him right on his threshold. Bracing himself, he stepped out, feeling icy lashes that made his pajama bottoms flutter and his balls swear. Snow attacked the flashlight's beam so he switched it off, realizing he didn't have any gloves on. Cursing himself, he fastened a hand onto the nearest length of deck railing, and pulled himself to the edge.

Peered in the direction of the Moseby home.

A broad expanse of snow separated the two houses, and Agatha had often sent him over to borrow sugar as fine as the frozen grain presently burying the land. Alice and Jacob were more Agatha's friends than his, but he got along well enough with the couple. They'd been at her funeral. Aggie—as she despised him for calling her—would want him to—

There.

A growl?

Ben squinted, snow stinging his ruddy cheeks. He raised a hand to shield his eyes. Goddamn storm made seeing worth shit. He flicked on the flashlight and aimed it into the night, not seeing any better.

Marie and Clifford Spree's place was only a baseball toss away, not as close as the Moseby's, but this weather made all but the closest properties disappear and feel far away. The wind shrieked and chilled his hands and legs. The timbers of the deck squeaked frozen notes when he shifted. He aimed the light to the right, in the direction of the Spree house, and held his breath even as he felt the blood in his limbs painfully crystallize.

Sensed movement made him whip the light back towards the Moseby's. The beam wavered for a moment, on space shimmering with falling snow.

Then a dog slunk into the beam of light. Muzzle first. A large, white terrier breed. The animal crept towards the deck, low to the ground.

"What the hell y'doin out?" Ben hissed, his words smoking out of his mouth in instant vapor, twisted by the gale.

The dog halted, raised its snout and showed its teeth.

Ben felt his heart stop, blocked with ice. He backed away from the railing, keeping his light on the dog skulking closer, liking the animal less by the second. His hand slapped against the side of his house, felt the gap of the door. The flashlight's beam revealed a monster of a pup, staring at him like he was a chunk of barbecued pork instead of a man. Ben's breathing quickened as if he'd been dunked in the deepest waters of the arctic flow.

The dog, a guard breed whose name escaped him, lilted his head between meaty shoulders. More dogs padded up onto the cold, slippery surface of the deck, black as rats, crowding in and cutting off any escape. A trio of the tiny little foreign yappers appeared amongst the bigger brutes, bouncing as if at a party, tongues wagging like pink ribbons. A terrier growled and bared teeth, distracting Ben.

The lead dog—the Rottweiler, Ben remembered in a flash—leapt at his chest. He dropped the flashlight and caught the dog, but his frail legs buckled under the weight of the animal. The beast snapped for his throat but Ben jerked back with a speed defying his arthritic frame. Then another went under him and upended his world. The old fisherman went down amongst almost a dozen dogs that had gathered upon his deck. They swarmed him. The Shih Tzus yammered shrill notes, like a trio of playground sidekicks in full support of the bullies.

One dog clamped down on Ben's hand, crushing the bone and making him spend whatever breath was left in his lungs on a groan of agony. Others fastened onto his pajamas and the legs beneath. Cloth ripped and the cold licked bare skin. Another feasted on Ben's right elbow, the arm protecting his throat. The dog jerked the limb away, stretching him out, leaving the old fisherman defenseless. The Rottweiler plunged forward, jaws flashing, tilted to the side, and attempted to take off his face with one bite.

It took three.

26

Max ate the last of the roast beef laid out before him in great gulps. Flossie stroked the animal's mane, feeling the water from melting snow. She still had a half a bag left of regular dog food, but that wasn't enough for this reunion. Her baby had returned home and deserved the good stuff. That initial rush of joy still hadn't released her and she knew she'd come close to strangling Max in her embrace. The main floor of the house had beckoned, where the wood stove radiated warmly, and she led old Max to the grill and its orange grin. She charged the dog not to move, and got to work welcoming him home, clapping and rubbing her hands as she went.

When Max finished eating, she delivered a bowl of water to him. Once he finished with that, she made him lie down and massaged his back with a thick towel.

"So good to see you. So good to see you. So good to have you *back*."

She kissed Max's forehead, accepted the weak kisses in return, before finally allowing the dog to rest at the warm heart of the house.

"You just stay there," Flossie whispered, sitting on the floor and stroking the dog's neck. "You're home now, so you just lie there and relax. Mom's gonna take care of you. Take great care of you."

With that, she leaned forward and planted another tender kiss on the German Shepherd's forehead.

The dog whimpered beneath.

*

Kirk heard an ominous crash to his left, smelled salt water, and took a moment to grasp Ross's arm. "Where's the sea?"

His companion pointed. "Ten or twenty steps straight ahead that way. Then a guardrail and about a fifty-foot slide. Or a thirty-foot drop."

Kirk felt his stomach knot. Knowing how close he was to a cliff, he made it a point to stay close to Ross's back. In the fury of a nighttime blizzard, a person could become disoriented in a second. That Ross instinctively knew where he was going amazed the warden.

"You okay?" Ross yelled back.

"Huh?"

Ross haltingly indicated his own face. Kirk took the hint, felt his mouth, and drew away fingers coated in ink. The sight of blood suddenly amplified the screaming of his crushed ribs. He wiped his fingers in his coat and started walking. Ross stopped him with a hand.

"You sure yer up for this?"

Kirk nodded. "Until I say otherwise."

"Whattaya mean?"

"Just keep going."

The woodsman's near-invisible face considered him before turning around and continuing on. He didn't walk far. Two driveways ran off either side of the main road. Ross paused at the juncture, allowing Kirk to catch up, before he chose the one on the left. Kirk walked in his knee-deep tracks, and even that leeched away his strength.

A tantalizing smell of fresh blood rode the air currents and pulled on Kirk's nose, hard enough to block out the skin-splitting cold and his battered body.

"Wait. Ross, wait."

Ross stopped, got whipped around by a ferocious gust, and disappeared from sight for all of five seconds. In that space of time, Kirk could smell the man, but couldn't see a damned thing, and Ross only stood five feet away. The slash weakened, the blizzard's breath spent for the moment, and a figure stood just beyond the length of his arm.

"Poof," Ross said. "I'm still here."

"You smell something?" Kirk asked.

"Smell what? My fuckin' nostrils froze up long ago."

Kirk winced at that. He pulled his knife and trudged by the Newfoundlander. "Keep close, and keep that thing ready," he said, meaning the shotgun.

A monstrous dune lay across the driveway, attaching itself to the two-story house like some great gray tendon. A car's bumper poked out from the under the slope. Something heavy slapped the ass of the dwelling. Ghostly whorls spun off snowy crests and broke against Kirk as he went around the scene, seeking the main entrance. He found steps to a deck, climbed them, and located the main door flapping in the wind. The first body lay on its back in the foyer, the crime almost erased by the storm. Ross appeared behind him, staring at the wrecked corpse, seeing the dull gleam of bone, the excavation of the torso, and how the sagging cavity had filled with snow.

"Oh Jesus," Ross said, slumped against the doorframe, wraithlike plumes whipping around him. The dropping temperatures slurred his words. Shock stiffened his features as surely as the dropping temperatures.

Kirk crept further into the house. The remains of a woman, only partially covered in white, greeted him just down the hall, splayed out on her back and missing a forearm. Missing a face. He glanced back at Ross, noticing how his boot prints left tracks of blood. Gore covered the entire floor, frosted by a veneer of crystallizing sugar, and the heady aroma of it all made him wish… just *wish*…

"You—you know these people?" Kirk asked.

"Yeah. 'Course. Small town. Name's Moseby."

"How many live here?"

"Just Jacob and Alice."

"Any children?"

"Not here."

Kirk stooped over the woman's body and touched her uncovered skull. "Blood's almost frozen, but not quite. We're close."

He started forward, deeper into the house, gleaming knife held at his waist and at the ready. Kitchen chairs had either been toppled or pushed away from a table, its cloth yanked hard on one side, spilling the decorative vase and some dishes on top like a failed magician's trick. Kirk found a flashlight and felt sticky blood coating the tubular length. He thumbed the tool on and waved the beam around the floor.

Dark paw prints cluttered the kitchen floor in a gruesome floral pattern. Some even went up the sides of wooden panel cupboards, the bulk of the dead refrigerator, even the stove. Half an ear lay near a chair, as if ripped off and spat out in disgust. What looked to be a huge, ravaged spider had been squashed near some cupboards, and it took him a moment to realize that he was looking at a hand.

"Anything?" Ross whispered harshly in the background.

"Yeah."

"What?"

"We're close."

"You said that already."

"Really close."

Ross didn't reply and Kirk didn't bother going into the living room. He walked back out into the hall where the Newfoundlander jerked to attention, his back pressed against the wall and shotgun pointed towards the open door. He visibly relaxed when he saw his companion.

"Jumpy," Ross reported, meaning it. The dead unnerved him. "I went into the kitchen."

"Yeah?"

"Found a phone but it's dead. Everything's down."

The wind rattled the timbers, releasing an eerie thump and crackle that made both men pause.

"Look," Kirk said, eyeing the flashing snow outside, creating the illusion that the house was spinning very, very fast. "Is this the closest house to the trees?"

"No, there's… there's one more. Cliff and Marie Spree. About fifty feet straight out from here. And then above this, further up on the hill, maybe another forty or so, it's Ben Trakers's place. We'll cross the Sprees' driveway to get there."

Kirk absorbed the information. "Okay, this is where we part."

"Huh?"

"Two of us won't be able to stop the pack."

"But you will?"

"No, but I'll be able to slow it down. You haveta go back there, and warn the rest of the town. Even better, get them to someplace safe. Staying behind locked doors isn't going to work anymore. I think—I think the dogs have a taste for killing now. I don't think they're going to stop. You get to a phone and call those cops if you still want to. I'll do what I can. Here."

"You sure?"

"Yeah, I'm sure."

"Listen. This is important. I'll do what I can but it's up to you to get whoever's in town to safety now. Shit's gone down tonight, and it'll get *worse* if we both don't do what we gotta do. Okay?"

Ross set his jaw, regarded the weather outside while firming up his grip on that intimidating piece of shotgun business. "Okay," he croaked, like a man suddenly realizing there was no bottom to this pool. "Okay. I'm outta here. You watch yerself."

"Yeah."

Ross turned to leave.

"Hey," Kirk said, stopping the man in his tracks. The Halifax native held up his knife. He studied it for a moment before offering the weapon hilt first.

"Take this. I won't need it."

"D'hell are you going to use?" Ross asked, horrified.

"Don't worry about me. You just get the rest of the herd to safety."

If Ross thought this choice of words were strange, he didn't show it. He took the knife, unzipped one lower leg of his snowsuit, and stuffed it inside his own boot. Once that was done, he took one last worried look at Kirk before hurrying off into the night.

"Yeah," Kirk said. He squinted at the man as he disappeared into the blizzard, wintry exhaust fluttering off his back.

Then he was alone.

He waited for a minute, very much aware of the storm, in part to ensure Ross wouldn't change his mind and come back. A bleak veil whipped past the open doorway and for a moment it resembled a portal to some alien, other dimensional place, one Kirk really wanted no part of. To go there, he knew he'd have to change over. Had to become that which he so reviled, and yet longed for.

Standing there, the tatters of his coat flapping gently, he studied the doorway. The moon's pull on him strengthened, like morning's first stretch of chest and spine. Despite how good it felt, how much he wanted to give in, he resisted.

Taking a winded breath, Kirk went deeper into the house, searching.

27

Brutus pulled free a single piece of the dead homeowner before darting inside the house, declaring his presence by pissing on items of interest. He ran upstairs, paws plodding on carpet, claws clicking off tiling. He sniffed and snorted through three bedrooms, rummaging for anything more, before returning to the living room and discovering that, in their frenzy, the pack had torn the near devoured owner apart. The top portion lay in the center of a rug, jerking with every feverish bite taken. Ignoring the feeding, Brutus jumped onto the sofa and lowered himself, presiding like a regal sphinx. Snow rasped at a picture window, drawing his brooding attention, while beneath him, his pack prowled and growled, fed and rested. The owner they'd killed wasn't overly large, but they weren't overly hungry. The dogs pulled the flesh from the bones of the dead not out of necessity, but because something drove them to do it.

Sounds of the feast lessened in Brutus's ears. The night outside the window captivated him with an increasing sense of urgency. Though he didn't know what was happening, he could feel the growing pull on his body. He stretched his jaws and whined once before snapping them shut and resuming his stare. The other dogs slowed in their feedings, sensing something coming upon them, something terrible, yet needed. The bloodhound sniffed at the air, trying to find a scent. The Golden Retriever, normally so sickly passive, whined and dropped the foot in its blood-caked maw. The Shih Tzus bounced and hyper-yapped as if demanding the others' attention. The rest of the pack, mongrels and half-breeds of terrier mixes, ceased what they were chewing upon. They tensed, searching for the source of what swelled within each of them, yowling in a blend of heat and uncertainty.

All looked to the ceiling of the living room, searched it, even as their organs began to bloat. Their bones moved with disturbing quivers. Their jaws suddenly ached, and many began stretching them, to release the building pressure in their ears. One of the terriers leaped into a sofa chair and bounded off its back where it crashed into a wall. Another hopped into the air, barking at nothing, yet *something*, as an unseen force took hold of them all, grabbing them by their necks and injecting them with a terrible energy, igniting their cores and expanding outward. The Shih Tzus pranced as if on a hot grill. The Retriever howled and placed its forepaws against a wall, spine arching, hair spiking, eyes bulging with fright. A

Bull Terrier clamped down on a plump cushion and ripped its guts free in a yellow shower of foam before shaking it across the other dogs.

A force took Brutus across the back and yanked as if trying to pull spine and skull out of his puckered asshole. He barked, whimpered, then settled into a low moan as his bones bulged against his skin, his organs inflated, and blood crash-flooded his veins like open fire hydrants attempting to bleed off internal stress. His jaws snapped shut and contracted in a firecracker of aching pleasure. His talons raked the stuffing of the sofa, clawing deep, before his skin split apart with fleshly cracks. Sinews stretched, pulled, burst with all the grace of a mighty yawn. Bones lengthened. Musculature grew powerful layers in seconds. Brutus's eyes blurred, shut, and cracked open, glimpsing the contortions the rest of his pack experienced. He blinked, eyes watering, when one of the mongrels, twisting and writhing on its back, thrust a leg into the air. The limb hyper-extended to its fullest, trembled, and *cracked* before bending impossibly in the other direction while its skin split and sloughed off, replaced by…

Man-flesh, glazed in muddy gore and dead peel.

The Retriever held its face with man-thing hands, clawing at its ears while its muzzle shrieked and its hairless chest grew stiffening nipples. The Shih Tzus rolled about the floor, sprouting limbs and hands that thickened before their still yammering but shrinking snouts. One black mongrel screeched with vocal cords that no longer belonged to an animal and bolted from the house upon two legs, disappearing into the livid depths of the blizzard. The Bloodhound pressed its length into one dark corner, fluid bleeding from an impossibly lengthening rack of teeth.

Then a burst of pain crippled Brutus, skewering his senses. The pack cried out with him and the sounds warped through his punished skull as if coming from the other side of the universe. Wind flattened his ears and a searing heat enveloped his body.

Darkness overcame him.

When he opened his eyes, he saw he'd been stretching *fingers* to their fullest, yet something wasn't quite right. Black veins rippled like sailors' knots under hairless flesh, snaking up past his elbow joints and diving deep into heavy cords of muscle. The urge to *push* took him and he obeyed, against his digits, willing, wanting the transformation to complete.

With a scream, long talons burst forth from his fingertips.

*

Flossie came awake with an odd feeling that something was not quite right. She lifted her head from the circular rug and realized that, in the warmth of the wood stove and the joy she'd felt for Max's return, she'd fallen asleep with her head against the animal's side. Her pet had gone, however, waking her up.

"Max?" she called, searching the room. "Max?"

The wood stove's fire burned low and she made the mental note to throw a few more junks into its mouth after finding out where Max had gone. Feeling sparkling needles in her knees and hips, she stood and made yet another promise to herself to get to a doctor and ask about joint replacements.

"Max?" she called again, but the kitchen area and foyer were empty. The front door surprised her, as Max made no qualms about letting her know when he had to go outside. The sound of snow raking against a nearby window caught her attention, and she watched it for just a considering second before wandering through the house, wondering if she'd been sleeping all along, and her missing companion had only been a dream.

A short hall off the living room led to carpeted stairs. A window spilled ghostly light at the top, illuminating the landing. The glass trembled and hissed from the attacking storm system, reminding her of mouthfuls of moon rocks. Her husband Rufus had been a sugar hound himself. It broke her heart when the doctor had informed them both that he had developed type two diabetes. The cancer followed only three years later.

"Max?"

Nothing. She stared at the dark beyond the top of the stairs, listening to the house groan under the constant pressure.

Thumpthump.

The sound tumbling along the floor rooted her in place.

"Max?"

Another stroke of winter hit the house, leaning it to the north.

"Max?"

Then the softest whimper. That got Flossie moving up the steps. "Max? You okay?"

She hauled herself up one step at a time, the old wood squealing with dissonant chords. Halfway up she heard another thump, which made her twist around at the hips, eyes level with the second floor. She gazed towards the spare bedroom at the end of the carefully handcrafted banisters, glowing in the absence of light. The beige door had been closed to only a pitch-black crack.

"You okay, boy?"

A distressing whine got her moving at top speed. She whirled around on the second-floor landing, eyes on the door.

Then a sound stopped her in her tracks, as solid as if she'd run into the wall of a root cellar. Sinews ripped, an eerily earthy sound, slow at first but quickening towards the end, followed by another *thump* not unlike a boot. Or a limb. Then a subtle squeal of something stretching to its fullest.

A dog's panting, choked by another nerve-twinging whimper.

Flossie's old heart ramped into overdrive. Her body above the waist lurched towards the room, but the rest of her refused to go any further. Rufus's thunder gun hung downstairs and she knew how to use it, but the rational part of her mind overruled this. Not in her house that her husband had built for her. And certainly not because of Max.

This pair of thoughts moved her feet forward. Her hand gripped the nearby banister as if worried about being swept away. She shuffled to the door, hearing the barest rumble, a rattle of bone, and placed her hand against the wood. Pushed.

"Max?"

In the darkness, what looked up from the floor, near the edge of the spare bed, wasn't entirely Max.

It was a dog.

But a dog whose grinning snout was retracting *back* into its head to the sound of crackling seashells, while chunks of flat blackness split apart, revealing ivory underneath, and dropped to the carpet in a dull cadence. Fluid dribbled. The jaws opened with the creak of twine stretched to its limit and the eyes, wide and horribly insane with fright, fixed on Flossie.

The room whirled, Flossie felt her legs go boneless, and the last thing she carried with her into the whirlpool of unconsciousness was an oil-soaked hand—half human, half paw—grabbing for her as the carpet rushed up. And her last received signal, before her brain went offline, was that of an explosion at the back of her head, where it hit the floor with all the force of a falling body.

Like a final nail being hammered into a coffin.

28

Kirk almost missed the lane leading to the Sprees' house, but the coy scent on the wind stopped him from going any farther. He stood there, on the snowy road, swaying and shying away from the storm's fury. A long-barreled shotgun, found in the last house and loaded with twelve-gauge shells, was clutched to his chest as if he were about to present arms. After finding those dead people, he decided that every little bit would help.

Screams coming from the Sprees' house had hooked his attention. The same screams had him staring off into the dark, up the hill, while winter thrashed all around. The sickening feeling of being too late seized him. Kirk wasn't even certain as to what he could do, but knew his non-existent plan had just changed. Though he resisted the hidden moon's magnetic draw, feeling it right down to the roots of his teeth, he contained it. Ability not easily learned. Being able to control the change, even stave it off if needed, was all part of his high status in the grand pack.

What felt no more than an electric buzz to him was probably more than enough to turn two dozen or so dogs.

Into something more.

Borland's grinning, canine jaws came into Kirk's mind. He remembered the feral eyes blazing with cruel intensity and evil mirth. Then the dogs at his house. Those in particular. Animals that had become men. The haunting song of the blizzard joined with an even more horrific chorus of voices, like a coven of banshees being exposed to daylight.

Or freakish *Weres* transforming for the first time.

Run.

The one word whispered at the base of his skull caused the length of his backbone to shiver. Even worse, part of Kirk admitted it wasn't a bad idea.

Then, like a grim portent, *her* eyes floated before his own in his pain-racked mind. Soft, staring, with the barest hint of scolding reproach. It was enough of a reminder to make Kirk feel a twinge of shame. His fingers, wrapped tightly around the shotgun, felt only one icy breath away from falling off, but he held the weapon with newfound conviction and waddled through the thickening drifts. The gun would slow down this new breed until…

He struggled through the thickening snow, following his nose. The blizzard slowed time like blood in a dying man's veins. The black steeple of a tall A-frame house loomed in the sorcerous folds of the storm, surprising Kirk by how close it was. He pumped the shotgun and damn near dropped the weapon when he braced the stock against his shoulder and felt the crackle of hot pain. His strength left him and he lowered the gun, stooped over as powerful gales washed over his frame. A moment later he pushed forward, the cold working its murderous poison deep into his being.

The door to the house slapped in the wind.

That brazen clap of wood on wood startled him, caused him to halt in his tracks and gaze ahead, scrying what he could out of the northern dark. A protective railing rose above a snow-smothered deck. The doorway beyond appeared as a black rectangle set into a face swathed in gloomy ice. Then he caught the smell. Strange, but not new. The same aroma wafting from Borland when he'd changed. From the dogs that had become men.

Kirk stopped, the deep freeze of the night suddenly balmy compared to the fear rooting him in his tracks.

A shadow stood in the doorway, a malefic black against the surrounding dark. A man stepped forward. A *naked* man, chest heaving but otherwise still, sheltered by the house, and no doubt every bit as aware of Kirk as he was of him. The wind rose in a blast, obscuring the figure in a dusky hail of granular white.

Kirk took the time to raise the shotgun, felt his cheek freeze on gunmetal when he lined up the sights.

The man-thing roared and slammed a heavy arm against the doorframe. Perhaps twenty feet back and Kirk could hear the splintering of wood as if he'd been slammed into it.

"C'mon then, y'fucker," Kirk seethed, breath exploding past clenched teeth. "I'll make it all better."

The wind dropped, enough to allow the curtain to sag.

Kirk's finger froze on the trigger.

Outlines detached themselves from the house, oozing forward like phantoms blurred by the swirling dark. The pack crouched, stooped, or otherwise stood, knee-deep in the drifts and leaning into the wind. Their naked shapes trembled, no longer protected against the elements with the coats they'd been born with. Mutters and squeaks of voices, attempting to growl warnings. Faces cowled by the dark, but here and there, haunting glimmers of light where eyes lurked.

All faced his direction, easily outnumbering him.

Limbs flexed and flapped as if being tested. One shade took a step forward and nearly toppled over, entirely unaccustomed to a two-legged gait. But learning.

A new breed of *Were.*

Kirk brought the gun to bear on the nearest target just as one screamed, unleashing the full extent of its altered vocal cords. That piercing shriek caused Kirk to jerk his aim towards the screamer—and he blinked. Small, quivering breasts dotted the thing's chest. Short bristly hair covered the head. The female took two unsteady steps towards him, its long legs sinking to its knees, and let loose a caterwaul of hellish ferocity. Protruding eyes fixed upon him. Claws hung from the thing's fingers, and a mouth craggy with canines gnashed the air. On the third step, the rest of the shadows screeched and advanced like drunken children.

Kirk shot the bitch in the chest, flinging her backwards to practically disappear in a snowbank like a gunned-down angel.

The uproar ceased, shivering forms suddenly paralyzed from the startling report of the weapon.

Kirk swung on another, pumped and fired, disintegrating a shoulder as if an invisible yeti had risen up behind the *Were* and chomped a huge section out of its flesh. The blast punched the owner through the gathered pack. Not waiting for applause, Kirk racked the gun once again, working fingers and hands made clumsy from sub-zero temperatures sharpened by North Atlantic winds. He took aim and the shapes scattered, vanishing into the storm. He fired at the thing in the doorway, exploding part of the frame into splinters and shards, driving the creature out of sight.

Cries of pain cut the night air. The female rose from the snowbank, torso shredded, unrecognizable gobs of pulped flesh dangling. She climbed unsteadily to her feet, heedless of her crippling wound, and moved forward.

Right at Kirk.

The warden backed up as the breed staggered closer. A glistening clump sloughed from her chest cavity and plopped into deep snow. The female got within an arm's length of him when he heaved the shotgun into her face. She flayed it aside, black eyes beholding him with a coldness only spiders might possess. He planted a boot against her chest and pushed her off balance, just as the second *Were* rammed into him, driving him onto his back. A claw flashed down, shredding his forehead to the bone. Blood drizzled his vision. A mouth gnashed at his polar-bear collar, the breath scalding. Something wet grazed his ear. The breed yipped into the fabric and Kirk seized the chin and twisted until bone cracked. The man-thing went into a violent seizure, its head flopping on its shoulders.

Kirk kicked it off. He staggered to his feet and away from the pair. Blood seeped into his eyes and he wiped at the gruesome barcode in his forehead, wincing at how the flaps of skin hooked into his sleeve and got pulled apart farther.

"Shit," he panted, attempting to catch his breath without disturbing his shattered ribs. Blackness dripped from his head. A gust of snow covered his face, and he squinted and sputtered against its force. The blizzard swooped in, masking everything, but Kirk could smell their alien tang. Heard them yelling in the dark, wondering what happened to their once majestic voices. The blasts from the shotgun had frightened them, but they hadn't run far.

Kirk's head began to spin and he stumbled to his knees. Snow kissed his cheek while a haunting screeching pressed in, sounding both near and distant. He reared back, woozy and only dimly aware of the slowing of time. The cries became distorted, echoing, confusing him. His hands buzzed miserably from the cold. Kirk plunged his face into the snow, bellowed into its smothering depths, and let the shock pull him back to his senses. Something clawed at the bottom of his boot and he kicked it away. He stood, nearly fell once again, righted his stance and got moving. Shapes circled the edges of his vision—*Weres* adjusting to their new bodies. He limped towards the house from which he'd taken the gun. The oddly human cries of predators surrounded him. Kirk didn't remember his own clumsy baby steps when he'd first changed, as the transformation had overwhelmed his mind utterly.

He reached the house and crashed through the open door. More shouts, cutting through the din of the storm, and Kirk felt his breath quicken. He placed a shoulder against a wall and pulled the door shut. It wouldn't close. Snow and the near-devoured foot of one of the corpses prevented it. More harsh roars, closer now. Kirk cleared the threshold with a boot and hooked a knee, pulling the foot inside. He slammed the door and locked it, felt for and found some old hook locks at the top and bottom, and fastened them as well. A thick inlaid pane of glass, cut in the shape of a sickle moon, was just below eye level. He stooped and scanned the blackness beyond, leaning against the wall for support, feeling lightheaded once again. Gritting his teeth, Kirk pulled his stocking cap down, covering his bleeding forehead and *willed* himself to remain conscious.

He spaced out anyway, losing all sense of time and just struggling to keep his legs underneath him. The moment passed and he rewarded himself with a deep breath before looking to the window. The face of a *Were* filled the glass, mouth open in a horrific display of fangs, feral eyes riveted upon his own.

Kirk staggered back. The breed's face screwed up and dropped from sight. A second later the door shook in its frame as something slammed against it. The wood held, built solid to withstand Newfoundland winters, but that didn't deter the *Weres* from trying to come through it. The barrier trembled again. Guttural chatter could be heard just beyond. Dark heads gathered and bobbed into view at the window. A hand, crowned with evil claws, slapped the glass and splintered it into cobwebs.

Big. They were as big as men, Kirk realized, knowing that when regular *Weres* took to wolf form, their mass almost doubled. It appeared that the same happened to the horrors on the other side of the glass—perhaps even more.

Claws raked and gouged the wood while a face actually attempted to bite through the window. Not too bright, but they were learning how to use their new bodies, learning how damn powerful they were. Kirk remembered Borland tossing him around like a wet pillow. He placed his back firm against a wall and slumped to its base, taking grim stock of his situation, witnessed the door *bulge* from a single blow.

He couldn't put it off any longer. He was hurting too badly.

With one last energizing breath, Kirk got to his feet, and staggered deeper inside the house.

Seconds later, a breed put its palm through the glass. A razor-sharp shard unzipped a deep line in its forearm as it withdrew for another strike. A cannonball blow finally split the wood down the middle, and a short, considering moment followed. One could sense the understanding of the besiegers, catching on to what they possessed. They were *stronger* than dogs now. More hands and even feet battered the door until bloody fists and heels burst through. They piled in, wrenching broken planks free. The door shuddered, tearing away from hinges. The storm penetrated the house.

Yelling cries of savagery and victory, the *Weres* entered the hall.

Kirk heard them come through. Heard the guitar-like whines and screams from the breeds as he felt broken bones shift. The dark floor of the washroom beckoned, the inky line where the bottom of the door grazed over the linoleum. Bones cracked. Eyes bulged. His jaw popped and unhinged, widened, then fastened tight. Power ripped through his back and when he arched it, vertebrae crackled like beach rocks in a cold surf. His senses exploded from a human's to the heightened set of the werewolf. The change wrenched free an aftermath of a memory buried deep in his mind, never to be revisited. A fleeting ricochet of dialogue as painful as a bullet to the face, and for a shifting second, he saw *her*, saw her pleading face as she explained to him she couldn't be his. Never be his. She wouldn't be with a man in denial of what he was, *resisting* what he was.

Kirk's own voice wailed in his head—he *wasn't* a wolf, he *wasn't* a—a flash of pain chewed the memory up and pulverized it into embers of nothing. He opened his glaring eyes, his mind settling in the ripple of the transformation. He always retained his mind, his sense of self, upon changing.

But he couldn't suppress the urge—the *need*—to hurt something.

The breeds dug at the remains in the hall, sniffing and puzzling over their diminished sense of smell. Some stepped over their companions on the floor. One tripped and landed in a heap, drawing the scalding attention of the others. A burly, man-shaped *Were* dropped and ravenously licked the bones of one corpse while its companions gathered in the living room. The group, seven strong, kicked and grabbed things. One tall brute grabbed the sofa, lifted it and jammed it through the nearest window in a cascade of twinkling glass. A female reached the stairs to the second floor, caught a scent, and peered upward with villainous eyes. She called out, the sound like a raucous of bare nails across a chalkboard, and got the attention of the others.

Sniffing and stretching their jaws, they padded up the steps to the second floor.

A short hall possessed four doors. Three lay open. The last one, at the end of a soft carpet, was closed.

The smell grew stronger, even frightening. It was a musky scent, thick and dangerously mysterious, leaking from underneath the closed door. The *Weres* crowded into the cramped space and inched towards the end of the hall. Their growls rose in pitch, their weaponized fingers flexed. Heedless of whatever lurked behind the door, not one backed away. They'd recovered from their shock of the shotgun, felt empowered by the impressive strength of their new bodies. Felt invincible in their numbers. Their black eyes as bright as polished coal.

Any fear they might have had quickly evaporated, replaced by a desire to kill.

Tentatively, one reached out with a single finger, tipped with a knife-like talon.

Kirk sensed them right outside the bathroom. He felt better, infinitely stronger, but far from healed.

A long, penetrating scrape started near the top of the door, on the outside, and dragged itself to the floor. Though the sound might've frightened a lesser soul, it had no effect upon the Halifax warden. Not now.

Kirk bared fangs as long as spikes and growled.

Just before bursting through the door.

29

Kirk slammed a paw into the face of one *Were,* pushing its skull back with enough force to catch and splinter a nearby doorframe. The brutish werewolf surged forward, its jaws crushing the throat of a nearby female and ripping it out in a wet flash of blackness. The other figures, stunned by the ferocity of this new monster, drew back, stumbling over each other to escape. One with a jutting jaw screamed and grabbed the shoulders of the great beast, plunging its nails deep into meat. Kirk threw his weight into his attacker, snapped the claws off at their roots, and put jaws through a once-solid wall. The werewolf leaped, landing on the fleshy back of a man, and raked him to the bone. The breed shrieked, forced to the floor. Kirk stomped, pulverizing the head like a bad melon. The body snaked and twitched until Kirk got over him and kicked off with both hind legs, flinging the convulsing *Were* into a far wall hard enough to leave an impression.

But then the remaining breeds recovered. One with pallid skin slashed Kirk's sensitive nose, almost tearing the tissue clean off his snout. Another jumped onto his back and drove both tooth and claw into his shoulders. Yet another grabbed for his head, stabbing claws into his neck, seeking to pull it clear of his torso like a stubborn cork.

The werewolf freaked.

Kirk rolled onto his back, crushing the ribs of the *Were* clinging to him in a burst of air and a crunching of bone. His rear legs came up, hooked and nearly ripped an entire arm from the attacker of his head, flinging the *Were* away in a note of rage. Kirk twisted onto his paws and plowed into the abdomen of the pale one, biting deep and tasting spine, buckling the breed in half while runnels of blood splashed to the carpet. The werewolf smashed the wilting ghost into a wall, three times in an eye blink, the final blow spiking the ragdoll through planks in a burst of splinters.

One breed fell over itself in its haste to retreat.

Kirk made to leap but something grabbed his tail and swung him into the wall, crumpling it, then the ceiling. Plaster rained down. The werewolf yowled and kicked, but the breed holding him—one with bulging eyes—stood just out of range. Eyes slammed Kirk into the floor with a *whump*, causing the wounded *Weres* to shiver where they lay. The breed jumped onto the sorcerous animal, biting for a jugular. Four wolfish paws caught the angry creature in midair and Kirk rolled Eyes into the wall hard enough to buckle wood. The Halifax warden twisted to gain the top of his recovering foe. The breed clawed and slashed, tearing explosive chunks out of the werewolf's hide before realizing its mistake of leaving its neck unguarded—a split second before Kirk's serrated jaws powered down on its throat, crushing the life from it. Kirk didn't release the creature right away, but when he did, he did so with whatever power he possessed in his neck and shoulders, tearing upwards in a grisly shower.

With no one left to fight, Kirk slunk from one moaning *Were* to the other, killing each with a single bite, shredding throats. He took no chances, even tearing out the gullet of the one whose skull he squashed, not wanting to discover if the thing could regenerate its head or not. Kirk remembered tales of werewolves who'd been decapitated in battle. They *could* grow them back, but the mind was forever gone, replaced only by a monstrous desire to deliver death amongst all. He'd heard stories of the hunts to put down such a creature, frantic races where the werewolves had to kill the beast before the human herds discovered them, and hoped he'd never have to partake in one.

When he finished the last, sinking his teeth as well as his growl into the breed's pallid skin, Kirk counted the dead. *Six*. He'd lost count in the fight but knew one had escaped. Not that it bothered him. He had more pressing concerns at hand. The holes and gashes the *Weres* had inflicted upon him throbbed and he licked each one with a whimper. His blood dripped upon carcasses while the blizzard approved with its own scream.

He stumbled into a nearby bedroom, feeling how the blood-saturated carpet squished beneath his paws. The battle rage faded. He crawled under the nearest bed and peeked out at the carnage left behind. Kirk knew he had a problem. The pack had crippled him even more, damning him from returning to a man. He needed to rest, for which he sensed there was no time. And he needed to feed. Food was critical if he were to heal.

Unfortunately for him, he'd collapsed only feet away from a huge supply of fresh, fragrant meat. The notion repelled him, eating the breeds, as much as feasting on humans ever did, but for a different reason. He didn't like people, as they reminded him of what he once was. What he had. And despite the years and the changes, he still thought of himself as a person. One living on the outside, granted, but still a person. Unlike Morris, who seemed to revel in his *Were* abilities, his *Were* curse.

A wicked aroma clung to the broken, unmoving forms. Tantalizing. Sweet. He should have left the upstairs, but something primal inside stopped him, kept him right where he lay, smelling all of that moist nourishment. Lifesaving, in this case.

Don't. Don't do it. It wasn't him. Wasn't like him. He was—he was a *person. Trying* to be a person. Trying to be… and his argument collapsed when it arrived at *a good person.*

Kirk whined. His mouth flooded with saliva. When he took control of himself, he discovered he'd crawled *back* towards the horrifying banquet.

The meat's tainted, he reproached himself in a weakening daze. His stomach rumbled, knotted. His ruined nose couldn't even keep out the now heady bouquet, blood sweet and thick.

Another short crawl, his resistance eroding by each punishing second. Agony. His body trembled, ached, bled. A voice grabbed his consciousness and whispered the one thing going to save him. The one *act* which would save the town. The people.

Kirk closed his eyes, knowing the truth of that low blow.

Sighing, he crawled another weary foot and prodded something with his muzzle. *Huffed* and whined one final time.

He didn't see what he bit into.

30

The storm gathered itself up and laid into the solitary figure struggling through its white rage. Ross endured and arrived at the first house he had to check on and, he supposed, the people he had to get to safety. *Safety!* The notion seemed more incredible with every passing second. Seems like he'd hope someone would save the town for years, but from a different, less horrific, fate. Amherst Cove had been quietly dying for some time now, as its people either moved away or expired of natural causes, but Ross had held onto his life here for as long as he could. The little coastal town was his home, and part of him believed he'd die here. And even though he'd only just made the decision to move, he wasn't going to abandon the townspeople this night.

And, God above grant him the strength, he'd do what he had to do to save every last one.

Ross hit the door with his fist, hammering the wood as if Lucifer's own hand were about to close about the scruff of his neck. He strangled the shotgun in his right hand, the metal frosted by the elements.

The door opened, and the barely distinct shape of Doug Cook stuck his head out, half a foot over Ross's.

"D'hell y'doin' out hare?" Doug yelled into the breath of the storm, holding his door with one great mitt of a hand.

"Doug, it's Ross Kelly."

"Ross," Doug declared, his tone softened by wonder. "D'hell y'doin' out hare? Jesus, b'y, y'happen to see it's snowin' out?"

"Doug, let me in. Gotta talk to ya."

"Jesus, yes, come in. Come in."

"Who izzit, Dougie?" a woman's voice asked.

"Ross Kelly."

"He know der's a snowstorm on?"

"Yes, Jesus, yes, he knows," Doug bawled back and motioned his visitor to enter. A moment later, the door shut out the freezing wail, and Ross composed himself as best as he could without sounding like a lunatic.

"We got a problem, Doug," he said, staring up into a face and form outlined by yellow light. In his sixties, Doug Cook was a giant in the bayside community. Deeper inside the house, his wife Dorothy held up a flashlight as if posing for a commercial. She was near as tall as Doug herself. Their male offspring was a behemoth, set to play pro basketball in the States.

"Wha's that, my son?"

"You got a gun in the house?"

"Christ Jesus, yes."

"Get it and get dressed. You got to leave here."

That was met by a stunning clap of silence.

"D'hell y'talking about?"

"D'hell he talkin' about, Dougie?" Dorothy echoed, coming down the hall with the flashlight raised like the mother of Nancy Drew.

"Walt Borland's dead."

"Whaaa?" Doug's face sagged with shock.

"Killed by wild dogs."

"What?" Firmer now.

"Yeah, and a pack of them might be heading this way."

Doug's thick brow, the only hair south of a dome that shone brightly in the flashlight's glare, crumpled as if his thoughts had been doing eighty into a dead end. "*This* way?"

"That's right?"

"Well, just close the door is enough, ain't it?"

"Yes, Jesus Christ Almighty, dat's enough," added Dorothy, supporting her man.

"No, that's *not* enough," Ross blurted out, knocking his shotgun against the wall. Doug and Dorothy Cook both focused on the weapon before regarding their insisting company in a new and wary light.

"He's got a gun," Dorothy whispered into Doug's substantial shoulder.

"Sawed off piece, y'got there, Ross," Doug said. "Where 'cha get it?"

"It's Walt's. Look, you got a phone?"

"Jesus, yes, got one. Dead, though. Y'been drinkin' Ross?"

I fucking wish. "No." Ross shook his head.

"Drugs?"

"No!"

The flashlight's beam blinded him.

"He doesn't look high," Dorothy said, completing her own inspection.

A gunshot thundered outside.

"D'hell is that?" Doug asked, eyes darting to his closed door.

"I don't know," Ross answered, also looking. "Might be a guy I know. He told me to get everyone back."

Two more cracks from a gun. The Cooks jumped at each report.

"Back?" Doug said, face screwing up with concerned puzzlement. "Back where? There's nowhere to go around here. There's nothin'. He a cop?"

Ross blinked.

"You don't know?" Dorothy asked, incredulous.

"No, I don't, but… but he knows stuff."

"He tell you about the dogs?" Doug questioned.

"He *saved* me from one of them dogs."

"Whaaa?"

"We found Borland dead in his cabin. Went to call the cops at his place but there were two of the animals there. They jumped both of us. Clawed up my arms."

Ross showed them both.

"Dey might have rabies," Dorothy whispered, gazing upon Ross as if he possessed the Bubonic plague itself. "Jesus, Dougie. Dey might have rabies."

The words made Ross's stomach lurch like a knob of ice in the Atlantic. *Rabies*, his mind panicked, prompting him to inspect his forearms with greater scrutiny. The terrible thing was his arms, more specifically the *cuts* in his arms, were *burning*. Everything below the elbow seemed hot and itchy.

"You haveta get to the hospital," Doug declared, nodding grimly.

"How can he get dere?" Dorothy asked behind her man. "De roads are covered. I mean *covered*."

"Who's got a snow machine?" Doug asked, pulling Ross's head up. Who *did* have a snow machine?

"Clifford Spree has one," Dorothy answered, hope in her voice.

"Not Clifford," Ross said, fearing the Sprees were already gone.

"Oh, Cliff and Marie will take you, guaranteed," Dorothy insisted.

"Tom Dawe's got one," Doug added, before his wife could continue on that thread of conversation. "Cathy and Bill Byrne, too."

"Yes!" Dorothy exclaimed. "Dat crowd's got all kinds of it over dere. Christ our Savior. Quads, boats, cars, trucks, you name it. You best head over dere."

Doug squinted and stepped by Ross to peer out the window. "Someone's comin' here."

"What?" Ross asked, leaning in to see, but Doug Cook's respectable mass eclipsed him.

"Jesus, whoever it is—" Doug's profile grimaced in the light. "There's—well, *Jesus!*"

A growing, maddening huffing from beyond raised Ross's hackles and paralyzed him until a fist smashed through the door. Doug shrieked. Dorothy squawked. Ross shouted *get back get back* a second before clawed fingers ripped into the shuddering hole, widening it. The glass exploded inwards and a second hand clamped down, jeweled shards slashing flesh. Someone growled outside, and the flashlight beam glimpsed a bulbous eye and a fanged maw.

Just before the whole door came off its hinges.

Jesus Christ, Doug thought while retreating in a raw shot of terror, lifting his shotgun. *There's* two!

A naked man charged into the hallway and straight into Doug Cook's bulk as its companion wrestled with the door. Doug raised a heavy arm but his attacker uppercut with a jackal's giggle of wicked glee. The big man fell to his knees, gurgling, as Dorothy stood and screeched at the sight of her husband going down. Ross raised the barrel in a rush and fumbled his shot, blasting the ceiling. The recoil and his own instinct for self-preservation combined to land his ass flat on the floor. Doug slumped over, took a breath, and kept on gurgling. A second hand closed around his neck and impossibly *yanked* all of him towards the maelstrom of the wrecked door. Dorothy turned for the hallway and that motion attracted the attention of the

Giggler, who was already deciding who to attack next. It streaked for Dorothy, slamming Ross into a wall. He glanced up to see muscular legs flash by in a wildly shaking beam of light. Clothing ripped and Dorothy *truly* began to sing. Ross got to his knees, pumped the shotgun, and aimed at the muscular back of the Giggler who was shredding the woman he'd known for twenty years. He fired, flaying a chunk out of the creature's flesh and flinging it farther inside the house. Ross started for Dorothy's form, now soaked in red, one arm propped up and twitching. A man-sized howl cut the air and Ross spun around to see the first freak heave Doug's sizeable lump into the blizzard. The doorway framed the beast in darkness for a heartbeat before Ross shot it in the ribs and blew the monster outside. He whirled to see the Giggler about to tackle him, baring teeth belonging to a nightmare. Ross pumped and pulled the trigger—

Empty.

The man-thing blared hatred and took two steps before diverting course and pouncing on Dorothy. She didn't cry out as a claw slashed out, draping the far wall in a thick arc of scarlet.

That was all Ross needed.

He bolted out the wreckage of the door, past the recovering horror that was lifting itself up out of the snow.

And ran for his life.

His hurried departure from the Cooks' residence carried him though growing mounds of snow. Shrieks and screeching of the beasts seemingly all around him merged with the wind. A hard blast of air staggered him and he fell to his hands and knees, almost losing the shotgun. With a choked cry he twisted over onto his ass, scanning the ferocious screen for signs of pursuit. A disoriented Ross stumbled to his feet, turned, and took three running steps before flipping over the guardrail shielding motorists from the cliff drop—the metal cutting him off at the knees.

A grunt of pain and fright punched past his lips as he went over the guardrail, knowing *exactly* where he was and immediately flailing with both limbs. The snow exploded into his face, smothering him like a freezing pillow. His body torqued to the side. He landed on his ribs, slid a foot, and clutched for anything to halt his slide a second before realizing he'd already stopped.

"Oh fuck," Ross whispered. His leg stretched out and felt air. The cliff's edge dropped away right at his left elbow. "Oh fuck, oh fuck," he panted, rolling into the guardrail and gasping for relief when the metal stopped him. His left knee felt unsteady from its rude hyperextension, and Ross favored it when he flexed, but far from broken. Not so far below and altogether too close for comfort, the sound of waves crashed upon beach rocks like titans bashing grand drums. A few wisps of saltwater even spattered him.

Images overwhelmed his mind, of things hauling big Doug out the door like a piece of carpet. The violent spray from Dorothy. Ross grimaced against the cold metal, bordered on losing his mind, and took quick, deep breaths that made him lightheaded, eventually getting his nerves back into line.

Then he discovered he'd dropped the shotgun. He sifted through the mini-craters of snow and nearly lost control once again when his gloved fingers grazed the barrel. He seized the firearm, drawing it up and wiping the stock as if it might magically grant a wish. *Ammunition* flashed in his head. He'd gathered up all the shells he could find on Borland's cabin floor. He groped at his pockets and thumbed three into the breech. The damn thing hadn't been able to slow the monsters down, however, remembering with horror how he had shot both the brutes with disappointing results. He'd wounded them, probably hurt them, and no doubt pissed the bare-assed bastards off, but he wasn't able to kill them.

Then he remembered the knife, Doug's silver knife now down his boot. He reached down and breathed a sigh of relief when he touched the pommel. That pig sticker got the job done. Silver. He clearly recalled the speech Doug had given him at Borland's house.

You a superstitious man? Believe in vampires, werewolves, that kind of thing?

He sure as fuck did now.

That knife of yours, that's silver, ain't it?

Yeah.

Yeah. Ross gripped the shotgun, no longer confident in its power but refusing to throw away its security, despite being lessened. If anything, it knocked the things off their feet for a few seconds, and the one dog he'd blasted the head off of back at Borland's house hadn't moved too fast either after the fact. *Head shots.* Head shots did some damage. It slowed them down, at least until he could stick the knife into them. Then a moment's sickness as he realized he'd *forgotten* he had the blade at the Cooks' house.

That smacked him cold, leaving him feeling pretty useless for a fleeting moment. Then he took a deep breath and swore not to make the same mistake twice. Not with the others. He'd die before someone else did.

The blizzard shoved Ross around as he got up and carefully stepped over the guardrail. The road lay under an ever thickening cream. It forked after only a few steps, up the hill and straight ahead.

Up the hill led to the next nearest house. Flossie Jones.

What time was it? The question lingered as he steeled himself and started up the incline, hanging close to the right side so he wouldn't go past her drive and walkway.

A great, skeletal tree took shape, thrashing as if it sought to escape the garden, and just below its frosted limbs lay the path leading to Flossie's front door. Ross got his new story straight. People weren't about to leave their house for a few wild dogs. They would if they thought it was something else. Walt Borland. Man was dead, anyway. Might as well get some use out of him.

He stumbled towards the dark shell of the house, feeling uneasy about the gloom, and spotted deep tracks filling in. Ross dropped to a knee and winced, noted the closed front door and the lack of a window. Horror gripped him, but he gathered his nerve, aimed the shotgun and proceeded. The tree, one that bore sweet cherries in the summertime, continued to head bang in the wind while a potato garden, ringed with beige beach rocks, slept under about two feet of snow to his left. Blackness surrounded all in a stormy background, making Ross feel as if he were on the very cusp of reality itself. The spectral scene could've decorated a wall as a mural.

Snow foamed at his knees and hadn't quite managed to erase the grooves of how Flossie had swept her door open in a wide fan, rivaling any pattern in a Japanese rock garden.

"Oh no," Ross moaned.

He tried the door, discovered its heavy bulk locked, but still managed to rattle it with growing fury.

"Flossie!"

The night screamed back.

"Flossie? You in there? It's Ross Kelly."

Nothing.

Then he sensed a sudden presence, permeating the wood like a bad smell, creeping him out enough to jerk back and point his sawed-off cannon at the door. Seconds passed and nothing ventured from the house. He glanced over his shoulder and saw the tree, how it waved, directing him to walk around the house.

Weapon leveled just in case something flew out of the storm, Ross followed the tree's directions, escaping the brunt of the wind, and discovered the coal-black mirror of a window looking in on Flossie's main floor. This he put his face to, cupping a hand to the glass. A small couch could be discerned in the dark, along with a fridge polished hard enough that it glowed. Weak light smoldered at the end of a hall.

The light abruptly flickered. Puzzling over this, Ross squinted and held his breath when a face flashed before his and the window fogged before teeth. Ross staggered back, fright electrifying him as the thing's eyes swiveled in its skull and fixed on him. Jaws snapped and a voice strove to be heard above the blizzard, coming across like raspy gibberish. Ross stumbled away from the window, heart crashing as if it had just taken a killer shot of adrenaline, abandoning his attempt at saving the widow, knowing it was too late.

He pushed on to the next home, following the map line to the southwest. Doug had said they would be forming into a pack. The guy was wrong. They were hitting houses in ones and twos. Perhaps even more.

Knowing he didn't have much time left, Ross staggered through the glacial drifts, each step like wading through fresh cement.

31

Max saw the man stumble away from the window. He cried out, hating the way his voice sounded, and pounded the wall with his newly formed hand. For the last few minutes, he'd been walking about on two legs, using whatever was nearby for support, trying to adapt to these new limbs. He'd hovered over Flossie's body upstairs, nudging and licking her face to no effect, and just feeling miserable in the dark of the house. He'd moaned and latched onto the shoulder of Flossie's sweater, attempting to pull, but only serving to stretch the material and bunch up the rug.

The shout below had given him a surge of hope.

Max had damn near killed himself in his rush to figure out the puzzle of the stairs, and in the end slid halfway down over the uncomfortable slope as if he'd just taken a dump, something he knew had to be done outside if the urge took him. Then he used his legs again in an awkward walk, supported by his arms, and navigated the rest of the way. When he spotted the face in the window, Max forgot trying and just *did.* He ran to the face—everything working in a burst of relief.

Only to watch the man run off, disappearing into the storm.

The Shepherd recognized the face, recalled memories of beach walks and saltwater mists with Flossie. He shouted as the man disappeared into the night. Max fumed in frustration, though realizing the greater control and function in his limbs. The dark enveloped him as he stood, flexing his hands in and out of fists, feeling the strength surge to his summons, but not quite grasping how to utilize it.

With a snap of teeth, Max ran back through the dark. His night vision was limited, but adequate to see Flossie's fallen shape, whereupon he experienced a mallet slap of helplessness. He pawed at her, discovered how his fingers gripped, hooking them into crevices of his owner and pulling her into a sitting position. As much as he disliked this new body, hated how cold everything felt, he was quickly appreciating its power. Testing his grip, he experimented clutching at Flossie's unconscious person for minutes until he wrapped his arms around her torso, facing him, and lifted her up until her head flopped over his shoulder, embraced in a drunken waltz.

Flossie felt very light in his arms and Max had no problem bearing her weight as he retreated back down the steps, one careful foot at a time. Upon reaching the ground floor and the dying warmth of the stove, he dumped her in a heap.

Sniffed the air. Scrunched up his face.

Something was coming.

Something not nice.

Max stepped into the foyer, smelling the various materials of leather and rubber, and regarded the closed dark of the door. A growl emanated from his throat. The door was something he couldn't open on his own and this time he was glad of it.

The smell grew, getting closer.

A voice screamed from beyond the wood. A voice not unlike his own, but deeper, dangerous. Max hunched over, glancing at Flossie's unmoving shape on the floor before a loud hammering jerked his attention back. A section of the door bulged, crumpled inwards, followed by another powerful blow that split the wood as if it were cardboard. The thing outside shrieked, and punched a fist through on the third strike. Talons pulled away the ruined fragments, and a single eye glared at him in the resulting hole. Another wild yell of anger.

Max could only blink and stare, watching the door being yanked from its hinges in a twisting whine of wood and metal. It came apart in a messy clatter.

The man standing in the doorway wore no clothing. Lean ropes of powerful muscle covered its naked body. A black bush of hair covered both its head and genitals. It stopped just outside, chest heaving, freezing, and stared wide-eyed at the Shepherd. The man-thing, as this wasn't exactly a man, snapped long dog's teeth in Max's direction, and blurted a message of nonsense. When Blackbush got no reply, he shouted in a louder voice that Max found offensive.

Then he understood with a chill.

It wanted to come inside.

Blackbush sniffed at the air, talons flexing, and moved to enter. Max blocked him, glaring at the creature with a forbidding expression. Blackbush glowered, drew lips back from his respectable set of jaws, and made a threatening display of them.

Max didn't care for the thing's aggressive overtones. He didn't like the posturing, and he sure as hell wasn't going to let some alien mongrel into his house. Blackbush came forward and Max pushed him back. The intruder tried once again, rushing the doorway, and this time Max put power behind his hands, shoving the beast hard enough to take it off its feet, sending it into the snow.

Nearly twenty feet away.

Blackbush sprang up from the drifts like a coiled spring and screeched, throwing its arms wide and clawing at air. Muscles flexed and he fixed Max with eyes as black as boot leather. Max wasn't impressed in the least. The Shepherd knew what was coming, but he stood on the threshold and shouted back as savage a warning as he'd received. Blackbush overrode the message with a guttural yell, laced with furious consequences if he wasn't permitted entry. Max puffed up his considerable chest and silenced him with a gruff response of his own.

You ain't getting in.

So fuck *off.*

A livid Blackbush hunched over, knee-deep in snow, buffeted by the elements. It rolled its meaty shoulders and shook out fingers ending in frightening talons. The night cloaked its hairless hide in a flat glow and for a moment, the creature seemed to weigh the gravity of the curt command. He regarded the bitter tempest all around, then Max's form, considered how far, how *badly*, he wanted into the house. The brutish creature then grudgingly hissed and ranted as he turned away and stalked off into the night.

Max licked his lips and stretched his jaws until he felt his ears pop. The smell receded. Relief warmed his chest and he stood in the doorway, blinking and breathing, snow pattering his face and body. That had been a near thing. A very near thing. But danger had been averted.

Max started back in, but stopped and faced the garden area again. His nose flickered.

Out there in the dark, the smell retreated but didn't dissipate.

It lingered, somewhere out there in the swirling veils, as stinging as a whip of frayed wires.

A second later, the smell grew.

Max tensed up, releasing a knowing *whuff.*

The blizzard churned as a black shape erupted from its depths, charging the front door with wrecking-ball speed.

Blackbush. Grinning insanely.

Less than ten feet out, the monster leaped at the unwavering doorkeeper with a roar. The attacking man-thing barreled into Max's midsection with a fleshy clap that flickered night into day. Max buckled. The Shepherd raked Blackbush's bare back, gouging grooves in his flesh even as he felt pain exploding in his guts. His attacker's momentum overwhelmed him and they rolled into the foyer, flailing with arms and kicking with legs, trying to bring their feet into play. It quickly became apparent that Blackbush was the more experienced with his tools. In a burst of stars and speed, Max absorbed three swats from heavily-clawed hands that minced his cheeks into ribbons and jacked his head from side to side. An eyeball popped. His throat let go in a gargle. His head got crushed into his shoulder, hard enough to feel vertebrate crinkle painfully, enough that all strength left him in a gush.

Blackbush got his hands into Max's armpits and heaved him into the low ceiling, flattening his skull in a grimace of teeth, before flinging the creature against the foyer wall. The house vibrated with the impact. Blackbush pounced and pistoned a series of hard knees into Max's chest, bone against bone, caving ribs in an explosion of agony. The knees stopped only to be replaced with more punishing blows to the face and head of the defender, opening up torrents of blood and leaving Max's face in ruined tatters.

Then, perhaps sensing his foe dead, Blackbush stood back. He studied the body at his feet, *whuffed*, and bellowed loud enough to split the latex paint covering the walls.

Blackbush's head jerked around, smelling fresher, more palatable meat just waiting. A dark mass lay unmoving, breathing ever so slightly, but still alive, and without the off-putting scent clinging to his enemy's hide. Blackbush hesitated a moment before flaying Max's face one final time, turning it into an awful grid. Satisfied he'd established dominance, he moved towards Flossie, flexing iron jaws.

Leaving the Shepherd slumped against a wall.

Somewhere, in a warm dream, Max was no longer a man. He ran through open fields, upon four strong legs, banking left and right at times, chasing one of Flossie's grandchildren through an overgrown meadow, while the old girl herself stood off and watched, shouting and clapping her hands at times. The fresh smell of dry grass tinged with a hint of saltwater and fir trees filled Max's nose. A young girl squealed and ran, her blonde hair bouncing and flashing like fine silk in the sun. A grinning Max chased her down as he'd done many times before. Occasionally she stopped with a giggle as pure as summer rain. She whirled around at the last possible second, hands bunched to her face in excited play before throwing her arms around his thick neck, accepting his kisses.

The sight sparkled as if the very sun blazed down upon the scene. Sounds echoed in his ears, those of happiness, while the pressure of a child's loving hug resonated around his neck. So good. So very good.

But then the carpet of grass slipped away with a tug of reality, replaced by the smell of blood and wood and decaying air fresheners. Max opened his remaining eye, distantly wondering why the other wasn't working. Pain burned through his chest and face like hot pebbles, and he knew he'd been hurt bad. Very bad. Perhaps onto death.

But then he saw the intruder standing over Flossie, remembered how her granddaughter ran to him in that swaying sward of twilight, felt again the embrace of a little girl's arms.

A little girl Flossie would see this spring.

Gritting teeth, Max willed life into his limbs, felt them move. On the main floor, Blackbush screeched, as if trying to waken the woman at his feet so that he could kill her. Max pulled himself along on bloody hands and knees, feeling the ruined bellows of his chest working, rattling, *grinding*. Blood pattered from his ears, his face, but his one good eye narrowed into a determined slit.

Blackbush reached for Flossie with a scream.

And Max's hand shot upwards in the graceful arc of an underhand softball pitch, grazing the flesh of thighs before clamping down hard, claws deep, on a rather bulbous set of testicles.

Blackbush's screech twisted into a singular note of surprise before tapering off into a paralyzing wheeze. His arms dropped and his legs gave way, but not before Max emasculated him with one ferocious yank. Blackbush mewled as Max crawled on top of his adversary's back. He pulled the dark mop of hair to one side, exposing flesh traced with arteries thicker than roots. Max chomped into these with whatever power he had remaining. Blackbush shivered underneath, quieted, and finally went still in a widening pool of bad wine. Max started chewing and didn't stop. Not even when he hit bone.

When Max drew back from the carcass on the floor, the neck, shoulders and a good amount of the upper torso had vanished.

Every breath flared embers of agony within Max's crushed chest, but he watched the man-thing bleed out, willing to pitch into that piece of dying meat once more if needed.

Blackbush did not rise. Instead, the creature performed one last feat of magic for his audience of one. The legs shortened, a snout lengthened, the skin oozed hair until covered, all in under a minute. Max watched the shrinking transformation with baleful eyes. And when all was done, a half-breed terrier exhaled gently, a blood bubble swelling upon black lips, and became still at the center of an expanding puddle.

Max passed out by Flossie's side.

32

The blizzard sought to upend Ross as he struggled through sorcerous spirals of snow, numbing him through his snowsuit. He sensed he was heading in the right direction, although at times he felt as if he were slogging through a wall of stinging gauze. A wooden fence appeared almost mystically. Ross grabbed it, lowering his head against the icy lashings, anchoring himself long enough to get his bearings. To his right lay a road and a cliff side. The hill was on his left. The house belonging to Caramel and Roger Moore stood somewhere ahead. As far as Ross knew, the Moore house could be ten feet away from him. Or it could have been buried right up to the tip of its A-frame.

A powerful gale bore down on him, a veritable avalanche of snow and cold, surprising even him with its strength. Ross held on, burying his face in his arm and hugged the fence for dear life. The length of wood trembled like a speeding train bearing down on a length of rail. Had to be minus twenty at least by now, and the temperature seeped through the layers of his snowsuit and gloves with insidious determination. The wind intensified, almost impossibly so, furious that something living defied its wrath, and seemingly concentrated itself upon the man with the goal of blowing him over the cliff or jerking him up and away into the night. Tightening his arms around the fence, Ross heard frozen fibers crack, stole a breath, and prayed.

Then the storm winds slammed into him with all the force of a tornado.

"Jesus H. Christ," he snarled into his sleeve, barely hearing the words, believing any moment the storm would flay the snowsuit from his back, just for starters, before *really* having fun. But then the nearly irresistible force subsided, as if debris choked the blizzard's windpipes. Ross, breathless himself, took the lapse to flip over the fence and pound feet in a direction he hoped was correct. The blizzard could alter a person's path by degrees, disorienting them enough to make one walk past their mark without even realizing it. For all he knew, after the blast he'd just survived, he could be in fucking Kansas.

Ross crashed into the trunk of a nearly submerged car. He stumbled around the useless vehicle, glancing once over his shoulder and seeing squat, before pressing on ahead.

A wall loomed out of the freezing gloom. The Moores had painted the house a light sky-blue, but the storm rendered it colorless. He pressed himself against frost-bearded lengths of clapboard and staggered along, until he found the front door. Ross slammed his gloved fist on its hide as if he were old Jack Frost himself, weary of the gale. He didn't stop until it opened a cautious crack.

"D'hell ye want?" Roger Moore demanded, his face twisting in the weather.

"Roge," Ross shouted back. "It's Ross Kelly. Can I come in a minute?"

Roger allowed him that, closing the door as soon as the milky figure stumbled inside.

Ross didn't mind Roger and Caramel Moore. Right up to his seventy-fifth birthday, Roger possessed a wicked sense of humor, no matter how many spy jokes the boys cracked at him. He went along with the fun, delivering secret service lines with a thick Newfoundland accent. Ross's own favorite had been, "I'se James Bond. Now, luh, give us a mar-teenie… and shake de living' shit outtavit."

Roger wasn't doing the spy bit tonight.

"Lard tunderin' and Joseph. What in de fokkin' hell is ye doin' out in dis shitstarm?" he said, putting effort into closing the door. Caramel, her hair colored so, sat in the kitchen nearby, leaning back from a rusted kerosene lamp. Candles, killed by the wind, smoked in strategic places all about a surrounding counter.

"Roger," Ross gasped.

"D'fok ye gots the gun fer? See a sick cow out dere 'er sump'in'?"

"Listen, you two have got to come with me now. I'm gathering up everyone and moving them to Tom Dawe's place."

This stunned Roger and his Irish-Scot lineage. He scrunched up his balding brow and bared a rack of teeth too perfect to be his own.

Ross took a breath and said the only thing he could think of. "A crowd of crazy folks shot and killed Walt Borland, Jacob and Alice Moseby, and I'm pretty sure they killed the Sprees and Ben Trakers, too."

Roger Moore's eyes widened, shocked.

"And whoever the hell they are," Ross said, staring hard, "they're coming this way."

"Who'll watch de house?" Caramel screeched.

"Don't worry about the house. As far as I can tell, they ain't after money or whatever. They're just bent on killin' people. The plan is to move over to Tom's place, shore up, and when they come for us, we blast the bloods-a-bitches."

"Blast?" Roger squeaked.

"*Blast.* Shoot the fuckers stone cold dead. I mean it. I can't tell you what they did to old Borland or the Mosebys but it was bad. They're using the storm as cover. Probably be well away from here by the time anyone comes along and clears the roads. Or gets the phone lines up. Kill them and let the cops sort them out in the end."

"Is dey terrorists?" Caramel squeaked, all set to move right there.

"Yeah," Ross answered her. "They're terrorists."

Roger exchanged looks with Caramel before they both scurried off, preparing to abandon their home.

Ross hung back at the door, shaking his head at nature's fury. He suddenly thought of Alvin, regretted leaving the guy, and decided to head back for him when he got the chance.

"Hurry," he shouted, and both Roger and Caramel popped into sight, moving at best speed and clothed in thick pants and sweaters. Roger carried a long-barrel shotgun, which he placed on the kitchen table before leaning over with a curse and hauling on his boots.

"De phones are gone," Caramel said, pulling on her own gear.

"Yeah," Ross said, glancing nervously outside. "I know."

When they finished, they resembled a pair of winterized bowling pins, complete with goggles.

"Leadondiniffinyergonna," Roger blurted through a thick homemade scarf, and swung his arm in the direction of outside.

"Stay close, stay together," Ross instructed them. "That thing loaded?"

"Goddamnrightshe'sloaded."

"All right," Ross said, and rubbed warmth back into his cheeks. "Let's go."

33

Feeling none too good about what he was about to do, Sammy bundled up in his winter gear under the fretful eyes of his wife, Mary, standing in the archway of the kitchen, her new hairdo slightly off kilter. He'd said he'd check on Harry, and by God, he meant to check on the old bastard. Sammy didn't have many friends left in the world these days, since most of his good ones finally succumbed to the relentless march of time, so checking on one of the last ones didn't bother him in the least. He should've done so as soon as Ross and his buddy had left the house instead of screwing around for an hour. Sammy scoffed at that. He wasn't really screwing around, but shoring up the old homestead for the worst of the blizzard. The years on his frame just made the work go slower.

Mary, however, was worked up about him heading out into nature's gullet. "He's a grown man. I don't see why you have to check on him. Why can't he check on us? He wouldn't do this for you."

Sammy rolled his eyes at this logic.

"You're really going out there?"

"No, I'm just dressin' up for fun."

"Don't you sauce me, Samuel Walsh. Don't you *dare* sauce me."

Sammy huffed, his patience wearing thin, but knowing full well the pointlessness of getting into an argument with Mary at this stage of life.

"You come back to me," she said, voice trembling and eyes moist. "Hear me?"

"I hear you, mudder."

"Don't give me that mudder shit," Mary scolded with heat. "You tuck that away. Be careful out there in that mess. You're not twenty anymore. Be careful and come back to me."

He straightened while pulling on a stocking cap. Once done, he faced her and let his arms drop to his sides.

Mary hesitated for a moment, then embraced him in an emotional hug. "You heard me, right?" she asked, her mouth muffled by the insulated material of his coat.

Sammy hugged her back. "I heard." He kissed the top of her head, smelling the apricot scent of shampoo.

He released her then and waddled to the door. The snow scraped like knives at the glass, eager to welcome another soul into its blustery fold.

Looking back once at his worrying wife, Sammy took a breath and cracked open the door.

He heard the gunshots halfway to Harry's house.

That *pop... pop-pop,* swallowed up by the wind, rattled Sammy's nerves, rooting him to the spot faster than the slop Mother Nature was slinging into his face. His bifocals matted with sticky fluff, Sammy stood and thought for a moment before carrying on to Harry's house. A gust nearly bowled him over a third of the way through the walkway, but he arrived safely at the front door.

Light flickered beyond the window and Sammy saw his friend moving inside his kitchen with a flashlight. He hammered on the door with his fist, startling Harry enough that he whipped around. His friend's shoulders drooped and a second later he strode over to unlock the door.

"Whattin' the hell is you doin' out in this?"

"You hear them shots?"

"Yeah, why?"

"Get ready and get over to the house. Bring your gun just in case. Wild dogs are loose."

"Wild *dogs*?"

"Yeaup. Ross Kelly and another guy stopped by the house. Told me to getcha. Which I'm doing. Them shots fired were for the dogs, I bet."

"Wild dogs?" Harry repeated in disbelief. "In Amherst Cove?"

"Worse, they gone and killed Walt Borland."

That silenced Harry.

"C'mon then." Sammy waved. "We'll hole up at the house til' this all blows over and the cops get here."

"Let me get my rifle," Harry muttered. He disappeared inside his house.

Sammy stood inside the porch area, glanced nervously at his snow-covered boots, and *humphed.* Wild dogs. Something about that story wasn't sitting well with him.

A weird vibe of menace overtook him in that instant, turning him towards the door.

Framed in the window and colored by night was a man.

A naked man.

Sammy blinked as a hand spiked the pane and fastened tightly about his neck.

Harry Shea heard the glass shatter and shuffled back into the kitchen at best speed, lifting his polished Lee Enfield rifle with as much self-assured grace as a competitive shooter. The stock firm against his shoulder, he signaled his deadly intent by working the bolt and chambering the first round of a ten-round magazine, making the gunmetal crack. He knew his weapon just as well as the curves of his dear departed missus, eight years in the grave, and knew what it could do.

A frigid stream of air smacked his face as he stood in his kitchen, squinting in astonishment at the missing window in his door. Sammy was also gone. Harry didn't call out to his friend, and he suppressed the flare of frightened concern, knowing it would do neither of them any good. With a hunter's step, he gravitated to one wall and sidled up to the ruined window, barrel first, peeking outside. Broken glass shone like smashed teeth, coated with blood and snagged pieces of woolly material. Harry swallowed. It was tatters sliced from Sammy's coat.

Grimacing, Harry saw tracks in the snow and though he knew he shouldn't, he opened the wrecked door and stepped outside anyway. The blizzard struck hard and cold, rendering him momentarily breathless. The tracks disappeared into the night. Splotches of what could have been paint drizzled drifts. Harry firmed up his weapon.

A naked woman and man materialized out of the storm like a macabre couple kneeling in prayer. Except, they weren't requesting heavenly guidance.

They were feeding.

On a man-sized clump of pale flesh, runny with curds as bright as pulped raspberries.

"You..." Harry whispered, morbid shock morphing into undiluted rage. "Bloods-a-*bitches*."

The woman glanced up, her eyes like dead headlights, mouth opened in an angry question, chin dripping.

Harry shot her through the head, exploding the skull like an old whiskey jug and dropping her flat. The man screamed before lurching towards him, revealing a set of chompers Harry had only previously seen in a late-night vampire flick. The bolt clacked and his rifle barked back, punching a hole through a good chunk of his attacker's gut. Harry primed his weapon again and fired three more times with devastating cadence, blowing meaty chunks out of the monstrous cannibal on the first shot and drilling two more into him just for spite.

Harry glanced at the flayed body that had been his friend Sammy, sadly realized these things had murdered him with their hands and teeth. Feeling increasingly evil himself, Harry decided right then to demonstrate just how surgical he could be with a rifle.

He took aim at the man's face, only faintly interested at how the jaws bit at air, and readied his rifle with an executioner's authority.

Out of nowhere, a hand seized Harry's throat, crushing his windpipe in a dazzling burst of pain. It lifted him off his feet. Choking, Harry struggled to bring around his rifle, only to have it slapped twenty feet away. His vision dimmed, focusing on the polished, volcanic rock of his killer's eyes.

Brutus didn't like guns. Didn't like the noise. Didn't like his prey using them. Blood from the man's ruined flesh ran in rivulets down his arm, the steam blown asunder. Cartilage crinkled like plastic. He brought the face in closer, noting the light quickly fading in the noisemaker's eyes.

Life.

To be *savored.*

Brutus held the man's face to his set of formidable teeth and chewed it off.

Once finished, he tossed it away and heard the eager yipping of the Shih Tzus jumping at his scraps. He considered the headless torso of what was once the Golden

Retriever, and while her loss didn't upset him, it did ignite a very dangerous train of thought. The matter of a dwindling pack. Several had gone off on their own, though he suspected not far, but the notion of strengthening their numbers, *adding* to them, took a firm hold.

Brutus stood, his powerful physique unmoved by the blizzard's fury, lording over the fresh kills, and smelled the air. His senses pulled him away from the house with the two men, across a road, and down a short driveway, following tracks being filled with snow. He stopped at a closed door.

A light winked from inside, compelling Brutus to place his weapon of a hand against the glass, feeling its cool surface.

*

Mary Walsh had seen some strange things in her life. Once, when she was a girl on the lower beach, her father and his fellow fisherman had hauled onto the shore a thirty-foot eel as thick as a man's thigh. She'd witnessed glowing lights over the bay, watched them seemingly pirouette in the sky as if on a cosmic stage before blazing trails towards the heavens. Even saw silhouettes in upstairs windows of a King's Cove house suspected to be haunted––same house had all possible entry points at ground level entirely boarded up.

But nothing was stranger, or more frightening, than watching a naked man with a bodybuilder's physique emerge from the swirling folds of the night, pushing towards her front door. It wasn't Sammy, and for a moment her heart fluttered as if dunked in a vat of liquid nitrogen. His dim outline marched by the kitchen window and around the corner.

She stood there, aware of the trembling in her limbs, and covered her mouth. Who was he? And more importantly, why in God's name wasn't he *dressed—*

Something bumped against the front door and Mary's breath caught in her throat. She stopped herself from moaning and placed her back against a wall. For seconds, nothing happened, and she hoped that the guy had simply wandered off. Perhaps he was drunk on some sort of wicked, mind-altering drug the kids had these days. All her thoughts dispelled when she heard a brittle tapping from the direction of the front door window. Mary held her breath, and against her better judgment peeked around the corner, into the porch area.

Near total darkness, broken by a window frame of night.

A face with angry eyes of coal appeared outside the glass. It grimaced with the cold, exposing a set of teeth no human being should ever possess. Mary barely suppressed a squeak of terror, her own eyes nearly swelling out of her face, and jerked her head back when the face beyond the glass froze as if hearing her. Her muscles seized up, and for seconds, she stood, staring, as rigid as a rabbit caught in the glare of oncoming headlights. *Oh Jesus*, her mind shrieked, *Oh Christ Jesus our Savior.* Oh shit…

Another bump from the front door, stronger this time, and Mary took off for the living room. When she bolted, there was a skipped beat before an ear-cringing clatter erupted from the doorway. Mary shrieked. The thing behind her shrieked. She ran through the darkened living room, powered by fear and flight, and smashed her shin into the corner of the coffee table. The impact drove her to her knees, and she sob-squealed into the dark, before crawling at best impulse power towards the archway leading to the upstairs.

Monsters. There were such things as monsters. And one was in her kitchen, sounding as if it just bounced a table off a wall. The jingle of falling utensils made her flinch.

"Oh no, oh dear," she sputtered.

A diesel truck of a man charged into her living room, kicking furniture out of its way. She glanced over her shoulder to see the mountainous frame. Mary squealed and leaped to her feet, the pain of her shin muted by endorphins, and ran through an archway, turned a corner and thundered up a flight of steps. She reached the top and glanced back to see three figures scampering up the steps in pursuit. Another piercing shriek left her, and she fled to the remaining refuge of her bedroom. Once inside, she closed the door and pushed a chest of drawers across to barricade it, sobbing all the while.

She made it only a quarter of the way when the door blew inwards.

Mary staggered and collapsed on her back, hairdo completely off-kilter, and stared up at the bare-assed fright easing into the bedroom. Other, eager voices followed it, figures filling up the hallway with midnight eyes and shark-like smiles.

Mary released one last wail and turned onto her knees, fully intending to smash her way through the sole bedroom window and praying the fall would kill her. A hard hand clamped around her ankle and pulled her back. She screeched as the invader held her up by the joint, the tendons in her free-flopping leg straining to the point of snapping. It shook her like a fish.

Then it slammed her against the wall.

*

Brutus dropped the body to the floor. He knew it was a female from its wailing, and slapped her against the wall to silence the noise. She gasped when he released her, not entirely dead as he first thought, but stunned. Brutus studied her shape in the dark. The female was an old one, he knew that from her feeble attempt at escape, but she might be of some worth. The instinct to breed, to replenish the pack, was strong in him, and if he wasn't killing, eating, or sleeping, he fully intended to impregnate any and all females he encountered. Memories passed through his mind, like slides passing through a light, other places, places filled with people, his owner mounting a female…

He paused, sniffed the air, and decided there was no point in attempting to mount this one. She'd been long infertile.

Brutus scoffed. He wasn't of the mind to eat her, either.

Behind him, the Shih Tzus gathered, eager to please. Brutus didn't care for the smaller breeds, but they followed him without challenging his authority.

On the floor, the female awakened and moaned.

Having better things to do, Brutus *whuffed* and walked away.

The Shih Tzus looked after him expectantly, their toothy maws slamming shut as the pack leader passed them, allowing them his leavings. They fidgeted and licked lips, eying him as he descended the steps. When he was out of sight, they regarded the crippled female with ravenous mirth.

And grabbed her.

*

Alvin couldn't see a goddamn thing outside his window.

The gunshots he'd heard—the second volley of the evening no less—got his attention almost as fast as his girlfriend's hand in his lap during a session of high school algebra. He hated to think Rossy could use his help, but also despised venturing forth into that particular cream-of-ass freezing soup. His watch gleamed 8:48PM at a touch. Night was only just beginning, and he bobbed on his heels like a kid in need of an exceptionally long piss. Restless, he roamed his house, checking doors and windows, thinking of the windows in particular as his castle's murder holes. That got him salivating over a sweet compound bow he'd seen on Amazon and how a few broadheads from one of those puppies would take the fight out of a hairy bastard real quick.

If only he'd ordered it a month ago.

But what were those gunshots about?

He'd completed his rounds around the house, anxious at the absence of gunplay, and came back to stand at attention at his picture window. C-Cup thumped away in the background, pulsing purified oxygen at a steady rate. On a good day, he could see Shea and the Walsh's houses just below. Nothing now, just a terrible black blur that crackled against the glass. He took a deep breath and adjusted his chest protector, then his cup. The cup in particular felt tighter than usual. Alvin sighed, fearing his fat pad had expanded without telling him. Damn thing felt like it was cutting off circulation down there.

Thoughts of his nearest neighbors flittered back. Harry wasn't his favorite person, but Sammy, despite being something of a philosophical butter tart and nut bar mix that just so happened to really enjoy his homebrew, was the more civil of the pair. And then there was his wife, Mary. Alvin shook his head, supposing he could at least check on her, and then do a quick patrol to make sure all was well along the outer perimeter. Having decided that, Alvin got ready. He forewent the winter boots but wore sneakers to accommodate his shin guards. Disconnected himself from C-Cup and hooked up his tubing to a portable oxygen canister and let it hang from his hip. Stretched a ski mask over his helmet. When he finished hauling on his winter coat (realizing he couldn't do up the zipper because of the protective measures, and mentally swearing at pizza fingers), he resembled a black-and-blue-padded practice dummy, like the ones used to train police dogs. With a broadsword.

"Fuck that K-9 ass up," Alvin muttered, slapping a shoulder.

Tightening his grip on the weapon, he approached his door like an astronaut about to embark on a spacewalk. The wind jumped him as soon as he stepped out, nearly tearing his door from his hand. He leaned into it to seal his home and, once done, shuffled around to face the bay––or at least the direction of the bay. Despite all his bundling, the cold still seeped through his ankles and legs, and his coat flapped around his ass like a ruined parachute. Using Ass Fucker as a dangerous cane, Alvin muddled through the drifts filling his driveway, and headed for Harry Shea's house. The blizzard targeted him, slamming into his padded mass with enough force to halt him at times.

Pushing through the dismal weather, a puffing Alvin found the corner of a fence and realized he'd gone off course a few feet. He followed the fence until arriving at Harry Shea's wooden gate, half open and buried in snow. Alvin glanced left and right before squeezing his bulk through.

"Goddamn fuckin' snow," he muttered, sinking with every step, hating every second of being out in the cold. The gloomy profile of the house crept into view, wintry ribbons flailing from its peak. Alvin continued on, locating sets of tracks leading straight to an unmoving mass lying on a bleary canvas. Snow had covered much of the blood pooled around the shredded man, giving the impression that he'd fallen from a great height and exploded upon contact with the ground. This wasn't the case. Alvin saw the torn winter gear and skin underneath and realized quite darkly that something had been feeding extensively upon the dead man. Then he saw the broken glasses, Sammy's glasses, and suddenly there wasn't enough oxygen in his portable tank. With the number of horror movies he'd seen in his life, one might think nothing would faze Alvin's desensitized sensibilities, but seeing his neighbor torn and sliced into red lines found a hole in his mental armor, and left him numb.

The wind dropped just a fraction, revealing a second body, headless, buck naked, and as frosty as a freezer burnt roast. The fact that it was a woman was lost on him, but then he saw a *third* body.

The urge to swear came upon him but Alvin couldn't spare the breath. Perhaps the new corpse was Harry. It might have been except there wasn't any real way he could tell. The gutted body had no face. No eyes. Nothing at all except a red skull collecting stardust, the brain pan cracked open, subjected to extreme pressure.

Alvin tried hard not to look at the filling inside.

He considered the house, shook his head, and plodded with numb feet along a mess of footprints to a door with its window smashed out. It wasn't locked. Alvin let himself in but went no farther than the kitchen, knowing the place was empty. All these years he'd been wishing for the deaths of the two Amherst Cove men, and now that it had happened, he felt the need to just sit for a bit and re-evaluate the universe.

Mary popped into his head.

Alvin hurried back out into the cold night at best speed. He arrived at the Walsh house minutes later, slowing when he saw the front door sticking out of a white dune, resembling a block of chocolate garnishing a sundae. The dark opening beckoned, drawing a cautious Alvin closer and chugging away on his oxygen supply. He brandished Ass Fucker with both hands as he stepped closer.

Jesus Christ, he thought in awe and prayer upon seeing how the Walsh's house had been violated. Hinges dangled by the barest fibers off the entryway frame. Alvin crept onto the porch, snow blowing inside, and felt his stomach take an unpleasant dip. Dark, so dark inside. The slate of pitch before him dotted by occasional gray squares of windows.

"Hey," Alvin said, dreading the very attempt.

Past the kitchen. Into the living room.

"Mary?" Alvin asked, a little louder, a touch braver.

"You here?"

The *thump* of something overhead, upstairs, stopped him just beyond inside the living room, his heartbeat suddenly loud in his ears. He scanned the darkness for a stairway, as he'd never been inside the Walsh's house, and had no idea about the layout.

Another thump, followed by the squeal of wood from above—a shrill note that made Alvin forget he was sucking up his oxygen supply by the bucketload. He didn't call out again. Something told him that Mary wasn't entirely... alive.

The urge to flee grew very strong.

The padding of feet over his head, like children running to the sound of a dinner bell, made him look heavenward. Voices, high-pitched and eager, squealed with sinister delight. Whoever they were rattled along upstairs, like a troublesome pipe. They stopped for a brief, considering moment before continuing toward what Alvin believed was the southern part of the house.

The voices became clearer in a rush, a meld of primitive cravings. Alvin didn't realize how hard his hands shook, as if Ass Fucker had abruptly decided to divine water underfoot. Ahead in the dark, feet crashed over steps, odd yips of anger, and the groan of wood.

The clamor drew his adjusting eyes to an archway at the far side of the living room, past dark shapes of overturned furniture.

The shape of a man materialized there, bare feet padding on carpet, and making Alvin almost piss himself like a racehorse made to drink from a fire hydrant. The figure had a short but stocky build, like a heroic dwarf without a suit of armor. That sudden, broken-spring appearance unnerved Alvin and his fear spiked, feet already drawing him back towards the kitchen. He brought up his sword, in case the dude wanted to dance.

Another shadow joined the first, similarly built. Then an identical third. They whined and growled, destroying whatever language they'd been born with, and homed in on Alvin's retreating form. One stepped into a beam of grayish night light and for a frightening second, Alvin glimpsed the curved teeth. Saw the startling black eyes.

All thoughts of fighting evaporated.

The three shadows charged.

Alvin didn't scream—he was too intent on getting out of the house. He ran for the ruined doorway, clipping the corner of a table and making his hip sing, whipping both himself and the piece of furniture around. The three dwarves crashed into the table's edge, one practically clotheslined. Alvin realized with a stab of fright that none of his pursuers wore a stitch of clothing, which freaked him out *more*.

This was the stuff of fucked-up nightmares.

He bolted from the house, broadsword swinging, breaking through the deeper drifts and spraying snow. The road and incline up his own driveway made him chug dangerously, and he clutched at the doorknob of his own house. Weak sounds of pursuit caused him to glance over his shoulder, panting like he'd just run a marathon tied to the back of a moving bus.

Nothing.

But then the three hunters scrambled out of the blizzard, their short legs pumping, faces lifted towards Alvin. Seeing those eager expressions triggered some childhood fear of being eaten alive, and he was certain if he were caught, the three evil triplets would feast on his bones while his heart still fluttered.

He opened and slammed the door, locking everything available, and remembered the other houses.

They were coming in, through the windows, whether he liked it or not.

Alvin rushed down the hall, hearing C-Cup breathe, reeling off the walls. Hands pounded against the house, causing him to glance back in terror. Images of mutilated Harry and Sammy flashed through his head. They'd been *devoured.*

Glass shattered at the front of the house, jacking his nerves as he charged into his bedroom and slammed the door. The length of tubing running from C-Cup down the hall got pinched under the door's edge. That hooked his attention. He then regarded the concentrator with deadly intent.

Oxygen.

A loud bang, inside the house.

Alvin rushed to C-Cup's side and yanked the tubing off the plastic nozzle, feeling the blood throb in his temples. He twisted the knob controlling the stream of oxygen up to five, and C-Cup went into overdrive, filtering nitrogen from the O2. Alvin then went to his closet, grabbed the dangling wrench and opened up the valves on the two back-up air tanks stored there. The compressed air screeched upon its release, venting into the closed-off room and scaring the man as much as the hunters in his house. Alvin swallowed, ran to his bedroom desk and fished a silver lighter from a drawer. He struggled, near breathless, up onto his bed, using Ass Fucker for assistance. Alvin inspected the sheet of glass, the storm outside, and gulped down whatever air his ruined lungs could manage. He felt as though his heart were about to explode.

Voices, talking evil nonsense, just outside the door.

Alvin kept Ass Fucker close as he opened the lighter, and placed his gloved thumb against the spark wheel, hoping to God there was fluid left in the shiny shell. He took a deep shuddering breath and saw his reflection in the dark, stormy depths of the glass.

Something slammed against the door, the sound puncturing the furious stream of air from the opened tanks. Alvin took the deepest breath of his life and, to the left of his reflection, glimpsed three grinning dwarves smashing his bedroom door. They fixed on him immediately. One ran right at the bed with a maniacal eagerness—

Just as Alvin flicked the lighter's wheel.

The bedroom exploded in a frightening gasp of fiery blue light, enveloping three figures with an apocalyptic fist. Hungry voices became peals of agony.

Suddenly blazing himself, a roaring Alvin propelled himself through a sheet of glass and tumbled, still smoking, twenty feet down like a meteor crashing to earth.

34

The flash from the top of the hill distracted Ross from the people ahead of him. He watched how the fire swelled with eerie delight, burning through the night's malaise. The conflagration was close to Alvin's house, if not the source of the blaze itself.

"Sweet Jesus," Ross muttered to himself, the words lost in the gale surrounding them all. If it was Alvin, he hoped the man survived.

"What was that?" asked Phil Crout, holding onto his wife, Jessica, both looking towards the top of the hill. The retired fisherman was perhaps the most stubborn to convince to move, if only until the storm died down and the power was restored, and they only managed to do it after he locked the property up. Roger and Caramel Moore's outlines stood huddled together only a stride ahead.

"Alvin's place," Ross bellowed into the storm, the tension making his nerves quiver like stressed wires. "Keep moving."

The little line Ross had collected crawled along the lower road, stepping into each other's tracks, heading towards the unseen home of Leo and Bertha Tucker, a retired couple from Lab City. Most of the community knew their history. Leo had retired five years ago as a well-respected geologist. Bertha had made a sizeable chunk of coin drilling wells in northern Saskatchewan before tiring of it. Like a few of the inhabitants, they'd discovered the little cove and fell in love with it.

Ross guarded the rear, squinting and holding his shotgun close. The night hemmed them into the smallest box of vision, and he hoped they would be able to reach their destination. Then the house materialized out of the night, snow-lashed and haunting. A steep driveway as groomed as a ski slope led to a corner that faded in and out of sight with every gust.

The four seniors ahead of Ross regarded him, features swathed in shadow, projecting apprehension. He'd rooted them out of their warm homes, and taken on the responsibility for their safety.

"Go on," Ross shouted. "Get to Tom Dawe's and hole up there. I'll get Leo and Bertha."

Hesitantly, like little children leaving the safety of their parents for the first time, they moved towards their final goal. Having sent them on their way, Ross trudged up the driveway. He turned a corner of the house and headed for the main door. Putting his shoulder and back to the wall, he elbowed three hard raps against the frame, aware of the tracks he'd left behind, painfully taking note of the shifting, tenebrous blackness licking at the house.

A flashlight beam shone through the glass. The door opened a moment later, and Leo held onto its edge with a rough hand. He stood eye-to-eye with a weary Ross, scowling his question as loud as any shout. "D'hell you want?"

"Let me in," Ross barked. "I'll tell you inside."

Tucker didn't budge. His eighty years had slumped his shoulders and shrunk his height, but he projected an aura of not to be trifled with at any age. Though a geologist, he'd also served with the military and seen action in the Korean War. Some even said that on some evenings, when Leo really got on the beer, he could be prodded for war stories and operations some folks hadn't even heard of before.

"Don't think so," Tucker replied sternly, gazing at his visitor over a pair of bifocals thick enough to protect his eyes from the glare of a welding torch. "I don't take kindly to men holding illegal firearms. In any weather pattern."

"All right, listen. You've been hearing the gunshots tonight? There's a bunch of crazies running around shooting the place up. They already got Walt Borland, Jacob and Alice Moseby and probably the Sprees. I think they're coming this way so I'm pulling everyone back to Tom Dawe's. Strength in numbers and all that."

A harsh blow of wind whipped around the corner of the house and almost ripped the open door out of Tucker's grasp. When he composed himself, he grudgingly bade Ross to enter, shutting the blizzard out as it droned curses.

"Now then, say all that again," Tucker ordered him, practically nose to nose in a short hallway.

"Who is it, Leo?" Bertha asked from somewhere within the house.

"Ross Kelly from up on the hill."

"Oh hello, Ross," Bertha chimed, her pleasant voice lilting. "Dirty old night out."

"Dirty is right," Ross agreed. "You both had better come along with me and leave the house."

"And head over to Tom Dawes's," Tucker said.

"That's right."

"Folks are barricading themselves over there."

"Yes."

"And who are these crazy people, you say?"

"Fuck, Leo, we don't have time—"

"Ross," Tucker interrupted in a schoolmaster's voice. "I'm eighty-one years old. Retired in two professions where it's either common sense or practice to clarify situations before proceeding into the unknown. A lack of intel is a lack of thought and purpose. I'm also bullshit-intolerant and I fucking refuse to simply move for no one unless given a damn good reason to, regardless if they come knocking on my door with a sawed-off shit flinger. So if it's all the same to you, and you aren't too keen on using that miserable piece of metal in your hand there, I'd appreciate you answering my questions."

Ross sighed. "I don't know who they are."

"Yet you know they've killed Borland, the Mosebys, and the Sprees?"

Bertha's dark outline shuffled into view at the end of the short hall.

"Yeah."

"I see." Tucker pulled back a bit, pointing the flashlight down and illuminating his furry slippers, complete with plastic claws.

"Alice Moseby is dead?" Bertha asked nervously.

"According to this shit disturber, she is. And a good many more." Tucker swung his attention back to Ross. "And you say they're heading this way? The crazies?"

"That's right."

"You know this for a fact?"

"Jesus, Leo."

"For a fact?" Tucker insisted.

"Yeah. Pretty much."

"You've seen them?"

"Only one," Ross said. "Over at Walt Borland's place."

"That's a long ways out in this weather."

"We figure they used the treeline, came down around to the cliff's edge and just headed for the closest house."

"Who's we?" Tucker asked.

"A guy I found at Borland's place."

"You don't know him?"

"No, but he knows what's going on."

"That him there?"

Ross blinked for a moment before spinning around. There, just beyond the glass, appearing out of the raging nebula of the storm, was the outline of a man approaching the door as if stalking prey. Tucker flashed the light on the glass, ruining the scene for a moment, but then the creature pressed its face up against the glass and snapped at it with teeth as curved as tusks.

Ross hissed his fright, raising the shotgun as a claw smashed through the glass, sending shards inside the hall. It grabbed Ross by the front of his snowsuit and jerked him forward, crashing him into the door and ruined window, once, twice, trying to bend him backwards as it pulled him through the opening. Bertha shrieked. The man outside garbled furious syllables. A blast of freezing air invaded the house. Ross tried to bring up the shotgun but a third yank bounced his forehead off the unyielding wood of the upper frame. The skin burst apart. A metal knob, half of a pair from which a parted curtain hung, missed impaling his right eye by a finger. The shotgun slipped from his hand. Then, the pressure on his snowsuit grew. In a daze he heard seams pop, felt his back extend three uncomfortable degrees past his limited arc of flexibility. Oddly enough, his feet suddenly became awash in orange light.

The shotgun pushed past his hip and fired point-blank in the attacker's face, scrubbing flesh from its skull and snapping the creature back. Ross dropped to the floor, gazing up incredulously at Leo Tucker, holding the smoking weapon close to his chest.

"Leo!" Bertha shouted as she pointed.

A long arm reached through the window, over Ross's head like the pallid underbelly of some vicious serpent. Leo fiddled with the dry shotgun. Claws swished the air, inches from the old man. Ross looked down, saw how the zipper of his snow pants had pulled back from his boot, revealing the hilt of the Bowie knife.

In a blur of speed where the eye, mind and body coordinate in near-perfect sync, Ross yanked the knife free and slashed at the forearm. The silver blade parted flesh and stroked bone. Something outside squealed hideously enough to split eardrums. The arm jerked and yanked outside as if torched. Senses returning, Ross scampered away from the window, joining Leo and Bertha in their kitchen. Back in the entry area, Leo's flashlight rolled on the floor where he'd dropped it, the light illuminating an oblong section of the door's base.

"I think we should do what Ross says," Bertha panted into her husband's shoulder.

"I agree," Tucker gasped, eyes on the smashed windows. Cries of horrific pain and rage echoed sharply from outside. "Get my semi."

Bertha left them.

"You got any more shells for this?" Tucker asked Ross.

"Yeah."

"Then here." He handed over the gun while Ross stooped to sheathe the knife. "We best leave out the other door before—*Jesus.*"

There, behind the door and framed in a ghoulish portrait of glittering crystal, the thing whose face had been surgically removed by Tucker's lead pellets slammed a heavy arm into the wood. The door bucked. The house shook. The force dislodged the flashlight on the floor, the beam rolling to partially illuminate the shotgun's shredding. The thing had no eyes now, and its nose was a ragged hole, but even robbed of its senses, the monster reared back its powerful arm and smashed the door aside.

Without thinking, Ross stepped forward and stabbed the beast straight through its raw nasal cavity. The thing squealed, a curt note not unlike a sneaker twisting on a basketball court, before convulsing and slumping across the threshold. An adrenaline-charged Ross extracted the blade and picked up the shotgun—not remembering even dropping it—though he no longer held any faith in the weapon.

Tucker's hand fell on his shoulder and pulled him back. The older man closed a second inner door, and withdrew both of them deeper into the house. "Tactical retreat," he breathed and shuffled towards a coat closet. Bertha appeared a few seconds later, holding a long shotgun by the barrel and placing it against a wall.

"Give him the shells," Tucker said, and Bertha held out a small box. Ross sheathed his knife first before taking it.

He ripped open the box and thumbed red cartridges into the magazine.

A resounding crash came from the kitchen, startling the three.

"Head to Tom's," Ross said, working the pump and turning away from the couple before they could say anything. Wiping his bleeding scalp in a sleeve, he edged up to the kitchen, and peeked around the corner.

One of the man-things was hunched over, standing in the wreckage of the inner door. Its arm dribbled blackness onto the floor. The face whipped towards Ross as he stepped around the corner and fired nearly point blank into its abdomen. The naked midsection exploded with a meaty *chuff,* driving it backwards. The walls spattered. The creature gasped and staggered into the entryway. Ross pumped the shotgun, charging across the kitchen in pursuit. He spun around the corner to find snow coating the floor, the gore-soaked remains of what looked to be a crossbreed of terrier basking in half a halo from the discarded flashlight. An evil, blowing miasma of ice and snow festered beyond the wrecked entrance.

Jacked up on fear as before, Ross kept his shoulder to the corner and peered out into the blizzard, fingers flexing on the gun, waiting for something else to pop into sight. The little body of the dead animal caught his attention for a brief moment, just enough to realize they reverted back when truly dead, and that only the knife killed them. He'd remember that.

Nothing tried to enter the house.

But something screamed outside, the sound eerily warped by the winds. It only took a few seconds for Ross to realize he was hearing more than one voice. Believing it was time to leave, he backed away and felt his way along the walls, through the now-empty house, until he found the second door and let himself out.

Into hell.

A savage wind blew Ross two steps towards the cliff side, some forty feet to his right. Snow snake-danced before his eyes. He righted himself and searched for tracks, couldn't see any, and decided to plunge ahead anyway. Voices yelled out somewhere behind him, some pissed off, some in pain, all sounding closer than he wanted. Worse, the feeling of a presence on his heels haunted him. He found the road leading up the hill and stopped in the middle, shotgun leveled at the freezing dark.

The wailing cut through the storm. Ross's teeth chattered.

A voice, closer now, but visibility was so poor that a dog-thing could be five steps away and he wouldn't know. Ross didn't want to fight out in the open. He got moving and a short time later, the glow from lit windows lifted his spirits considerably. The house slowly took shape, and he rounded a corner to find a deck facing the bay. A set of stairs climbed the side. Recent boot-crushed drifts told him that the folks he'd gathered up had arrived in one piece. He stumbled up the steps, collapsed against a wall, and slammed a fist on the nearby door.

It opened and a bushy Tom Dawe, the silver-haired uncle to Bigfoot himself, reached out. Faces crowded over his shoulder. Flashlight beams flooded the deck.

"Tom," Ross muttered.

"Get in quick. My God," Tom said, arm still outstretched, mouth hanging open and pointing a flashlight beam. Ross glanced back and felt his stomach drop somewhere around ankle level.

There, bathed in the artificial light and mottled with possible frostbite, stood a naked man appearing risen from a dismal grave. It squinted in the harsh beam, retreating from the lowest step, while frozen tatters of flesh and blood adorned his face and neck.

More faces crowded over Tom Dawe's plaid-checked shoulder, their voices cooing startled amazement. Tucker was one of them. Roger Moore stepped out onto the snow-caked deck, holding an additional shotgun at the ready. Caramel stood behind him, covering her mouth with a very old hand while shining a powerful flashlight at the newcomer.

The creature, looking as if it had been mauled and left for dead, wavered, *whuffed*, and, with a growl, held up the very dead-looking Flossie Jones. Its arms, spotted with gruesome frostbite, faltered for a moment, then firmed up long enough to ease Flossie onto the deck. That single marble eye blinked away snow, appeared wary, but also sadly exhausted. A tongue licked at its lips for a moment, and in a startling display of affection, the creature leaned in, and nuzzled Flossie's cheek with its nose. The human onlookers heard a deep, solemn note from the thing's ruined windpipe, before backing away.

Ross didn't aim at it, distantly surprised that Roger didn't, either.

Screams rose off in the distant dark, and the man-thing's attention split between the sounds, the people with the firearms, and Flossie.

A flood of disbelief coursed through Ross. "Max?" he said softly. "Maximilian?"

The figure hesitated for a moment, as if recognizing its name. Then it lurched off into the night, moving only as fast as its near frozen limbs would bear it.

Jessica and Bertha went to Flossie's side.

Ross allowed himself to be led into the house.

*

Max stumbled off into those freezing, swirling, ebony veils that chilled him to his very core. He wanted to sleep, very badly in fact, and despite feeling sad for leaving his owner amongst people, he also felt relief in being able to do so. He'd returned his wonderful owner to her own kind, to relative safety, which was what he'd set out to do since leaving their home. And like all dogs, he sensed his time drawing to an end, but unlike most, he was winding things down the best way he could, with what he had. All he really wanted to do now was perhaps find a place out of the cold. Get comfortable. Perhaps even give his balls one last lick. They certainly earned it. Having something to eat was an idea as well, before closing his eyes for that final sleep. From which there was no waking.

Leaving the warm glow of the house behind, Max lifted one heavy foot after the other, rubbed at his hairless arms, and walked into the heart of the blizzard.

35

Brutus called out into the night, marshaling his pack while his remaining companion, the bloodhound, with its long and narrow face, led him down the hill towards an unknown destination. Their flesh shivered with the intense cold, but they drove on into the drifting sheets, relying only on their sense of smell. Long Face's nose was superior to Brutus's, and they moved through the screaming wind until the cold became far too great for even them to bear. A house rose up out of the night, and Brutus and Long Face stomped towards it. The door was closed, so Brutus smashed out a window before gripping the wood and wrenching it off its hinges. They tore into the house, ran through every room before deeming it safe. Brutus returned to the entrance and yelled again into the face of the storm.

Like echoes in a bad dream, the others shouted back.

And soon, slinking towards him like frozen children, came the remaining breeds. They moved as if in pain and quickly sought shelter within the house, greeting their leader with a quick growl and a sniff before retiring inside. After minutes of this, only Brutus stood outside. He heard no other sounds. His once mighty pack had been decimated to only seven, including himself.

Seven was enough.

In truth, he only really needed one to breed again.

He stomped through the darkened halls of the house, stopping at a comfortable couch and barking at the mongrel shivering upon it. The breed dropped to the floor, and Brutus curled up on its length as the others milled about close together, gelling for warmth. A male and a female grappled and whined at each other before the male finally mounted her, filling the rooms with the sounds of their rough coupling.

Brutus lorded over it all, watching the act with gleaming intellect. More of *that* was needed. And as the mating concluded rather noisily before him, his thoughts turned towards how he might find more females to impregnate.

In short time, he believed he had the answer.

*

Back at Borland's cabin, Morris woke and smelled the breed before he saw him.

It reeked of strangeness, alien in origin yet somehow oddly familiar. He'd gotten a whiff of it before. Off Borland, he believed, before the old prick went crazy.

Morris cracked open an eye and lay very still. The cabin floor had become a blackboard sprinkled with knobs. The destroyed doorway lay bare, filled with gleaming snow while the world beyond twisted as if dropped out of the cosmos.

Then he heard the scratching. A long, drawn out rake of claws on wood, somewhere around the back of the cabin, taking its time rounding the dwelling. Morris flicked his ears and realized he was still in wolf form. Feeding. He remembering gorging himself on Borland's remains, didn't have to look that way to know he'd chewed off both of the man's legs before dragging himself to a section of the floor where the blood hadn't pooled.

A growl outside, from human vocal cords but strikingly off. The sound of claws lifted, like a needle coming free of a wobbly vinyl record, before resuming, heading for the open door.

Morris studied the dark interior, tracking the noise. Something cleared its throat, and the raking lifted once again. The smell grew stronger.

A shadow of a man stepped into the doorway, the wind frazzling his hair as if a million volts coursed through it. Eyes twinkled in a face of black. A slit of a mouth unzipped in a hiss. He was big, lean and powerful looking, and wearing not a stitch of clothing. A hand gripped the frame and he pulled himself inside, over the threshold.

Morris growled, letting his visitor know where he was.

The man-thing, spawn of Borland, and reeking of that offensive half-smell of dog and human, tensed. It centered its focus on the wounded wolf lying on the floor. The thing's chest expanded and deflated, fearless, flexed knives atop its fingertips. Brimming with confidence.

That was the creature's first mistake.

The second mistake came when, instead of retreating for the hills, the breed actually zeroed in on the motionless wolf in the cabin.

Morris waited until it was close enough.

Then lashed out with all the force of a sprung bear trap.

*

"All right me son, you're inside now," Tom Dawe reassured a shivering Ross Kelly. He was sitting at a kitchen table and surrounded by what looked to be everyone still alive in Amherst Cove. Two of the men carried a still unconscious Flossie Jones into the living room, while the women fluttered about for blankets and hot tea. Heat flooded the house and, for a moment, Ross just closed his eyes and let himself thaw. He'd said it many times before, how he'd much rather come in from the cold and warm up than come in from the heat and cool off.

"What the Jesus was that thing, Ross?" asked a gruff Leo Tucker.

"I wanna know if'n there's more of the hairless bastards," Phil Crout said.

"Them the crazies y'talk' about?"

"Oh, she's froze, she's froze," one of the women folk wept from the living room.

"What is she, dead?" Tom called out.

"No, she's alive. Just froze."

"Don't mind her," Tucker said in that old voice of iron. "You just gather your thoughts and let us know what's going on."

"Tha's right." Tom spoke with a voice that could still carry a baritone note.

Mutters of agreement.

Ross faced the old men of Amherst Cove, ranging from the mid-sixties to their eighties. Tradesmen most, with the exception of Leo Tucker. Fishermen and carpenters, farmers and sea hands. All of Irish, Scots, or English lineage. Some with little accent, and others with various degrees of thickness meshed into something altogether unique. Tom Dawe leaned in, holding his semi-automatic shotgun by its long barrel, the stock firm on the floor. Only then did Ross realize the lights in the place were on. Tom had a back-up generator tucked away in his shed, and a blazing wood stove in his living room.

"Now then," Leo muttered with an investigative tone. "Start talkin'. That thing that dropped off Flossie Jones. Contrary to what I've heard, that didn't look like some crazy fucker shootin' the place up."

"And what's this about wild dogs and then terrorists?" Tom asked. "Cause that thing out there was neither."

"No," Ross admitted, feeling both mental and physical exhaustion take hold. "Look, I don't know much, but the crazy fucker part I made up. Had to, because that thing out there is one of the reasons to get you moving. You wouldn't have gone anywhere if I'd said there were monsters out there in the snow."

The gathered men, Tom, Leo, Phil and Roger, somber in the lit kitchen, supposed the younger man was right.

"So what is it?" Leo Tucker asked, holding his semi-auto shotgun by the neck.

"I dunno," Ross answered. "The guy I was with—he knew, but he wasn't saying much. They're shaped like men but they have teeth. Like dogs. Wolves. Fuckin' claws, too. You saw that thing that brought Flossie over. You saw the eyes on it. They're all like that. And I wasn't lying about Walt Borland. They killed him. Practically ripped him apart. Him and the Mosebys. Maybe whoever else who isn't here right now."

Ross didn't see the need to tell them he was the one who released the dogs into the wild. That was one mistake he meant to quietly correct if he could.

"The worst thing is," he carried on, "that I don't think guns will kill them. It hurts 'em, but doesn't kill 'em. This does."

He pulled out the Bowie knife, the silver shining.

"Jesus, Jesus," Roger Moore whispered.

"What's so special about that?" Tom asked. "Besides being a big-ass knife."

Leo Tucker held out his hand and Ross handed the weapon over. Leo hefted it, inspected and scratched its surface. "Silver."

The others regarded each other with growing trepidation.

"This thing's silver," Tucker declared. No one questioned Leo Tucker, the man who'd made a life of studying rock.

Tucker passed the weapon back to Ross. "You could've said it was a werewolf."

"A what?" Tom Dawe exclaimed. "What did you just say?"

The group heard some scuffling from the entryway, breaking the discussion. "S'up, my buddies," a short Burt Hill said, with an equally short Chris Hallet in tow, coming through the archway, leading deeper in the house. Both men waddled, as if they'd had surgery to bow their knees. "The women folks're all straightened away."

"Ross here says we gots a werewolf problem," Roger Moore announced.

"Not a werewolf," Ross said.

"Well, what is it then?" Tucker asked. "The damn thing's killed by silver. That sounds like a werewolf t'me."

"Can't be a fuckin' werewolf." Tom Dawe waved a hand in exasperation. "That was a goddamn man. Buck-ass naked and with big fuckin' falsies."

"A breed of wolf, then?" Phil Crout asked, rubbing his chin.

A loud hammering on the kitchen door snapped everyone around, sending more than just a few heartbeats through the roof. Tom Dawe and Leo Tucker both brought up their weapons with a speed defying their years.

A figure was at the door, cupping a hand to the glass. Man-shaped, and wearing a hockey helmet.

"JESUS *CHRIST* don't shoot!" Alvin bawled loud enough to be heard all the way to Newman's Cove.

"Christ almighty," Tom breathed, lowering his gun. "Sure as fuck *somethin's* out there to get his ass outta the house."

Phil Crout allowed a frosty Alvin to enter. He slapped a broadsword on the kitchen table, pulled his partially-melted helmet from his head, and collapsed in a chair across from Ross. The man's winter clothing had been terribly burned, as if someone had doused him in gasoline, ignited it, and then proceeded to stomp the flames out only after a full minute of cooking.

"Howya doin' b'ys?" he huffed at them all. "Jesus Lord our Savior, me nuts are froze off."

"No fuckin' wonder yer boys are froze," Tom accused. "Look at how yer dressed. Y'look like yer chemistry set blew up on ya. Y'been on some of that medicinal wacky tobaccy from upalong?"

"Could use some of that right now," Roger Moore said from behind. Phil Crout nodded in mute agreement.

"Wish I had, me son," Alvin said. "Just blew me fuckin' shack up."

"Saw that," Ross said grimly. "Sorry to see it go but glad to see yer all right. What happened?"

"Fuckin' *gremlins* is what happened!" Alvin pealed, his face freckled with soot. "Stocky little shits about yea high, cocks swinging and balls a danglin'. Little fuckin' bareback bastards killed…" At this, Alvin uncharacteristically choked up, shocking everyone, even Ross who couldn't remember ever seeing his friend become emotional. "They killed Harry Shea. And Sam and Mary."

Stunned silence.

"I told them to stay… inside," Ross muttered weakly, remembering asking Sammy to check on Harry.

"They did, but those short shits tore the doors off the houses. Gutted them like…" A gasping Alvin trailed off at that point, shaking his helmeted head while his portable air tank puffed exclamations. "They're dead. I went down to their houses to check on 'em. The three naked cocksuckers were at Mary's house. Then they chased *me* to mine and fuckin' almost had me too before I blew the back-up air tanks in my room. I had to jump through me own goddamn bedroom window and when I came to, the whole house had gone up. And you know the freaky part? The sure as shit, ball-grabbing freaky part?"

The enraptured townsmen waited.

"When I got to me feet I looked around. The whole place was lit up like a deadly fireplace. Deadly wicked! Daresay they could see it on the other side of the bay. Well, one of them pricks that was on my tail was hanging out the window. I figured when the tanks went up, they just started running anywhere to get away. One got to the window but only got halfway out before dying. It was a man first. A man. I want to make that clear 'cause I know ye'll think I'm off me medication. But as I watched, sure as God is my witness, that bare-assed, strung up fucker, he… he fuckin' *morphed* into a little fuckin' *dog*. A tiny goddamn poodle, and he dropped off the window down into the snow like a big fat flanker. Then I heard *other* voices screechin', just fuckin' *screechin'*, all over the goddamn place, and that was enough to pucker my asshole. Fought through that bitch of a blizzard to get here and I tell ya b'ys, that was no pork barrel of pussy either. I'm *shitbagged*."

It was a good thing Alvin only worked with a quarter lung power. He was the type to throw violent gesticulations into the storytelling once he got going.

"Y'didn't see anything out there?" Leo Tucker asked, the first to recover from that verbal salvo.

"Saw dick all out there. Snowin' so bad I'd need a map to find me own tackle."

"Daresay y'need a map at the best of times," Tom Dawe smirked.

"Hardee fuckin' har," Alvin blazed back.

"All right," Ross said. "Here's what we do. Phones are still down?"

"They are," Tom answered.

"Then one of us needs to take your snow machine and drive it outta here."

"And go where?" Leo Tucker asked. "Bonavista's twenty klicks away."

"Well, then, that person goes twenty klicks to the cops. And they come back with guns or whatever. Whatever the hell they'd use in a situation like this."

"The hell they gonna do with regular guns?"

"Can't do it," a dour faced Tom Dawe commented. "Took the track off the machine yesterday. Worn out. Had to replace it. Had Bill helping me."

"Y'didn't finish the job?" Ross asked.

Tom shook his head. "Got the track off. Ain't no tickle to do. So when we finished we got on the beer and watched a hockey game. Never figured we'd be fucking invaded."

"Montreal and the Oilers?" Roger asked, off topic. "I watched that."

"Good game," Tom stated.

"*Fuck* the hockey," Leo Tucker blurted out with military authority, silencing the men. "You can't get the track back on?"

"Yeah, we can," Bill Bryne spoke up in a rusty chuff of a voice, his weathered features swaddled up in a blue scarf and stocking cap. "But it'd take an hour or so to get the new one back on."

"If that." Tom straightened. "Everything's out back in the garage. Not like it's outside or anything."

"Putting a track back on would be no trouble for you," Ross pointed out.

To this Tom smiled slyly. "Me dad used to say, 'Flattery is like handmade soap—fifty percent is lye.'"

"Well, can y'do it or not?"

"You up for it, Bill?" Tom asked his buddy.

"Sure ting, sure ting."

"Okay, that's done. Who'll drive it?" Leo Tucker put to the group.

"I nominate one of the young guns here," Tom said, nodding at the two men sitting at the table. "I'm sticking around here. Protect what's mine. Besides, who here wants to leave their wife behind with them things out there? Besides Phil, that is."

They grinned at that, except Phil.

"I can't do it," Alvin huffed. "Never drove one before. Runnin' low on oxygen as it is."

"Hospital's in Bonavista," Tucker pointed out.

Alvin looked across the table and Ross saw the fear on his pleading face. The man had been through enough and probably would have to go through more before the night was done. But to travel all the way to Bonavista on an exposed snow machine, in the dead of night and at the height of a storm, was too much to place on his shoulders.

"I'll do it," Ross said with finality. "I'll go."

Tucker appeared pleased. "Good. That's settled then. All right, what's next?"

Tom adjusted the semi-auto under his arm, pulled Bill away from the group, and the pair of them left for the shed. The remainder stood about with their assortment of old weapons, suddenly quiet, while the women chattered and fussed in the living room.

"Load up whatever guns we got," Ross said. "It don't kill 'em, but it hurts 'em all the same. Maybe enough to keep 'em away."

"And man the windows," Roger Moore added.

"And man the windows."

They had four shotguns and three rifles amongst them. Four boxes of shells got plopped down on the kitchen table and arthritic fingers dug into them. The air *clicked* and *clacked* with the act of filling magazines and working bolts. Gun sights were lifted to cheeks and checked. And all the while, Ross could only marvel at how these old-timers, all in their twilight years, set about preparing for war with such a grim determination that he didn't possess.

Cocking a single eyebrow, Leo Tucker caught him staring as he put his cheek to check a gun sight.

"Y'think we are? Bunch a pussies?"

36

Kirk cracked open his eyes and saw broken claws littering the carpet, gleaming like snapped knives. They had been in him and his body had pushed the things out during the healing process. Still in werewolf form, he growled and pushed himself up on all four paws. He sniffed the air, thankful that his nose had healed. Bodies of slaughtered dogs surrounded him. One was missing both legs, and most of its lower body. Another had its belly dug out and Kirk turned away from it before seeing any more. At one point, during the feeding, he'd stopped thinking and had only consumed until passing out, whereupon his body broke down what it needed for repairs.

His shoulders and haunches ached, the bones shifting and grinding together like ill-fitting steel pieces without grease, but he was alive and standing.

The dogs around him had been torn apart. Only now could he fully appreciate the destruction wrought upon their forms.

He left the carnage upstairs, willing his still healing body to work. The wind pulled at the house, making it creak like a merchant ship's rigging. Kirk padded to the destroyed front door, sniffed at the air, and took a moment to reorient himself. His nose led him outside, where the storm slammed into him in a shock of freezing snow. He hunkered down and sniffed around the house, searching for the road. The cliffside. Snow pelted him, turning his fur white. The road, he soon found, ran to the southwest in a wavering line. The drifts, smoking around him with each step, rose to his underbelly.

The barest of scents pulled him through the storm, to a ravaged corpse almost buried in the snow. A man left to freeze, gutted and turned inside out like a slab of fish. A smashed doorway yawned open in the swirling night, and Kirk padded into the house. The breeds had violated the home, spoiling it with their stink, with their spoils. A woman lay on her back, sliced into runny bits. Both arms twisted out of her sockets. Kirk didn't sense the enemy in the house, so he turned about and stopped at the doorway. Another scent caught his attention and he recognized it as Ross's. Kirk hoped the man was still alive.

Trotting back into the storm, the trail led to a guardrail. Kirk inspected it for a moment, hearing the awesome crash of surf below, pummeling the shoreline with watery slaps.

He plodded a few steps more and halted, baring teeth in a hiss of steam.

There, just ahead and on its knees, was a man.

Kirk sniffed. *Not* a man. Another breed. Unmoving in the snow. Growling, Kirk crept forward. The breed lifted its hairy head and whined. Fear filled its single blackened eye, the other one destroyed, puzzling the warden. The creature appeared to have been run over by a machine. Half of its ribcage had been crushed inward in a gruesome cavity. Blood and huge, dark splotches of frostbite mottled its skin. It knelt, leaning into the shoulder of the guardrail, and Kirk wondered if the thing had frozen onto the metal.

The breed whimpered again, cold beyond cold, and fixed the werewolf with a suffering gaze.

Kirk stepped in close and nuzzled the man-thing, growled in its face, but the breed didn't respond. The warden studied the creature's face, the wounds on its naked body.

This one, shivering, cuddled up like a child, was different.

Who knew what dark magic Borland had practiced to bring about this change? Who knew the full, warping effect upon its helpless test subjects? Here, in the depths of the storm and dark, Kirk sensed that this… dog… was *aware* of what it had become. Knew it wasn't natural. It was still a dog, despite its shape, retaining all of its intellect, its sense of noble self, and its personality. It never asked for any of this, yet here it was, shivering to the bone, stricken and alone. Forever changed.

For the worst.

And because of that, Kirk knew what had to be done, no matter how much he dreaded it. No matter how much he wished things could have been different for a madman's victim. The dog looked at him then, its one good eye simmering an understanding.

Pity welled up inside Kirk.

I am not a monster. I am NOT…

Weakened beyond thought, feeling the elemental burn deep in its hairless flesh, the man-thing, once known as Maximilian, watched through narrowed eyes as the werewolf nuzzled his bare cheek and did the absolute last thing the German Shepherd expected.

It licked him.

The wonderful, warming heat from that intimate contact closed Max's eyes, in gratitude, squeezing the last few drops of unfrozen water from them which ran down his cheeks. Only as long as it took for the wolf to lick them away.

Tender enough that the dog actually *smiled*, weakly, unaware of its facial muscles actually forming it—simply reacting to the contact it so desperately needed.

Then the kisses were over, the heat lingering, dissipating.

Max no longer whimpered.

And Kirk ripped out his throat in a sudden, glittering arc.

37

"Y'sure them things are out there?" Phil Crout asked, sounding a little too eager. He hunched over, peering out a window with one corner curtained with snow, a hunting rifle at the ready. Tom Dawe's kitchen and its many windows faced a junction of the cliffside road and the lane heading up over the hill. Visibility remained poor as the blizzard continued, but every now and again, the wind dropped out just long enough to see a short distance.

"They're out there," Ross answered, still seeing the corpses of the Mosebys in his head. Remembering the deaths of the Cooks. "Guaranteed."

"You see for shit anyway, Phil," seventy-five-year-old Chris Hallet muttered, the newest addition to the company after Ross fetched him and his wife Sophie from their nearby house.

"No need for that, Chris," Leo Tucker admonished. "No need."

"Didn't mean it," Chris muttered. "Phil knows that."

"He's been giving me shit for most of me life," Phil said, still scouring the night. "Course, it's only shit he can't say in front of his missus."

That lifted the tension amongst the men in the kitchen. The wives remained in the living room, tending to the revived Flossie Jones. A wood stove pushed heat throughout the house. The first words out of Flossie's mouth concerned the whereabouts of her German Shepherd, Maximilian, to which the women had no answer.

The back door opened, allowing the outside temperatures to suck out the warmth. A few seconds later Leo Tucker trudged into the kitchen, not bothering to kick off snow and appearing as if he'd just dug himself out of an avalanche.

"Tom's got the track back on," he reported, making Ross exchange looks with Alvin, who had clothed himself with a few items from Tom's wardrobe that just fit.

They hurried to the shed.

*

Brutus woke on his comfortable throne and considered the dark forms in the living room. A female had climbed up on the couch with him, and he'd welcomed her body heat as currents of air swept through the house, coming from the ruined entryway. She'd also pulled a thick blanket over them. The temperature inside had dropped significantly. Now, however, after their brief rest, his own primal urges brought him to his feet. A breed slept under the carpet, sheltered from the cold, and Brutus stepped on the beast, getting a shocked yelp. He shouted at the rest of the sleeping pack, rousing them to stretches and complaints of the cold.

Snarling and flourishing claws, Brutus marched to the picture window and shattered the glass with both forearms. The wind buffeted his bare flesh, summoning shivers, but he sensed that fresh meat was close.

He intended to find it.

*

Rising out of the blizzard's might, hunched over and unflinching, Kirk stalked the house just a few leaps away. He'd gotten a little lost in the depths of the storm, wasting time in between the ravaged houses he did find, until coming upon the latest. The front door lay smashed open and the stink of the breed hung off it with malefic menace. But the real clue was the throaty yelling from within.

Kirk sniffed and crept downwind of the open door, head hanging low between his shoulders. From somewhere inside, the sound of breaking glass perked his ears.

Baring his canines, Kirk slunk inside, intending to end the monsters.

Or die in the attempt.

*

A baleful hue of light hung over the gathered snow, emanating from the garage with its doors thrown wide. All manner of handyman equipment hung from peg walls or were piled up on workbenches, giving the interior the cluttered feel of a flight hangar. The single headlight of the snowmobile blazed a cone across trampled white. Tom stood over the machine, one leg on its seat, revving the engine and listening. Ross and Alvin trudged over a raised wooden walkway that led to a side door in the garage. The snowmobile's rear, resting on top of some cement blocks, greeted them upon entering.

Tom turned around, stepped away from the machine, and pointed at it with a smirk. "All done and ready to haul ass."

"Didn't take you too long," Ross said.

Tom shrugged, a motion that seemed incredibly weary. "Yeah, well, the rest is all yours. Lift the ass off the blocks there and put her on the ground. You can drive her right outta here."

Ross did just that, lifting with his legs and dropping the weight with a thud. It was an Arctic Cat model, sleek and painted red that shined under the garage's lights. A Plexiglas windshield would take the edge off any gusts. Thick hand muffs covered the handlebars for greater protection against frostbite. It was a low-riding slingshot, capable of reaching well over a hundred kilometers an hour, weighing nearly a hundred and fifty kilograms. Story had it that Tom bought the racer off a dealer friend in Clarenville.

"She's too much woman for ya, Tommy b'y," Alvin said, huffing as if he'd just run a marathon.

"Go fuck yerself." Then to Ross, "You still gonna head out? Been thinkin'—probably better to stay in the house and wait them out. Phones be up in the morning. If they come, we fight."

"Problem is, they don't wait for very long," Ross said. "They'll come right in here and start killing people. Already done it. Everyone could be dead by morning. No, the best chance is getting to Bonavista tonight and bringing back reinforcements. Here."

Ross handed Alvin the silver knife. "I'll keep the shotgun, but I'd feel better if y'had this."

Alvin took the weapon and studied its length, wishing it was broadsword sized.

The engine rumbling, Ross climbed astride the seat as Tom held out a red helmet. Ross put it on, slapping the visor up and facing the two men.

"You get back to the house and hold out. Shoot anything naked. I'll be back in two hours at the most."

"Follow the roads," Tom yelled. "Enough snow on 'em. You'll be in Bonavista in thirty minutes or less. That animal y'got underneath ya can fly if I didn't say so before."

Ross nodded, slapped the visor down, and slipped his hands inside the handlebar muffs. He squeezed the throttle and eased out of the garage bay, the single headlight illuminating the way. Once onto snow, he gave the machine a greater shot of gas and roared away in a spray of snowy surf. Ross knew how to handle a snowmobile.

He slowed down while getting around Tom's swamped Ford F150, and cut a path onto the road.

Once on the hill, he cranked it.

*

Brutus pulled back from the glass, smelling the draft blowing through the house. The wind changed direction, coming from behind and carrying with it the unmistakable scent of something very dangerous. The other breeds smelled it as well and they turned to see a shadow barely contained by the pitch-black hallway. The werewolf showed teeth that blazed in the dark, and growled a challenge.

Drawing himself up to his full, ominous height, his musculature rippling, Brutus growled back. He had no fear of this challenger. None at all.

Then, the darkness outside was abruptly split by a single staring eye of bright light, distracting both parties for a deciding instant. Brutus's growl ended with a questioning grunt as the snowmobile charged out of the blizzard and turned.

Before shooting up over the hill.

Sensing something of importance was escaping, Brutus had the inexplicable impulse to chase it. He screamed and leaped through the window, snow rising well past his knees upon landing. The breeds shouted after him but he ignored their cries, fully expecting them to follow on his heels. Yelling every step, he bounded onto the snow-filled road and charged after the roaring light, the smell of exhaust in his nostrils.

He did not look back.

*

Kirk squared off against the pack, already facing him as he crept down the short hallway. It didn't matter. He had them all in one place, and before the next minute was done, he intended to kill every last one. The largest of the pack, a brutal beast towering over the tallest breed and corded with heavy muscle, screamed and threw down a pose meant to frighten Kirk.

Brutal.

Kirk remembered the brass tag affixed to the leather collar, back in Borland's store.

Brutus.

A comet flash blazed through the picture window, washing the walls in fleeting light. The deep grumble of the snowmobile engine ripped through the living room as it sped off into the night. The tall brutal one turned around as snow lashed about him. He hesitated for all of a second before leaping out after it.

That one motion distracted the remainder of the pack.

Kirk lunged forth, jaws biting down hard on the naked neck of the nearest monster, pinching flesh and bone together like an aluminum can and leaving a rag doll at his feet. A single piercing squeak cut the air, frightening enough to get the full attention of the remaining breeds in the living room.

Then they were on him.

Kirk slammed one with his two paws, sending him flying backwards to crash into a wide-screen television against the far wall. He tore the face off another with a flash of claws, yanking the jawbone from the skull and leaving his victim thrashing on the carpet. Something landed on Kirk's back while a breed swiped the side of his face, slashing his neck down to his collarbone. The creatures screeched and mobbed him. Kirk roared back and chomped an arm in two. He torqued his entire frame, swinging the breed with him, bowling two others over before biting clean through the limb. The man-thing on his back bit into his shoulder, crushing bone and soaking fur in a spurt of blood. Kirk howled and kicked, disemboweling a female just behind him, the thin flesh of her washboard midsection firm one second, then spilling a nest of eels the next. Claws sunk into Kirk's chest, stabbing deep, pushing past bone. He twisted onto his back, squashing the air out of the breed riding him. Kirk untangled himself in time to face the man-thing missing its jaw bone. Jaw Bone shrieked pure rage at the werewolf, its single line of curved teeth all the more frightening against its ghastly wound. They leaped at each other at the same time, colliding like a fleshy gong, before Kirk's superior strength pushed the breed against the wall. He slammed his paws against Jaw Bone's thick shoulders and raked his talons downward in grisly runnels, right to a pair of bare upper thighs, sapping all fight from the creature. Kirk ripped its throat out in a black starburst. A breed grabbed his legs and slammed him into a doorframe, nearly breaking his neck in the process. Claws grabbed the werewolf, sinking into his flesh, hooking his ribs. Kirk twisted, snapped, and glimpsed a screaming, white face and swelling eyes. He swatted the head, flattening it to the shoulder with an audible *crack.* The creature—the female he'd gutted only seconds earlier—staggered back, suddenly wanting nothing to do with the werewolf.

Kirk pushed ahead and caught her skull in his jaws, crunching it like a knob of hard candy.

He dropped the dying breed and placed his back to a wall, facing the last man-thing as it climbed to its feet. The man's chest had caved in, and Kirk recognized him as the one who had clung to his back. A bitter wind cut between them, whisking away the steam snaking out of the dead or dying. The thing, visibly crippled and hurting, was barely able to stand, yet seethed undiluted anger at Kirk.

The remaining breed, the Bloodhound, fixed its harsh eyes upon the werewolf's dripping shape and bared a shark's maw of teeth. Its posture screamed hatred. Despite feeling mind-numbing pain and unable to fill its punctured lungs with air, Long Face wheezed, and in one final, defining moment of defiance, lifted its extended talons to attack.

Kirk charged in a brushstroke of fur and fangs and clamped down on the breed's neck, dragging it effortlessly to the floor, shaking it until tendons snapped and it fell lifelessly from his jaws.

When it was dead, Kirk limped to the nearest moving body and tore the throat out of it. He killed every breed still clinging to life this way, and once he was done, he resisted the urge to sit on his haunches and howl at the hidden moon. Once again, the pack had taken a bloody toll on him, inflicting punishment the likes he'd never experienced in his life. His shoulder rattled and burned when it flexed. The urge to just feed and slink away to recover settled over his mind, but there wasn't any time for that. Kirk regarded the shattered picture window. Brutus had taken off into the storm… and as long as one of the breeds survived, there was a possibility of this happening all over once more. That was something he couldn't allow. Snarling with pain, Kirk willed himself to move. Every step left prints of blood. With a weary *whuff*, he crossed the soaked living room carpet and leaped into the blizzard.

Intent on finding the one that got away.

38

The Arctic Cat climbed, spitting snow in its wake. The machine plowed over and through rising drifts, at times jarring Ross from his seat. He huddled behind the windshield, concentrating on the shifting surface ahead. Twisting coils charged the single headlight, muting the beam just enough to illuminate the edges of the road, and no more than ten to fifteen feet ahead at best. Bonavista. He had to think it was a damn fine time to head out to the coastal hub. A damn fine time. Thirty minutes. In this storm and with reduced visibility, thirty minutes looked to be doubled. Christ. He hoped there were people left to save by the time he returned with the RCMP. But part of him, the guilty part, felt relief with his decision to get away.

The road ahead unraveled under the snowmobile's light, and Ross leaned over the handlebars, absorbed with the task at hand and wondering what had happened to Doug. The man was missing in action.

A blustery gust of near-arctic air, blown from the icy lungs of Old Man Winter himself, damn near erased the road ahead, as if both of Ross's corneas had been shaved from his eyes. Then the curtain dropped and the headlight revealed a massive wolf, bent over on all fours, with a blazing rack of teeth. Ross jerked the Arctic Cat to the right in reflexive fright, but the monster was simply too big to completely avoid. The front slammed into the animal, sweeping it off its legs. It rolled over the hood and plowed through the windshield with a fibrous *crack.* A mass of fur crashed into Ross's upper body, sweeping him from the seat. His head was rudely pushed back on his shoulders. The Arctic Cat left him and he floated, weightless, for all of a split second before bouncing off a firm mattress of powder. The animal landed on top of him. The roar of the snowmobile ended with a boom somewhere in the blizzard, the engine dying as if speared through its heart.

Stunned, Ross merely stared up at the blackest night, unaware of what it really was holding him down. Then a great weight rolled off him. Ross shifted away from the monster, got to his hands and knees, too dazed to move any further. The Arctic Cat rumbled weakly in his ears, choking to death. His eyes squeezed shut and he fought to reorient himself, wanting air, *needing* air, seeing that shocking beast in his mind's eye. That was no regular wolf. It was something escaped from a lost age. A *sorcerous* age. The back of it alone had to be the width of a refrigerator.

A low growl cut through the blizzard's squall, prompting Ross to turn his head to the side.

"Oh," he breathed, feeling a spike of fear lancing the length of his spine. His breathing abruptly stopped, then started up again in great gulps. The wolf, or an honest-to-God *werewolf*, crept into sight, appearing none too happy. Ross backed away, speechless, awestruck by this miasmic apparition fading in and out of sight. He glimpsed the Arctic Cat on its side, impaled on a picket fence. The werewolf slunk through the streaking snow, behind the overturned snowmobile, until only the arch of its back could be seen. Its snout came around the front of the machine, while the beast's haunches were *still* visible at the other end. It moved funny, and it took him a heartbeat to realize that the wolf was missing a paw.

The wolf from Borland's cabin.

Movies had the hero muttering something cavalier at being confronted by such a beast, but not Ross. A sputter of monosyllabic sounds croaked from his throat as he backed off in a frantic shuffle of hands and legs. The movement caught the monster's attention, and it curled its impossibly huge head around the Arctic Cat. Images of being eaten *alive* flooded Ross's mind in a white-water rush that damn near paralyzed him to the core. Then fear gushed into his limbs, powering them with energy. He did at least fifty in reverse, charged entirely on adrenaline. In his retreat he flipped himself onto his feet and, with arms cartwheeling for balance, shot off into the storm, bounding through snow drifts that swallowed his legs to his knees. The urge to look back struck him, but the fuzzy dark spared him from spotting his pursuer.

But, as God was his witness, Ross swore he sensed it, keeping pace just out of sight.

The second time he glanced back ended with him falling down an embankment in a man-sized avalanche. He whimpered, got to his feet at the bottom, reached for his shotgun and realized it was gone. Wheezing fright and knowing he had to get away or at least hide, Ross sprinted into a small clump of stunted trees. He dove inside, hugging the drifts as if they offered protection.

Then he heard it. Something stomping through the snow, feet punching deep, the hurried breathing and a harsh growling. The night swirled and sped by like black static on a television, coating his visor in a misty slush. All concentration went into tensing for a quick sprint if needed. The smell of chilled fir needles cut across his nose, disrupted at times by the winds. Ross hunkered down and peered into the night, waiting for a shape to materialize, letting his breath out in a controlled wheeze that tortured his racing heart and lungs.

Trees behind him cracked. Ross stopped moving, making side eyes, and finally looked over his shoulder. Something huge forced its way through the firs. Ross moaned and exploded from his hiding place. He huffed it through the whirling clouds of stinging white, focused only on getting away, getting away now, but expecting that terrible set of jaws to clamp down on his ankles or neck at any second. Perhaps rabbits felt the same hot rush of terror before the crushing pinch of predatory teeth.

Ross staggered on blindly, arms burning, chugging at his sides, until a length of metal took him full across the chest and planted him on his ass. For a moment, he lay there, feeling the burn in his torso, not quite realizing what had just happened. He propped himself up and stared ahead, discerning the pole rising up out of a snow drift. Then a second pole, joining at the peak like an upside down V.

A swing. A swing set for kids.

I'm on the playground, Ross realized in a daze. The old playground just at the edge of town. His flight from the top of the hill had him backtrack at an angle, until he rammed into the metal swing set with a full head of steam. The playground itself was over thirty years old, left to rust and ruin as the children grew up, departed the coves, and weren't replaced. When the wind subsided, he heard the old groan of joints and chains swinging.

Ross gripped the pole and hauled himself up. To his right was the curve of a dome- shaped jungle gym.

This he stumbled towards, hearing his boots break through snow and his own ragged breath. He crumpled to his knees and crawled through a triangle of metal bars, drawing his legs in as if being outside of the protective dome meant death. As far as he knew, it meant exactly that. Ross surveyed the radius of the metalwork and positioned himself right in the center, sitting on his freezing ass.

He felt like a chunk of meat in a shark cage, waiting for his stalker to materialize from the deep.

A moment later, his heart stopped.

A sound of heavy breathing and, from out of the dark, partially obscured by night and blowing snow, came a man. Except… it wasn't a man. No sane person would walk naked through a blizzard's bite, carrying himself as Atlas unleashed. Hands ended in talons as long as knives, just as the rows of curved teeth, far too large for lips to cover. It walked right up to the edge of the jungle gym and snarled at the pipes. Ross blinked, shuddered, no longer feeling the maddening burn of his wounds, and just stared in wide-eyed shock at the monster not six feet away. Evil eyes transfixed on Ross, and a malevolent smirk of the monster's features cleared up any doubts as to the thing's intentions.

Seeing only an easy meal, the thing pushed against the bars of the jungle gym, and reached through with one mighty arm. Ross shuffled on hands and feet towards the opposite side, tripped and actually fell flat. A claw grabbed him by the ankle and yanked forward, hoisting him off the snow. Ross got a leg up, braced it against a pipe, but the pulling force crimped his knee out at a punishing angle.

Before stopping.

The thing had Ross dead and center, but it hesitated. Still holding onto his ankle, it turned, and looked off into the night.

Three seconds later, an eternity, the werewolf with one paw limped out of the dark, growling low. Loops of saliva hung from its muzzle.

Brutus yelled at the intruder, warning it away, but the one-pawed wolf did not retreat. The pack leader bared his teeth and slashed at the air with his free hand, making a display of his gifted weaponry. The werewolf circled the best it could on three functioning legs. The drool stretched onto the snow, and Brutus saw that it was, in fact, blood. Snarling, he released the human in his grip, allowing him to drop. The breed extracted his arm from the metal lattice and faced the wolf, roaring aggressively, his entire form rippled with power and authority.

The werewolf stopped circling and growled like an idling engine, feral eyes locked on, sending a message that there was no retreat from this fight.

That suited Brutus just fine. Then a second scent caught his attention, causing him to turn to his right.

A second wolf slunk out of the storm, appearing every bit as determined as the first.

Kirk came out of the night, led by smell and sound to the playground. He stepped carefully through the space between a low-riding merry-go-round, which had seen better days, and a buried row of decayed elephants and horses mounted on coiled springs. Morris eyed him, and the sight and scent of his fellow warden gave Kirk strength. He faced the imposing figure of the last breed, the one he believed to be Brutus, and showed his teeth in a guttural growl. The smell of his own blood filled his nose as Morris's did. Both werewolves had seen action and had taken punishment. The breed appeared practically newborn and rippling with angry power.

Neither Kirk nor Morris could allow it to live.

Brutus sensed this as well, yet showed not a drop of fear. Not to ones such as these. It yelled at the werewolves and swiped claws through the frigid air. He howled and stomped, summoning up a fury that damn near made its hairless hide shimmer in the night.

Morris voiced his own intentions, making it known that only one species of *Were* would leave the playground this night.

Kirk growled agreement and, on a mental cue, they slowly moved closer.

Brutus's yelling ceased. As much as he loathed the sight of these two challengers, and despite sensing a curious bond right down to his bones, he also agreed with the thrumming vibe coursing through the playground. Only the superior breed would walk away.

The pack leader eyed both werewolves, seeing how their blood stained the porcelain brilliance of the snow. Snarling viciously, Brutus waved them into his embrace.

No longer growling, the wolves edged in closer.

And Morris leaped.

With a speed thought impossible for his battered body, he shot through the air straight at the two-legged monstrosity with jaws wide open, seeking throat.

Brutus brought his powerful arm up and caught the werewolf by the neck, halting its flight in midair and choking a surprised gasp from its windpipe. The breed *leered* at the poor attempt.

Infuriated, Morris swung his hind legs forward but, before he could rend flesh, the monster whipped him around and smashed his body into the dome of the jungle gym with a frightening clatter. Snow fell like confetti. Pipes groaned and bent to the point of breaking.

Powerless to only watch, a shocked Ross damn near shat himself from the connection.

Kirk jumped and landed on the breed's back, sinking his teeth deep into its right shoulder and crushing bone. Brutus howled and simultaneously flung Morris into the wailing depths of the blizzard while twisting and slamming Kirk into the bare pipes. This time, metal broke apart. Kirk dropped from the breed, ripping away a huge chunk of meat from the monster's shoulder. He landed in a crest of snow, the impact dazing him. He righted himself and checked on his opponent an instant before unforgiving claws slapped his face, cracking Kirk's head to one side and opening bloody runnels to the bone.

Brutus tried lifting his right arm and screamed when the limb barely responded. He reached out with his left and sunk his nails deep into the scruff of the werewolf's thick pelt, hooking bone, lifting the creature off the snow like an empty suitcase.

Kirk felt those pointed appendages drive through flesh and hook into his spine.

Then Morris charged out of the night and barreled into the breed's midsection, snapping at unprotected flesh.

Brutus released the wolf and fell onto his back, brought his legs up and kicked the one-paw attacker across the muzzle, sending its black mass flailing into the night.

Kirk stood and circled, blood dappling the snow. Brutus charged him, driving him back on his haunches before Kirk forced his muzzle underneath the thing's left arm and bit down hard into an armpit, immediately tasting hot blood.

Bone crunched. Brutus howled. He grabbed Kirk by the scruff and yanked him free, whipping the battered werewolf into the swing set, breaking both of his hind legs in an explosion of blinding pain. Pipes bucked inward. Kirk dropped into the snow.

Seeing the wolf hurt, Brutus swiped a heavy claw across its face, ripping out an eye. He backhanded, opening up flesh to the jawline. He whacked it again, across the top of the skull, hard enough to shatter the brain pan of a man, but only driving the werewolf's bleeding head into the snow.

The *Were* didn't move. Breathing hard, Brutus unsteadily knelt and scooped it up by its throat, holding it high by its weakened left arm.

Morris sprung from the blizzard's depths and chomped down on the breed's right knee, crushing it.

The monster screamed and dropped to the snow on its side, releasing Kirk.

Morris ground his teeth, jerking the limb left and right. A hard claw smashed his snout, and his nose flew away in an eye-watering explosion. Blood flooded his sinus cavity and pain buzzed his entire skull as if a circular saw had gnawed on it from an angle, but he didn't release his adversary. With whatever strength remained in him, he held on and pulled back, not allowing the breed to get free. A fist hammered Morris's head, summoning stars across his field of vision. The second punishing blow broke several teeth but he held on, the breed's blood running down his throat. A third blow ripped an ear off. A *fourth* one pounded his neck, nearly breaking it and almost transforming the werewolf into putty. As it was, the connection still stopped Morris in his tracks.

The shrieking breed twisted into a sitting position, eyes blazing a fury that could've melted glacier ice, and drew back talons dripping with blood as thick as tar. For a split second the connected pair locked gazes, exchanging a message of animalistic hatred.

Brutus roared and that shovel-sized hand ending in knives flashed downward.

Knowing what was about to happen yet near delirious with pain, Kirk summoned every last ounce of power he possessed, channeled it to his intact front legs, turned himself back toward the fight, and pushed himself up and forward. His jaws snapped shut on the breed's hand, catching and crushing it into a squirting pulp.

Brutus released a screech that flamed into a breathless wheeze.

Kirk fell back to the frozen earth, pulling the limb with him, mindless from the agony in his broken legs but forcing his jaws and forepaws to obey. He rolled, twisting himself to the side, every movement a furnace of suffering, stretching the monster out on the spattered platter.

Brutus flailed at the wolf with the broken legs, but could not put any strength into his ruined right arm.

Morris released the mangled knee and sank teeth into the upper thigh, crushing it like an industrial compactor. Brutus bucked, kicked, but could not draw his remaining leg back far enough for a deciding blow. Morris reared back, refusing to give any quarter, feeling the breed weakening.

Kirk chomped into a muscular forearm, worked his way to an elbow. By the time he got to the bulging bicep, a snarling Brutus was relaxing, oily geysers erupting from torn flesh, thick sprays that ebbed into dribbles.

Morris had chewed through a thigh, his muzzle caked in a bloody slush.

Nearly collapsing from exhaustion and his own wounds, Kirk pulled himself up to the breed's shoulder. His nose stabbed its ear. To his surprise, Brutus ceased struggling and turned its softening snarl in his direction. All that could be heard was the wind. In the falling snow, their gazes met. No longer was the breed spouting hate-laced screams. The angry light therein had muted, dissolved. It blinked.

Not in fear, but in weary resignation.

That look made Kirk pause for all of a considering second. He didn't know what the breed had seen in his eye. He *whuffed* in its ear.

And tore out the creature's throat.

From inside the protective shell of the jungle gym, Ross sat and stared, witnessing the shadowy werewolves hunker over the fallen man-thing. Exhausted growls and whimpers cut through the wind. One of the beasts skipped away from the others and approached Ross. As it drew close, the dripping wreck of its face and missing paw were fully revealed, horrifying the island man.

The werewolf stopped outside of the bars, its battered and bleeding head hung low between wide shoulders. The sheer mass of the creature paralyzed Ross. *To the victors, the spoils,* or something to that effect, shot through his mind. Being stared down by a monster refusing to die did nothing for his recall of exact quotes.

A yowling from the other werewolf distracted the creature at Ross's cage, and the animal lingered for a moment, vacillating on what to do. To Ross's bowel-loosening surprise, the werewolf turned and limped away. Leaving bloody prints, it struggled back into the storm, snow clinging to its pelt, where it sat on its haunches for a moment and blocked Ross's view. There it stayed, unmoving, as snow lashed into its considerable bulk.

And after a short time, it hobbled into the dark, out of sight entirely.

Ross pulled himself to his feet, considered the bars for a long time before easing himself out of the jungle gym. The blizzard sung its melancholy verse, freezing him more than he realized and, in the pallid shimmer of the ground, he saw the tracks of the lone werewolf, the battleground, and the stains being hidden with fresh snow. Part of him wanted to bolt right there, just run for the nearest house. His own place was only ten minutes away from the playground, just up over the hill, and if he'd known that when he first collided with the wolf, well, he probably still wouldn't have made it back home. He'd heard tell of it before, but now he knew—fear, when it took you, when it really *grabbed* you, overrode all else.

He heard it then, hoarse panting.

Cringing and *knowing* he should be running in the opposite direction, Ross walked towards the ragged breathing. Plastic elephant heads bobbed in the wind, the squeak of their coiled springs oddly comforting. There, lying on all fours in the snow, lay one of the wolves. Smaller than the hellish thing that had sized him up as if he were a meaty treat. This one let out a whine that thawed the chill in Ross's chest. The animal's hind legs were on the snow, angled in a direction they were never meant to go. Ross had seen enough wounded animals in his time, and he knew this one was done for.

"Easy, boy," he breathed, finding both pity and strength in understanding what needed to be done. "Easy now. I'm… I'm going to make you better here, okay? You just lie there and—"

As he spoke, Ross dropped to the beast's side and reached out hesitantly, made contact with the wolf's back. The animal whimpered. Weak. Waiting.

"There you go, you take it easy now," Ross continued in a reassuring drone, easing a hand over its head. Down underneath the chin. The wolf licked its bloodied chops and closed an eye. Ross shook his head in disbelief. The *size* of the animal…

"You are somethin'," he marveled, hating himself for doing what had to be done, wondering if this animal *was* a werewolf, or just a freak of nature. He gripped the chin while positioning a hand on the back of its skull. Ears flattened in submission. Ross sighed. One quick twist would answer his questions.

Then he realized what he was attempting to do, and that the knife might be a vastly improved choice of tool.

Something growled in his ear.

The one-pawed wolf, hideously mauled and bloodied but still very much alive, snarled in Ross's face, rendering him unable to do anything except shake in bug-eyed terror, his mouth opened like a newborn bird waiting to be fed.

The werewolf in Ross's grip twisted free and bit down on his hand underneath its muzzle. Scalding teeth sunk into flesh, breaking bones like thin icicles.

Ross's mouth opened all the way before a scream, momentarily shackled by surprise, ripped loose.

39

The blizzard moved off just after seven o'clock the next morning, and the sun peeked out shyly, almost embarrassed to gaze upon the buried land. Monstrous drifts tethered themselves to houses like the gleaming strands of musculature, while long, dune-like crests filled the roads and rendered them impassable. Nothing moved in the dawn's revealing light. Not even a breeze.

The telephone lines opened up, and Tom Dawe called the RCMP detachment for help on behalf of the remaining residents. Overworked snow plow operators cleared the single road to Upper Amherst Cove by the afternoon, and three police cruisers followed. The law officers greeted the townspeople gathered at Tom Dawe's residence, and learned for themselves of the horrific carnage wrought by a pack of wild dogs. Upon the recovery of several of the dogs' bodies, officials discovered that while some of the animals possessed fatal gunshot and knife wounds, all had their throats ripped out, which puzzled the authorities to no end. Initial thoughts included a possible rabies outbreak, prompting the bodies' removal and subsequent tagging for further study at the wildlife department located in St. John's. Later reports would prove the rabies theory inconclusive, and the case would perplex experts for months, before more current investigations with clearer resolutions piled on top of the case study, never to be revisited.

The people of Amherst Cove took a week to mourn the souls lost on that horrific night, and arrangements were made with the local Anglican and Roman Catholic churches to coordinate closed-coffin funerals on a single afternoon three days later. The passing of folks like Samuel and Mary Walsh, Harry Shea, Kate and Karl Gibbs, to name just a few, all familiar faces of the tiny community, had left the survivors with a sense of loss so great, many said that the town itself had stepped into a grave. Never to pull itself out.

But, that all happened in the days following that first afternoon, after the snow had fallen, and a police cruiser stopped on the main road. Bundled for the cold, Officer Elizabeth Sheard trudged through snow that went past her knees in places, homing in on the little, green bungalow high on the hill. From the road, a snow-swamped deck could be made out, one that faced the ocean and offered a lovely view of a bay as polished as silver, glutted in places with pans of ice.

When she closed within ten feet of the front door, it opened.

"Morning, Officer," Ross Kelly greeted, wearing pajama bottoms and a beige fisherman's sweater.

"Mr. Kelly," Elizabeth greeted. "You okay?"

He looked pale, as if he'd been on a drinking binge the night before. "Ah, no, just recovering from last night."

"I've heard," Sheard stated. "You saved some people."

Ross didn't immediately respond to that. A growth of beard bobbed as he swallowed. "Not all, though."

"But enough."

Ross glanced towards the waters.

"May I come in?" Sheard pushed. "And get a statement from you?"

"Oh. Sure." He backed into his open door. "Come on in."

He led her through the porch and into the entryway, past a short hall that led to the bedrooms, and gestured for her to sit at a kitchen table where the air was redolent of coffee and bacon. Patches of water, as if wet mugs had been set down, dotted the linoleum. Elizabeth made a quick study of the kitchen, saw the old-fashioned cupboards and a sink full of dishes. That and the little puddles were the only things that marred the otherwise tidy interior.

"Bachelor's life, huh?" Elizabeth smiled faintly, sitting down.

"What? Oh, yeah." Ross scratched the back of his head as he sat opposite her. She noticed how his other hand had been bound in medical tape, enough to look like a tight mitten. "I let it pile up for a couple of days. Unless I get a meal of moose on or something and I'm forced to clean up. But I don't let things go too far."

Something thumped down a hall. Sheard heard it and Ross noticed.

"My dog. He, ah, kicks in his sleep."

"He stayed in last night?"

Ross nodded. "I think he was the only one."

"Lucky him." Sheard became professional. "Mr. Kelly, can you tell me what happened here in the last twelve hours?"

Ross took a deep breath, and relayed to her everything that had happened, from him discovering the ravaged corpse of Walter Borland below the hill, right up to crashing Tom Dawe's Artic Cat and the subsequent fight on the old playground between a mad dog and what looked to be a couple of wolves.

"Wolves aren't native to the island," Sheard pointed out.

Ross could only shrug at that. "Might've been a breed. Coyote mix."

Sheard supposed that could be the case, as only just a year ago a local shot and killed a coyote-wolf crossbreed. She moved on to other things of interest in the investigation, asked her questions, and finished up well within an hour. As far as she could see, Ross Kelly wasn't lying to her in the least. Battered and sickly he might be, but a liar he wasn't.

"If we have any further questions I'll be in touch," Sheard said as she stepped outside.

"I'll be here," Ross informed her. "Not going anywhere for a while. Not until my nerves are settled a bit."

Sheard regarded him for a moment, thinking on those last few words, but ultimately letting them go.

"Thank you for your time, Mr. Kelly."

Ross waved and closed the door. Through the door's window he watched the officer trek all the way back to her cruiser, white against white and strips of red. Only when the car moved off did he return to his kitchen.

There, sitting at the table in a robe that barely fit him, sat a glowering Morris, missing a nose and a hand.

"We need to talk," Morris said.

"About?"

"Us." Morris fixed him with cold eyes. "You."

Ross hadn't told Officer Sheard everything. That would open a can of worms he didn't think would ever close, and Doug's (or Kirk, as Morris called him) warning on the matter rang clear to him. *Let it pass. Just let it pass.*

"What about me?" Ross asked and coughed. He didn't think it was a bug.

"Bring him in here," Kirk called out from the spare bedroom, causing both men to turn. Morris gestured for Ross to lead the way. They entered the room where Kirk rested, splayed out over the mattress with roughshod splints on his legs. His chest was bare, and the silver gash simmered and sucked in light, never to completely heal. Kirk regarded Ross with his one good eye, as if he'd settled on what to say only just an hour before. Ross tried very hard not to look at the frightful hole already filling with a stomach-turning opaque sheen.

"You know what we are," Kirk said.

Ross swallowed and nodded.

"You know… you're one of us too, now."

"Because of this?" Ross lifted his bandaged hand.

"Yeah. Because of that. You feel it, right?"

That not unpleasant burning sensation all the way down to his testicles? "Yeah."

It was Kirk's turn to nod while Morris stood behind Ross, blocking any exit as if he expected the man to lose it. So far, the man had been rattled, but he hadn't rolled. Not yet, anyway.

"You have until the next full moon," Kirk informed him. "Then, well, your life's gonna change. Some think for the better. Some, for the worse. But you saw the dogs. What they became. Who knows what their bite might've done to you. But I'm pretty sure my bite will… overtake theirs."

"So… I'll be like you?" Ross had seen Kirk change from wolf to man last night, in the early-morning hours as the storm finally moved off over the Atlantic. Considering everything else that had happened, it didn't freak him out as much as it should have.

"Yeah. You'll be like us."

In that space of time, silence buzzed.

"So, what then?"

"Life's gonna change," Morris rumbled from behind.

"Your life's gonna change," Kirk repeated. "Morris and I have talked about it. I'll make a phone call a little later, with your permission, but Walt Borland wasn't all that you thought he was. And now that he's dead, well… a position's opened. Neither of us are from around here. We think, given the circumstances, you might be the best choice to fill the opening."

"Doing what?"

"Being the law," Morris stated before Kirk could answer.

"Being the law," the Halifax man echoed.

Ross stood there, appearing uncertain with everything, but still holding it together. "For how long?"

For life, Kirk wanted to tell him, knowing that he'd no longer age as a regular person, and, sooner or later, he'd have to move to another part of the island, assume a new identity, and live there until it was time to move again.

Again and again, to hide how the years no longer changed him. Not like the human populace.

But that would be overload right now. He could see it in Ross Kelly's eyes, smell it in his pores. Saw the way he held the hand Kirk had bitten. In the time between now and the next full moon, when Ross underwent his birthing transformation, there would be a lot of talk. A lot of drinking, too, no doubt. But Kirk and probably Morris would be around, just to ensure Ross didn't do anything stupid. In the aftermath of the brutal night they shared and fought, Kirk sensed a softening of Morris's attitude towards him. He could smell it when the Pictou warden had returned to Ross's house after the chore of sniffing out the dead and the near-dead breeds during the predawn hours, ensuring that all the abominations were killed.

When Morris had reverted back to his human form, the big man had actually smiled weakly at him.

It would do.

Ross, however, was another matter entirely. Kirk *believed* the Newfoundlander was all right, but bringing a new wolf into the grand pack had its own set of rules to follow.

A wolf that would be a warden from the get-go, no less.

Thinking back, as a recovering Kirk had done for most of the morning, there'd been no other way to save Ross's life. The breed had infected him. Even in his bloodied state, the taint hung about Ross like bad cologne. Kirk could have killed him, but instead decided to transfer the curse—a strain he hoped would overpower whatever invader was in Ross Kelly's system—and thus save his life.

At least, what was left of it. Only time would tell if Kirk had made the right choice.

Only the passing of long, long years would reveal if Ross would come to hate him.

When ye reach my age. Ye'll see. The lies. Jus' wait. Borland's voice rose up in the back of his mind. The memory had invaded his thoughts and now bothered Kirk incessantly.

I'm not a monster, he projected, into the silence of the newest werewolf's unanswered questions.

Kirk regarded the floor as a chill caressed his flesh.

I'm not…

Am I?

About the Author

Keith lives in the wild hills of Canada, on the island of Newfoundland.

Try these other titles by Keith C Blackmore:

Horror

Mountain Man

Safari (Mountain Man Book 2)

Hellifax (Mountain Man Book 3)

The Missing Boatman

Cauldron Gristle (novella—contains *Mountain Man* short story "The Hospital")

Heroic Fantasy

The Troll Hunter

131 Days (novella/ Book 1)

131 Days: Ten (Book 2)

White Sands, Red Steel

Science Fiction, Fantasy

The Bear That Fell from the Stars

One-Shot Short Stories

Ye Olde Fishing Hole (also in *Cauldron Gristle*)

The Hospital (the first Mountain Man story, and also found in *Cauldron Gristle*)

Children's

Flight of the Cookie Dough Mansion

If you enjoyed this story and have the time and inclination, consider leaving a review.
It's good advertising for me. :-)
Visit www.keithcblackmore.com for news and announcements.